"In centering her thriller around a main character who is
... ench
... Aubert set herself a difficult task, and she acquits
herself brilliantly ... ... ghts, together with
... ogue of the people she encounters and her
... and often humorous commentary on their one-sided
conversations, fuels this dazzling whodunit ... Never
stooping to melodrama or pity, she uses Elise's marvelous
sense of humor and intellect to create an unforgettable
character." —*Publishers Weekly*, starred review

"[A] strange, suspenseful thriller ... This canny novel
evokes suffocating feelings of dread for its appealing pro-
tagonist, who has not let her infirmities dim her intelli-
gence or her sardonic sense of humor ... Her insights ...
are neat and nasty ... [An] unorthodox whodunit."
—*The New York Times Book Review*

"Surprisingly scary ... Aubert does a chilling job of
telling the story through Elise's limited senses, trapping
the reader along with the injured narrator in a blind tunnel
of whispered revelations and icy fear."
—*San Francisco Chronicle*

"A beautifully constructed tale that gets scarier by the page."
—*Kirkus Reviews*

"A unique and unlikely heroine ... [A] frightening tale ...
An engaging puzzle." —*Booklist*

"The perfect heroine ... beautiful, funny, and brave ...
The book reads like romantic suspense from thirty years
ago, with the finely tuned hysteria of an Ursula Curtiss
mystery ... Wonderfully sly ... An expert mix of wryness
and tension ... Fabulous." —*Salon*

"The portrayal of an intelligent, blind, mute quadriplegic is
refreshing, and Elise is a spunky and engaging heroine."
—*Library Journal*

DEATH
FROM THE
WOODS

BRIGITTE AUBERT

TRANSLATED BY DAVID L. KORAL

BERKLEY PRIME CRIME, NEW YORK

THE BERKLEY PUBLISHING GROUP
Published by the Penguin Group
Penguin Group (USA) Inc.
375 Hudson Street, New York, New York 10014, USA
Penguin Group (Canada), 90 Eglinton Avenue East, Suite 700, Toronto, Ontario M4P 2Y3, Canada
(a division of Pearson Penguin Canada Inc.)
Penguin Books Ltd., 80 Strand, London WC2R 0RL, England
Penguin Group Ireland, 25 St. Stephen's Green, Dublin 2, Ireland (a division of Penguin Books Ltd.)
Penguin Group (Australia), 250 Camberwell Road, Camberwell, Victoria 3124, Australia
(a division of Pearson Australia Group Pty. Ltd.)
Penguin Books India Pvt. Ltd., 11 Community Centre, Panchsheel Park, New Delhi—110 017, India
Penguin Group (NZ), Cnr. Airborne and Rosedale Roads, Albany, Auckland 1310, New Zealand
(a division of Pearson New Zealand Ltd.)
Penguin Books (South Africa) (Pty.) Ltd., 24 Sturdee Avenue, Rosebank, Johannesburg 2196, South
Africa

Penguin Books Ltd., Registered Offices: 80 Strand, London WC2R 0RL, England

This is a work of fiction. Names, characters, places, and incidents either are the product of the author's imagination or are used fictitiously, and any resemblance to actual persons, living or dead, business establishments, events, or locales is entirely coincidental. The publisher does not have any control over and does not assume any responsibility for author or third-party websites or their content.

DEATH FROM THE WOODS

A Berkley Prime Crime Book / published by arrangement with Welcome Rain Publishing.

PRINTING HISTORY
Welcome Rain hardcover edition / August 2000
Berkley Prime Crime trade paperback edition / April 2001
Berkley Prime Crime mass-market edition / November 2005

Copyright © 1996 by Editions du Seuil.
Translation © 2000 by Welcome Rain Publishers LLC.
Cover design by George Long.
Cover illustration by Dan Craig.

ISBN: 0-425-20733-1

BERKLEY® PRIME CRIME
Berkley Prime Crime Books are published by The Berkley Publishing Group,
a division of Penguin Group (USA) Inc.,
375 Hudson Street, New York, New York 10014.
The name BERKLEY PRIME CRIME and the BERKLEY PRIME CRIME design are trademarks belonging to Penguin Group (USA) Inc.

PRINTED IN THE UNITED STATES OF AMERICA

10 9 8 7 6 5 4 3 2 1

A MAN WALKING IS A MAN DYING;

DEATH FOLLOWS HIM LIKE HIS SHADOW

———

BAOL PROVERB

ONE

IT'S RAINING. A THICK, HEAVY RAIN POUNDING THE windowpanes. I can hear the gusts rattling the doors and windows. Yvette is puttering around, closing shutters and bolting them tight. In just a minute, she'll be bringing dinner. But I won't touch it; I'm not hungry. She'll insist. She'll get angry. She'll say, "Come on, Elise, you're being silly. You've got to eat, you know, if you want to get back your strength." Bullshit. The only strength left at my disposal is that which maintains my internal plumbing in its present state. As far as everything else goes, I can't even start my wheelchair by myself. I'm what you'd call a quadriplegic. And as if I weren't happy enough to lose the use of my limbs, then I really hit the jackpot when I lost my sight and ability to speak: "We're experiencing technical difficulties." I'm mute and blind, and can't move. Frankly, I'm a living vegetable. Yvette's here, I can hear her rapid steps.

"Dinnertime!"

My dinner consists of strained vegetables and proteins, which are crammed into my mouth with a little spoon. It's too hot and I try to turn away. I can imagine Yvette looking exasperated. I remember her round, cream-colored face,

crowned with blond hair. For thirty years or so, Yvette, the
widow of a railwayman, sixtyish, with sturdy legs and a
powerful frame, has been working for my family. She re-
members my mother better than I. Of course I was only
five when Mom "went up to heaven." When my father died,
seven years ago, I came to live here, and Yvette continued
to take care of the house for me. Now she takes care of me.
The nurse taught her how to give me all the proper treatments. Poor Yvette; she has to wash, feed, and clean me. I
wonder how many times she must have wished me dead.
How many times have I wished death upon myself?

I wonder if it's dark. It's the end of May. I can't remember whether or not night falls at around seven or eight
o'clock this time of year. I can't ask Yvette. I can't ask anyone anything. My central processing unit is down.

I was on vacation in Ireland last fall when it happened.
With Benoît. October 13, 1994. I remember what he was
wearing that day: navy blue pants, a matching sweater, and
blue sneakers. I was in jeans, with a round-necked white
sweater. And very clean white high-tops. Now I've got slip-
pers on my feet, and I'm almost always in a nightgown.
And as far as the color of my nightgown goes, well . . .

Benoît and I took advantage of what time we had to
make a quick jaunt to Northern Ireland. The Giants'
Causeway. Belfast. That morning in Belfast, we decided to
stop in at the bank to cash in some traveler's checks. I can't
quite remember the bag I was carrying that day. Was it the
blue leather bag or the one with the multicolored back? It's
details like these that just drive me mad. All I saw and
didn't retain! And now I need images so badly.

To make a long story short, we showed up in front of the
bank and I pushed open the glass door. That's when it happened. The explosion—a car bomb, ten yards away. The
driver died, of course, as well as four passersby. And
Benoît. First there was a noise; the explosion was just enormous. It felt like being thrown into a furnace. Benoît
grabbed me by the arm and threw me to the ground. We
were caught in a whirlwind of metal and glass. I saw the car
as it exploded, I heard the screams, but didn't understand;

no, I really didn't understand what was going on, that this was really happening to me, Elise Andrioli. People were shrieking. I saw a shard of glass embedded in Benoît's throat, and blood spurting out—did I understand then that this was blood? I was shrieking, too. Something struck me over the head. I closed my eyes. And never opened them again.

For nearly two months I remained in a coma. When I regained consciousness, I was in France, in Paris. It took me a moment to understand that this was not a temporary situation. I would never get up or see again. I couldn't speak to the nurses or doctors. Only through listening to their discussions did I understand how serious my case was. I didn't want to believe it. And still . . .

They put me through a battery of tests before deciding that, even though my spinal cord did not seem irremediably injured, my motor centers were seriously damaged. "Motor cortex . . . the cerebellum regulation center . . . perhaps a catatonic state . . ." In short, a breakdown. And it's the same story as far as my eyes go: the optic nerve is intact, but something in the brain is out of whack and they don't know if I'll ever regain my eyesight. The doctors aren't sure whether I can hear or understand what they say, so they talk to me as if I were some doddering old fool. Everyone else does the same, except Yvette, who insists—and with good reason—that I'm perfectly conscious and that one day I'll spring from my wheelchair like Lazarus, back from the dead.

So there you have it. I'm thirty-six years old. I used to ski, play tennis, go walking and swimming. I liked the sun, going for drives, traveling, and reading novels about love. Love . . . Now I'm buried inside myself and every day I pray to die completely.

Often, when I hear Yvette fussing over me, I think back to a film I saw on TV one night. It was the story of a poor soul like me, but what's more, his arms and legs had been amputated—basically, he was a blind, mute human torso, trying to communicate with his nurse to convince her to kill him. Benoît and I almost cried. We were happy and healthy, sitting comfortably on our sofa, with a cup of something at arm's reach. All set to shed tears over someone else's sorrow.

Yvette's scolding me. I'm trying to swallow, but it's hard. Every day I wonder why some muscles function while others don't. Why is it that my heart goes on pumping blood and my neurons reason logically? Why has my skin remained sensitive to the touch and capable of shuddering? Every day since I've regained consciousness, I channel every ounce of will, with one single goal in mind: to move. Move, move, move. Two months ago I managed to blink my eyes, and last month I was able to lift my left index finger. I can also move my head, but these are uncoordinated movements I can't quite control. Raybaud, my doc, says I'm making immense progress. And then he goes off windsurfing. Raybaud's not exactly what you'd call sensitive. He thinks I belong in a special institution. An aseptic dying place, an electronic victory garden for human vegetables.

Dinner's over. Yvette's taking everything away. She's turning on the TV and doing the dishes. *"A crane toppled over on a building in Bourg-en-Bresse."* Sirens, screams, coverage. The anchor's overexcited voice. Better yet, there was a police snafu in Lille. *"A young Beur was shot down by mistake, all because of a car theft. The minister of the interior . . ."* What the hell were we doing in front of that goddamned bank? Is there such a thing as destiny? *"The police are still looking for Michael Massenet in Yvelines . . ."* If this is to be my destiny, then how am I to bear it? What good is it to complain? *"The anticyclone in the Azores. . . ."* The commercial thunders at me. I'm listening to enthusiastic voices vaunting the merits of diapers, mattresses, detergents, cars, toilet paper, batteries, perfume, cheese, and frozen food. It all seems so far away. The program Yvette has chosen has just started—a debate on drugs and delinquency in schools. I listen piously.

Debate's over. No one agreed on anything, but everyone's congratulating himself. Yvette sighs and rolls me to my room. She flops me onto the bed. The masseuse should be coming tomorrow. She'll pull on my dead limbs, anoint them with oil, and knead them interminably, wondering if I can feel anything. And I won't be able to answer.

"Good night," says Yvette.

Good or bad, it's always night.

THIS MORNING YVETTE TOOK ME WITH HER TO THE supermarket, as she does every Saturday since the weather became mild. It's not far, so she walks, pushing me in my wheelchair. Marvelous Yvette, who persists in treating me like a being with thoughts. Yet one more opportunity to remain seated. At least I'll have the pleasure of feeling the sun upon my face; hearing birds, car horns, and shouts of children; breathing in exhaust and the scent of freshly mown grass; guessing at the colors and movements of a whole world around me. Yvette put dark glasses on for me. She claims the sun might hurt my eyes. Personally, I think it's so that children won't be frightened by my constant stare. Hurt my eyes . . . For whatever that's worth! Sometimes, I jokingly tell myself that what I miss most is being able to look at myself in the mirror. It's futile, of course, but am I still pretty? Is my hair properly set? I'm moderately confident in Yvette's talents.

Yvette set me up by the tree—she told me so. Nice and calm, and not far from the guard in case some little hooligans take it into their heads to make off with me. I can imagine the headlines: "Ravishing Quadriplegic Raped by a Gang of Antisocial Youths." Yvette's gone inside to do her shopping. I'm waiting. People exchange comments on the weather, the elections, unemployment, and so on. Before I was a vegetable, I used to manage the Trianon, a small movie theater at the edge of town—correction, the new urban zone. Three brand-new screening rooms. My father left it to me. I'd carved out this arty, trial-run niche for myself, which offered the opportunity of being invited to a number of festivals and to go to Paris often. Film, theater—all over now. No, I mustn't get started on self-pity again.

Something has just fallen on my hand. It's humid.
Above my head, I hear something cooing. Fucking pigeon. The very thought of guano on my hand disgusts
me. I can't stand being unable to use my body anymore. I
can't stand this powerlessness—

"Why don't you wipe it off?"

Someone has spoken to me. A child. A shy little voice. I
say nothing, obviously.

"Ma'am, a pigeon's just made a cocky on you."

The kid must be wondering why I'm not saying anything. He's getting closer, I can hear his breath nearby.

"Are you sick?"

Perspicacious little kid, isn't he? I gather up all my will
and raise my index finger.

"You can't talk?"

No, I can't. I raise my index finger again. I don't even
know if the kid realizes this.

"My name is Virginie."

It's a little girl! I definitely haven't acquired that overde-
veloped sense of hearing of the blind. I feel her placing her
hand over mine—a cool little hand. What's she doing?
Ahh, she's wiping my hand. I can feel the contact of either
a napkin or a Kleenex.

"I'm wiping your hand, ma'am. Do you live around
here?"

Index finger.

"When you raise your index finger, does that mean
yes?"

Index finger.

"I live around here, too. I came to go shopping with my
dad. He doesn't like me to speak to strangers, but it's not the
same with you because you're paralyzed. Did you have an
accident?"

Index finger. It's the first conversation I've had in
months. I wonder how old she is.

"My father works in a bank. My mom's a librarian. I go
to school at Charmilles. I'm seven years old. You want me
to tell you a story?"

I raise my index finger, thinking. Seven years old. Her

whole future in front of her. To say that I was seven and had sworn that I would do great things . . .

"Once upon a time there was a little boy named Victor. He was the son of the tobacconist. He was a very bad boy, and so one day he died in the woods where, it so happens, he was forbidden to go."

What's she talking about?

"The police came, but they didn't find anything. After Victor, Death from the Woods took Charles-Eric, the son of the lady who works in the post office. The police came, but they didn't find anything. And then there was Renaud. And ever since yesterday, Death has taken Michael, by the edge of the stream."

This kid's crazy. What an idea, to be making up such stories! She leans on my forearm and whispers, "But I know who killed them."

What?! First of all, where does she come from? Where's her father?

"Because I saw the murderer. You're listening?"

I raise my index finger. What if this were true? No, it's ridiculous. She must be one of those kids who watches too much TV.

"Since then, I've been scared all the time. So my schoolwork's not that good, and they all think it's because Renaud died. Renaud was my big brother, you understand?"

I raise my index finger. This girl has a totally morbid imagination.

"I saw when it happened to Renaud. In the little shed at the back of the garden. You know, those sheds for kids—they're made out of cloth and have windows painted on them. Renaud was inside and—"

"Virginie!"—a deep, warm masculine voice—"I've been looking for you for a quarter of an hour. I told you to stay by the kiosk. At least she's not bothering you, is she, miss? Oh, excuse me . . ."

People always say "excuse me" when they realize what condition I'm in.

"Say good-bye to the lady, Virginie."

"Good-bye, ma'am. We come to do our shopping every Saturday."

"Virginie! That's enough! Excuse us . . ."

He has a young voice. Nice tone to it. I can see him as a big guy with short hair, in jeans and an Izod Lacoste.

"Is there a problem?"

That's Yvette.

"No, no, it's just Virginie, who came to chat with the lady. I hope she hasn't bothered her."

Out of all the things that bother me, this is really the least painful. Yvette's whispering. I can only imagine what she must be telling him. "A terrible accident, yada, yada, yada, crippled, lost her sight, her speech, horrible, isn't it, blah, blah, blah, so young, and her fiancé dead, too; poor girl, no hope, the doctors are pessimistic, life's so unfair . . ."

Into my ear, Virginie breathes, "If you come back next Saturday, I'll tell you the rest."

"Okay, let's go! Say bye-bye."

I imagine her father tugging her by the hand, rushing to get away.

Yvette places the plastic bags filled with pointy things upon my knees, hangs some others from the arms of the wheelchair, and we're off. As she walks she talks to me as she always does when she takes me out. She's gotten into the habit of giving these monologues. She told Raybaud that, in her opinion, I could understand her. And it's true. Raybaud replied that she shouldn't harbor too many illusions. It's too depressing. The only one who showed any real interest was Professor Combré, the neuropsychiatrist from the hospital. He's a brain surgeon. In three months he should be seeing me again. Sometimes I start to dream that he'll decide to attempt one last-chance operation. But how would I convince him? Yvette's talking nonstop.

"And to think they raised the price of sole again. You've got to be a billionaire if you want to keep eating fresh fish. I know you don't care a whit, but still . . ."

I don't know why, but Yvette has always insisted on being so formal when she speaks to me. She addressed my parents in the third person, and I was Miss Elise. There's something about it that's slightly retro. Now she's talking about Virginie: "Quite a pretty little girl, yes. Her father, too, a nice boy. Good people, it shows. The little girl was well dressed, neat, and polite. And he was very elegant, wearing a pale green polo shirt, a clean pair of jeans, but modern still, you know? It's a shame you don't get any more visits. I know you're not thrilled to hear that, but still. To wind up all alone like that . . . oh, you might even say your friends just let you go. But, like I say, people nowadays only like you when you're of some use to them."

My friends . . . I never had many friends. I could count them all on the fingers of my hand. Frank and Julia live in Paris, Cyrille was just transferred to just outside Grenoble, and Isabelle and Luc live in Nice, near where my uncle lives. Since I'd met Benoît, I saw practically no one, and most of the time, the few acquaintances we went out with lived in Paris. At first my friends called. In shock. Benoît dead, me crippled . . . Then the phone calls became few and far between. I understand; it must be annoying, so they preferred to forget me.

"Did I remember to get Ajax Window Cleaner?" Yvette suddenly wonders aloud.

On and on she goes, recapping her purchases. I'm not listening anymore. I'm thinking about what Virginie told me. Now that I think about it, I remember this little Victor very well; he was the tobacconist's son. Everyone was talking about it. Strangled near the canal. It must have been at least five years ago. . . . And then there was that other one, the one whose name was a real mouthful . . . yes, I remember, I was discussing it with Benoît. He was also strangled, I think. The police suspected an uncle, but came up with nothing. But this sort of thing goes on so often . . . people talk about it, then time goes by and they forget. And what about this little Michael? Was this also very recently? Didn't I hear that name on the news last night? I've got to listen to the TV news tonight. That is, if Yvette leaves me in the living room. Sometimes she rolls me into my room and leaves me there like a bundle of dirty laundry until dinnertime. I'm supposed to be resting. Resting from what, I wonder. She puts on the radio or music. She fumbles through my CDs, eliminates anything that might be jarring, and force-feeds me classical music or popular waltzes. I must have listened to *Riquita, Java's Pretty Flower,* two hundred times, and often I dream of strangling Riquita, beating her to a pulp.

Yvette has put all her purchases away. She's left me in the living room, in the sunlight. It's starting to get hot; Yvette has opened the windows wide, and I can feel the wind on my forehead and smell the flowers outside. I can't tell their fragrances apart, but I can smell; I breathe in the scent of spring in the flowers and avidly embrace the sun.

Someone's ringing at the door. It's the masseuse. A torture session awaits.

Fate has smiled on me. As she goes to work on my distended limbs, Catherine—the physical therapist—suddenly shouts to Yvette, who's busy in the kitchen, "Did you hear? They found that kid, strangled."

"What?" Yvette replies, turning off the faucet.

"Little Michael Massenet, from La Verrière. His mother sees me because of her neck. She had whiplash last year. They just found him in the woods. Strangled."

It's Yvette's voice now, closer. I imagine her wiping her hands on a cotton-print apron—pastel-colored spring flowers. "What kind of times are we living in?" she says with indignation. "How old was he?"

"Eight years old. A pretty little blond boy, full of curls. I just heard it on the three o'clock news. The body was discovered at the edge of the stream by some fisherman returning to his car, at the stroke of noon. They say he was dead at least twenty-four hours. You can imagine what a shock it must have been for that guy. If I had any kids, I'd never let them outside now. You realize this is the fourth one in five years?"

"The fourth?"

"Yes! At first they didn't make the connection, but now . . ."

"Is there a trail? Any clues?" Yvette interrupts, all keen on crime novels.

From the sound of her voice, the Great Catherine must be making a face. "You'd think! They're fumbling around in the dark. Just like her. Just look," she adds, pinching my calf.

Yvette must have cast a disapproving glance, for right away the Great Catherine explains, "In any case, she's making progress. It's incredible!"

But Yvette won't let herself be distracted. "But tell me, wasn't Michael Massenet that cute little boy who played piano at the cultural center?"

"Yes, that's him. Very polite, very precocious for his age . . ."

They continue on this theme for a while and I don't miss a crumb. Michael Massenet, eight years old, a student at CE2 in Charmilles, the new school in the new urban zone. His father was an instructor at the auto school, and his mother's a secretary. He's a good student, from a strong family. "Well, the crime must have been committed by some sadist," Yvette concludes.

Now I'm stretched out on my bed. Yvette has turned off the television. It must be eleven o'clock. At around three in the morning she'll make a round to see if everything's okay: Am I thirsty? Do I need to pee? Is it warm enough? . . .

Saint Yvette. I hope at least my guardian is paying her a generous salary. My uncle was named my guardian. My Uncle Fernand, the brother of my deceased father. He heads a masonry firm near Nice; he's what they call an honest man.

But that's not the subject of the day. The subject of the day is this murder business. We listened to the eight o'clock news. By chance, when Yvette grows passionate about a subject, she'll leave me next to her so that she'll have someone to whom she can make her comments. Surely they spoke of the little Massenet boy. Strangled. They've tied this to other crimes dating further back, perpetrated within a thirty-mile radius: Victor Legendre, strangled in Valençay in 1991; Charles-Eric Galliano, strangled near Noisy in 1992; and Renaud Fansten, strangled in his parents' backyard in 1993. No one had ever solved these murders. What's more, and as the anchor has pointed out, different teams were working on each case: the police were assigned to the first two, and the homicide division to the third. To make a long story short, the Michael Massenet murder has kicked off more investigations. Yvette hasn't stopped uttering exclamations, railing against the cops and people with sexual obsessions, who really ought to be given lobotomies.

An owl hoots in the distance. I'd like to turn over; I'm sick and tired of being on my back. One night I'm on my back, another on my side. Yvette wedges me in with pillows, placing cushions between my knees and ankles, as Raybaud recommended, to avoid points of compression that could lead to bedsores. Now, that must be a pain in the ass, propping me up like that every night. Stop it! I can't get started with these complaints again. So that little girl was telling the truth. Several children, including her brother, were murdered, or so she says. Terrible. I can understand how she would feel the need to talk about it. But there was something disturbing about her tone of detachment when speaking about these murders. She must be quite disturbed. . . . I would very much like to see her again . . . well, really, what I mean is, to hear her again. Charmilles? Isn't that the name of the school where she said she goes? That big glass thing surrounded by trees that someday must grow?

I dozed off, but just woke with a start. How did little Virginie know about Michael Massenet? She said, quite distinctly, "And ever since yesterday, Death has taken Michael, by the edge of the stream." However, the Great Catherine was quite specific when she said that the body was not discovered until noon today. How is it, then, that this little girl could know about it at ten o'clock this morning?

Because she saw it. She saw the body.
Or the murder.

That's why she was so knowledgeable. Perhaps she was walking around there and saw everything! She wasn't lying when she said she knew the murderer! And to think I don't even know who she is. Virginie. Now I'm jogging my memory. I saw plenty of kids parading by at the movie theater, but there are lots of new housing estates—people are moving in every day. The only Virginie I remember was a chubby little girl, around ten years old, who used to pig out on bonbons. This Virginie told me she was seven, so the two don't match. And then the other one had a loud, squawking voice, whereas this one had a calm, gentle voice. Cold.

If this little girl had seen the murderer, something ought to be done. But what? Obviously, I'm unable to notify the police. And even if by some miracle I could, what would I tell them? To go looking for a seven-year-old girl named Virginie, a girl I know so little about that I don't even know if she lives here or in one of those "residential communities" surrounding the woods?

All I want is to make it to Saturday.

TWO

TODAY'S THE BIG DAY. I GOT UP VERY EARLY. I KNOW so because I waited a long time for Yvette to show up, lift me, wash me, pass me my basin, and dress me. I'm happy I can control my bladder, more or less. It's reassuring. It leaves me with some hope that one day I'll be able to recover some of my autonomy. I'd be happy to just move my arms, nod my head, or smile. So much for sex. So much for talking. But to see. To see again. To communicate with other people. Why won't anyone give me a voice computer? Because let's face facts—I'm not rich or famous or brilliant.

The bed is specially equipped with a device that allows Yvette to slide me into the wheelchair. So now I'm settled in. Whenever we go out, she gets me dressed—an arduous task. A T-shirt, which corkscrews into my back. And a plaid skirt. She puts on those never-ending sunglasses and ties a scarf around my neck, which confirms for me that it's nippy outside. But I'm dying from the heat. Off we go. Fortunately the house leads out onto a small garden that lies at the same level. It's details like these that spared me from being placed in a special home. That, plus the money my uncle made off the sale of the movie theater, and which he

now manages for me. I remember his visit at the end of
January. He placed his hand on my shoulder, and his voice
became low and serious: "Listen, little one, I've been doing
some thinking. You need money, and you need someone to
take care of you. I've decided to sell the movie theater. I'm
sure Louis would agree. (Louis is my deceased father, who
founded the business.) I know you were very attached to it.
But you can always buy back a movie theater. You can't
buy back your legs. You've got to devote all your strength
to getting well. And that's going to cost a lot. I want you to
have the best care. The best there is. The best wheelchair,
everything. You understand? So that's why I've sold it. To
Jean Bosquet." I was furious. Bosquet! That fat bastard
who drives around in a Jaguar, who made a fortune in
porno during the seventies. He's got the dingiest, oldest
theaters around. What's he going to do with my Trianon?

The wheelchair bumps along on the sidewalk, jolting
me from all these memories. Yvette is talking nonstop,
commenting on everything she sees: that new raincoat on
Mrs. Berger, the teacher, who'd be better off if only she
gave up wearing such long clothing; you might say she
looks just like a barrel. And then there's poor little Sonia's
positively frightful hairstyle—she thinks that manicurist's
certificate of hers has elevated her to the status of starlet.
And so on and so forth.

Then something she says has caught my attention.

"Oh! There's that poor Mrs. Massenet. She's the mother
of that poor little Michael, you remember him, don't you?
Little Michael, the one they found in the woods last Saturday, that little boy with curly blond hair . . . he was always
so polite. . . . Ah, she's so sad! Rings under her eyes. So
brave of her to come out and do her shopping. Personally, I
would have changed supermarkets. Well, here we are. I'll
leave you here. The security guard isn't that far away. I'll
ask him to keep an eye on you. Be back soon."

I can hear her mumbling something as she ambles off,
looking for change for the caddie.

I'm on the lookout. With each approaching footstep, the
muscles in my neck get jittery. Will she come?

Suddenly she's here.

"Hi, lady. You all right?"

Index finger.

"You want me to tell you the rest of my story?"

Double index finger.

"The police found Michael. In the woods. He was dead for a while. I knew they were looking for him, but I couldn't tell them where he was, or else they would have asked me how I knew. You understand?"

Oh, boy, do I understand!

"I knew because I left to go play fishing with him. We don't fish for real, just tie a string around a stick and pretend. His mom didn't want him to go playing by the stream, but he lied and told her he was going to ride his bike. I was sick and tired of fishing, 'cause he told me that he caught all the fish and I couldn't catch anything at all, so I told him I was going home. I went away, but I found this pretty mushroom, and when I looked up again I saw that he met Death from the Woods."

Even at arm's length, I feel like shaking her. Met who, goddamn it!

"And then I knew he was gonna be dead, like all the other kids, because that's how it always is. I wanted to run away, but I stayed, hiding behind a tree. I wanted to see it."

Her little voice is so flutelike as she coldly reels off her litany of horrors.

"Michael said hello, and then I saw his face change. He took a step back, and then another, and another, and then he fell down. He was done for, you know? He tried to get back up, but it was too late. Its hands tightened around his neck, and shook him, and then he went red, then purple, then his tongue stuck out, and he fell down to the ground. His eyes were wide open. I didn't budge. I was hot, you know, and sweating, but I knew I shouldn't move. Then the hands let go of him and . . ."

"Are you still here, you little chatterbox? Can't you leave the lady alone?"

Her father must be very close. A brisk, pungent scent of eau de toilette. I don't feel the sun anymore. He must be standing in front of me. His voice seems close, and suddenly is very quiet: "Listen, it's not that I don't want her to speak with you, but I don't know if it's bothering you. Oh, hello, ma'am. Virginie slipped through my fingers to come here."

"Don't worry about it. Miss Elise always liked children. I don't think that's changed. She was always happy when they came by to see cartoons. You know, at the movies, the Trianon . . ."

"Oh, yeah, I know it. We used to live in Saint Quentin, but we've just moved to Boissy, the Merisiers."

Saint Quentin! That little boy Renaud, whom they were talking about on the news, was killed in Saint Quentin!

"Oh, that's right near us. We're neighbors! Well, that's a coincidence for you! Miss Elise used to be the owner at the Trianon."

Why does she need to tell everyone my life story like that? Now he's going to take me for some desperate old maid who would force-feed Eskimo bars to kids, patting them on the head.

The bags go on my knees. The wheelchair shakes. And the conversation between Yvette and Virginie's father continues. Terrific!

"Your little girl's so cute!"

"You'd think she's an angel, but she's really a little demon. Right, Virginie?"

"Do you have any other children?"

"I . . . uh, well, I . . . I had a son, but, oh, there's my car. I'll let you go. Listen, I'm sorry I can't offer to drop you off, but the wheelchair . . ."

"That's nice of you anyway. Anyhow, it'll do me good to walk a bit," Yvette replies, not insisting, yet full of tact.

"Bye-bye, Elise! See you next Saturday!" Virginie calls out in her clear, crisp voice. "Bye-bye, lady."

"Good-bye, Virginie. I think it will make Elise very happy if you come by to say hello . . . of course, as long as it doesn't bother you, sir . . ."

"Oh, no, not at all! All right, let's get going, Virginie. Mom's waiting. Bye-bye."

The car doors slam shut.

Yvette and I hit the road.

"I don't know what he meant with his son, but it was weird. I guess he didn't want to talk about it. There must have been some tragedy in that family. In any case, the little girl likes you. It's a pleasure to see children with heart. I remember, for example . . ."

Yvette's launching into a long digression on the rotten, sneaky kids she's known throughout her life. I'm no longer listening. Virginie had claimed that her own brother was dead. Her father's attitude would lead me to believe this is true. Already this is a point in the kid's favor. I just need to know if her brother's name was Renaud. But in this case, if Virginie really was present at little Michael's murder, then *she's in danger*. Certainly, the murderer will decide to get rid of her. Unless he didn't see her. How can I know? I can't stand being so powerless. I'm suffocating, suffocating—I feel as if I were wrapped up in a straitjacket, begging some mad doctor to please let me out. But no one will ever let me out. I wish I could scream. Raise my arms. Simply raise these fucking arms.

"Oh, my, look how you're sweating! Wait, I'll take off your scarf."

That's it, take it off, make it into a noose, and hang me from a branch, so at least I'll die standing up, I'm so sick of this! But I mustn't let myself slip into this type of thinking. Got to hang on to what's real. Virginie is real. And she's got problems. Big problems. I've got to know who her father is, what his name is. I've got to intervene. I've got to move!

THE GREAT CATHERINE COMES BY EVERY DAY TO LAV-ish her powerful treatments on me. She's a tall blond . . . Thin, athletic, aerobic, with a ponytail and synthetic shorts. Before the accident I used to see her from time to time at the movie theater with whoever she happened to be dating. She goes out only with big, husky guys with razor cuts who have a hard time walking without rubbing their thighs together. I knew her only by sight, as I never had any need for her services, and never found her to be all that nice. It's hard to admit that I'm in her hands, hog-tied, and that my reeducation depends on this dork whose opinions come to a stop at a red light, and who seems to be forever reciting the latest TV news broadcast.

But in this case she is useful. Very useful. Though incapable of keeping quiet more than five minutes at a stretch. I'm surrounded by big blabbermouths. They're addicted to conversation. Now, isn't that a blessing! In situations like mine you would thank God for inventing concierges. Yet, contrary to what you might think, I have absolutely no desire to withdraw into a noble silence to ponder the relative existence of the cosmos. Personally, I feel like living. I'm alive!

And so the Great Catherine is an inexhaustible font of information. She and Yvette are the "special suburban edition." I'll find out through them who Virginie is.

"Have you seen the news?" the Great Catherine calls out as she pulls on my forearm.

"No. How come?" We had lunch in the garden. It was so nice out.

"Can't be easy making her eat," Catherine murmurs pensively as she kneads my triceps.

Why, yes, my dear girl, but I feed the little cripple anyway. So sorry it offends your profound sensibilities.

"They spoke about little Michael again," she continues. "The same report as last week, the woods, the fisherman who found the body, et cetera, because now they're sure it's some kind of maniac. This would be four he's killed. Four children in about eight years, murdered! All within a radius of thirty miles. And to think he's out there, on the loose!"

"Didn't they pick up anything? Footprints? Tire tracks? Traces of cloth?" Yvette inquires, all ready to lead the investigation.

"Nothing. Not even that! All those poor little babies were strangled."

"And . . . uh . . . sexually assaulted?"

"No, not even that. Just strangled."

"Strange," Yvette mumbles as she putters about the room.

(She has to "dust.") "Generally, there's always some sexual motive when children are murdered."

"Really? Well, anyhow, they didn't say anything about that. The worst thing is that I know at least three of them, the mothers. One works at the post office in La Verrière. The second one's a tobacconist at Leclerc. And the third is Mrs. Massenet, who was one of my patients, like I was telling you."

"What about the others?"

"I don't know those people. They were saying on TV that the father worked for a bank. They didn't want to go on camera."

They're the ones! It's got to be them! If only the Great Catherine could have known them . . . But what would that have changed? She'll never realize I'm not a vegetable. To do that, she'd have to take a look at me. So I imagine I'll have to try to send her a message that's just as complicated. . . .

DR. RAYBAUD HAS COME. DOING VARIOUS TESTS, more drawn out than usual. That's normal—it's raining, and there won't be any rides out on the lake today. He palpated me all over, and I seized the occasion to raise my index finger several times in a row. He called for Yvette and asked her if I did that often. She answered that she knew nothing about it. He told her to pay attention to it. I blinked my eyes and tried to turn my head, but it didn't get the expected result. He thought I was having an attack, and they held me down on the seat until everything was all right. Raybaud's conclusion: it would seem that I've recovered some traces of movement. He's going to speak to Professor Combré about this. "But don't get your hopes up," he made it clear. Perhaps these are only reflex reactions, mechanical jolts, "contractions," as they say.

It's eight months now since the train of my life is rolling through this lightless tunnel. If only . . . No, mustn't get my hopes up.

"Miss Elise! Yoo-hoo! It's me!"

Don't worry, Yvette, I haven't gone anywhere. I'm still sitting in this wheelchair like a package waiting to be opened.

"You'll never guess who I just met! Right in front of the post office. Virginie and her parents! It's too bad you haven't got the movie theater anymore. We could've given them some free passes. They're showing *Jungle Book* this week."

The elephant patrol is marching all over my heart.

"I showed them the house, since we were nearby. . . . Her name's Hélène. Very pretty woman—thin, dark brown hair, with big blue eyes. Her skin's so white. His name's Paul. Paul and Hélène Fansten."

It's them! Virginie was telling the truth—her brother was murdered.

"He's so elegant, with a handsome face, à la Paul Newman. Really nice," Yvette goes on. "So manly. The same kind of guy as . . . well, hmm . . ."

I know. You meant to say the same kind of guy as Benoît. Is that possible? Benoît was one of a kind. And, what's more, he looked like Robert Redford, so . . .

"We got to talking a bit, and I asked them to come over one night for an aperitif. After all, we're neighbors! And you know what? They accepted! They'll be coming over Wednesday night with their little girl."

Well, hip hip hooray for Yvette! What she must have done to make them feel sorry for me to succeed at getting them to come over!

"And I was right about her son." Yvette lowers her voice, as if we were in church: "He died two years ago. He was one of the unfortunate who were strangled, did you realize that?! Virginie's mother told me they didn't like to talk about it, so I didn't insist, you know me . . . To lose a child is always difficult, but to know that he was murdered . . ."

Obviously, details like these are not the kind one would feel like speaking of at length. Renaud Fansten. I traveled a lot in '93. I was a judge at several film festivals, and then, I no longer remember why, but it was a time when there was quite a bit of friction between Benoît and me. No doubt, that's why I paid no attention to that murder. Hélène and Paul Fansten. Paul. It's a name that goes well with his voice. A man who's sure of himself. Are his eyes light or dark? Does he have brown hair? I imagine him with brown hair. And Virginie's blond, with long doll-like hair. Will handsome Paul and his little girl be coming to visit? I doubt it.

I WAITED FEVERISHLY FOR WEDNESDAY TO COME. I had the impression that time no longer moved forward. Once again, I found myself in a state of anxiety that reminded me of my first few dates with Benoît.

And so here we are. I feel as if I were sitting on a battery. It's ridiculous.

Yvette's been making herself busy all morning. If I know her, she must have prepared a lunch worthy of Buckingham Palace. She washed, dressed, and coiffed me (agony!) as if I were a schoolgirl getting ready for graduation day. I'm all prim and proper, dressed in a cotton summer dress (please let it not be one of hers), and set up in the living room, next to the open door. I figure I'm still brunette, thin, and petite, but I must have hollow cheeks, which lengthens the nose, and certainly I must be as white as an aspirin. What about that stupid hair growing beneath my chin? "Absolutely invisible," Benoît used to say. No way! It must be on my knees by now. They won't be disappointed to have made a trip to see some skeleton in a gingham dress with a giant hair coming out of her chin.

Yvette's rushing around. I swallow my saliva. I'd love to be able to look in a mirror to see how I look. Rapid footsteps, then slower ones, and a dash toward me.

A crisp little voice says, "Hello, Elise."

I raise my index finger. Virginie places her hand over mine. Hers is warm. Someone else is entering the room.

"Hello."

The deep voice. It's him. Paul.

"Hello."

A calm, gentle voice. It must be Hélène.

"Oh, please, sit down," says Yvette, over the creaking of the rolling table.

The leather sofa sighs. They must be sitting down. I imagine they're discreetly looking over the entire room: the club chairs, Grandma's cherrywood sideboard, the buffet with the stereo, the TV stand, the low wooden table, the shelves lined with books, and the rolltop desk where I used to keep all my papers. . . . I hear Virginie's little footsteps as she walks around the room.

"Virginie, don't touch anything!"

"No, Mommy, I'm just looking. She's got the whole Bécassine collection."

I have them from my father. I had kept them, thinking someday I would read them to the child I would have with Benoît. But we didn't have the time.

"Can I read one?"

"Of course, my pet. Here, why don't you sit down there?"

Yvette settles her into the big armchair next to me.

"It seems so huge, doesn't it?" Hélène calls out.

"Oh, yes. Come, I'll show you around."

They've all gone off, chattering. Virginie jumps out of her seat just as soon and comes over. In my ear, she whispers, "At school, my teacher yelled at me because I didn't know the lesson. But I can't learn anything, 'cause I'm scared. It's dumb, I know, because only boys are dying, but you never know. What if Death were to change its mind? Did you ever see the movie *The Meaning of Life*? My dad rented the video. All of a sudden, Death shows up at some people's house who ate some poisoned pâté to convince them that they're gonna die."

She must be talking about that Monty Python film. Boy, did I see it! It was one of our favorite films—I screened it at least ten times. She's leaning even closer, I can feel her warm breath.

"I'm scared of Death. Its face is horrible. I wish so much I could live in Disneyland, in Sleeping Beauty's castle."

Even if I knew how to respond, I could not. Yvette and the others are returning; their footsteps are resounding on the varnished parquet floor. They're talking about the weather, the high cost of living, and houses. Nothing terribly gripping. Virginie isn't saying anything. I suppose she's reading Bécassine, because I hear the pages turning regularly. Hearing her peaceful reading right after she's told me such abominable things, and while the others stand around chatting, gives me an odd feeling of unreality. In fact, I'm having a hard time accepting that what she's told me is *true*.

Paul's warm voice comes as an abrupt surprise: "We're not disturbing you, are we?"

"No, no, I'm certain she's happy. Miss Elise has always loved having company," Yvette answers for me.

Paul sighs as though something were suddenly making him sad. Might I be a romantic figure? Will he think about me at night, lying in bed, when the moon eats up the sky with its whiteness? Anyway, I'm almost certain I'll be thinking of him, or of the picture I've made of him: he's a slender man, with very short brown hair, a thin frame, long legs, and a resolute face, with big light-colored eyes. . . . Is it perhaps because his voice is reassuring, giving me confidence again? I feel so alone. Hélène, too, seems nice. I would certainly have been pleased to meet them before . . .

Hélène, Paul, and Yvette are buoyantly discussing politics in the new town.

Virginie is getting up so that she can put down her book. She's right beside me again; the heat of her small body is giving off the scent of bubble bath.

"I don't think Death really likes its work. But, you see, it's forced to do it," she whispers in my ear. "All of a sudden it gets the urge, just like that, and *psshht!* it needs another child. There's this policeman, the captain, he's called, and he's questioned me several times. I think he's got a clown head. I call him Bonzo. He's got this big yellow mustache, with straw on his head. He wants me to tell him what I know, but I can't. I can't tell, not anyone, except you, because it's not the same."

It's true I'm as silent as a tomb. So the police are interested in Virginie. As they would be in any kid from the neighborhood likely to have seen something, no doubt.

"Renaud didn't know; he wasn't careful about Death from the Woods, so Death got him. I told him not to play in the cabin. Because I saw Death circling him, smiling at him. But he didn't listen to me. Are you listening?"

I raise my index finger. I'm a bit dumbfounded from it all.

"Virginie, what are you doing?"

Hélène's voice, sounding nervous.

"I'm talking things over with Elise."

Nervous coughing.

"Don't you want some tea? Or some hot chocolate, sweetheart?"

"No, thank you, ma'am."

"Virginie, I want you here in two seconds, please."

It's Paul.

Virginie wearily sighs, "Can't they ever leave me alone?"

I smile. Or at least I feel as if I'm smiling. I don't know what expression my face is making.

"Is something the matter, Miss Elise?" Yvette inquires.

Well, okay, it wasn't exactly a smile.

"We'll have to be going," Hélène explains. "Some friends have invited us over to dinner. Ready, Virginie?"

"You really must come back and see us again. You know"—Yvette's lowering her voice—"I'm getting the impression she's doing a lot better since she's met you and your daughter. She's so alone. . . . We'd be very happy to have you back."

"Well, we'll see what we can do. You see . . . if my husband . . . he has quite a few obligations, don't you, Paul? Anyway, we'd like to thank you. It's been very nice. Are you going to say good-bye, Virj?"

"Good-bye, ma'am."

Then she rushes over to me.

"Bye-bye, Elise. I like your house a lot. And I think you're very nice."

She gives me a big kiss on my cheek. I swallow my saliva.

"Do you think I'm nice?"

I raise my index finger.

Whispers, and then Yvette's heavy footsteps.

"Miss Elise?"

Index finger.

She leans close and speaks very loudly, articulating everything: "Do you hear me? If you hear me, raise your index finger twice."

I raise my index finger twice.

"My God! It's true! She can hear us! The doctor thought she could! I knew it, I really did, that she could understand everything!"

"Extraordinary," Hélène murmurs.

I'd love to leap from my wheelchair and join in all this general rejoicing.

"What is it?" Virginie asks.

"Miss Elise can hear. She can hear us and understand us!"

"Well, yeah. If she couldn't, how do you think I could be talking things over with her?"

"Listen, Yvette, we've really got to be going, and, well . . . what I mean to say is, we're very happy for you two. . . ."

Hélène is still speaking. Paul must be very shy.

There's a din in the vestibule, then the door shuts. Yvette is already on the phone. She hangs up and triumphantly says, "The doctor will be coming by this evening."

I'm not unhappy that I've spoiled her party this way.

RAYBAUD CAME BY. HE SHORTLY GOT YVETTE UNDER control. The fact that I seem to hear and understand does not mean that (1) I'm 100 percent the same mentally as I was before; (2) that I'll regain movement. It's been seen, or so it seems, that people have gone for thirty years without moving an ear or a toe. Always encouraging, that Raybaud.

Basically, as far as my neurons are concerned, his advice is that I take a new battery of tests.

And, *whoosh!* Bye-bye, he has a dinner to get to, friends, impossible to be late—this guy's a real breeze. I don't even know what sort of head he has. I imagine him as some sort of hairy bodybuilder in waterproof coveralls with a stethoscope slung over his shoulder.

Yvette uncorked a quart of champagne, has me taste a drop, and knocks back the rest as she calls my uncle in southern France with the good news.

I spent a restless night. Well . . . so to speak. I couldn't think about anything besides what Virginie told me. And Paul and Hélène as well. They must think I'm repulsive. I can't understand why Virginie refuses to turn in the culprit. Because I'm convinced she's not lying—she knows who it is. But she's protecting him. It's incredible!

THREE

MY LIFE HAS CHANGED. I CAN'T SPEAK OF MIRACLES, but still it's fantastic. Professor Combré hinted right away that perhaps my paralysis stemmed more from a state of shock than from any real effects on my motor centers, as the nerve fibers in the spinal marrow were not severed. Without wishing to give me any false hope, he said he thinks chances are good that one day I'll recover some movement. Efforts toward my rehabilitation have intensified. Sometimes it feels as though I'm vibrating like an airplane about to take off.

Then Hélène came back several times, with Virginie. I get the impression that she feels very alone. Often she complains how Paul works too much. He has a high-power position at the bank with impossible schedules. She's bored. She sits down next to me in the living room and speaks to me in a low voice, about the weather, fruits, flowers, the color of the sky, and the approach of clouds. I feel I've found a friend. Virginie, on the other hand, is hanging around with Yvette in the kitchen. She seems to be avoiding me, and no longer talks to me about anything.

My diagnosis is that what we have here is a fine case of jealousy.

I don't know how to make Hélène understand that Virginie may be in danger. Of course, on an afternoon as sweet as this, sitting in this lovely sunshine, all these murder stories seem so far away. Perhaps Virginie is just a very imaginative little girl.

In any case, when Hélène is around, time seems to go much faster. Today I'm alone. I imagine I'm by the pool, getting a suntan. But it's hard to concentrate because there was an assassination attempt in Paris. I wished Yvette would lower the sound—I could hear frantic accounts and ambulance sirens, and thought of the splattered blood, the terror, the incomprehension. I thought about myself. My panic. I thought about Benoît, and how his life was so brutally cut short. With every news item like this, I'm plunged back into the past, especially when I'm trying to avoid it at all cost. I'm starting to understand people who refuse to listen to any bad news.

The doorbell rings.

Surprise! It's the famous police captain Virginie told me about. Yvette lets him in. I don't know what he's up to, I can't hear anything. No doubt he's looking at me.

"Miss Andrioli? I'm Captain Yssart, from the murder squad."

Ah, so Bonzo's name is Yssart. His voice is cold, with a touch of affectation. No trace of any identifiable accent.

"She can't respond, I told you so," Yvette informs him.

Ignoring the interruption, the captain goes on, "I didn't know you were ill. Please excuse my showing up so unexpected."

For a clown-face, he is positively well spoken.

Yvette, who must be stamping her feet by his side, can't help calling out, "The captain's here because of that investigation of the murder of Michael Massenet. I told him we didn't know him."

"Please be assured, madam, that if Miss Andrioli can hear us, of which I'm certain, then she can make out the sound of my voice as well as yours. If it would be all right with you, I'd like a moment alone with her."

"As you wish," Yvette replies, leaving the room and slamming the door behind her.

Coughing. I'm waiting. This guy may be my only chance for getting any help for Virginie.

"As you must certainly know, we're currently investigating the murder of Michael Massenet, as well as other, older murders; to this day, whoever's behind them has not been identified. Do you have any way of expressing yourself?"

Now, here's an efficient fellow! I raise my index finger.

"Okay. I'm going to give you their names. If you know one of them, raise your finger."

He recites the kids' names. When he gets to Renaud Fansten, I raise my finger.

"You knew the Fansten boy?"

I don't move. He coughs again.

"I see. We're having a slight problem communicating. Do you mean that you heard about the Fansten boy?"

I raise my finger.

"On television?"

I don't move.

"From someone who was close to him?"

I raise my finger.

"His mother, perhaps?"

I don't move.

"His father?"

I don't move. This is getting a bit tedious.

"Virginie?"

I raise my finger.

"Do you know Virginie Fansten?"

Here we are! You dirty hypocrite! You know very well that I know her, and you're more interested in her than you are in me. Which is fortunate, anyway.

"Listen, Miss Andrioli, I'm not going to waste your time with any roundabout verbal twists. I'm going to ask you flat out: Did Virginie give you the impression that she knew something about this matter?"

I'm about to raise my index finger when a thought holds

me back. Do I have the right to betray Virginie's secret?
But what if her life is in jeopardy? I resolve to raise my index finger.

"Did she tell you she knew who was behind these
crimes?"

I raise my index finger.

"Did she give you his name?"

No index finger.

"Did she give you the impression that she was in some
way mentally unbalanced?"

Suddenly I understand with amazement what he's getting at. He thinks Virginie's crazy. No index finger.

"Listen to me. She's a charming little girl who was seriously traumatized when she discovered her half brother
murdered.

Her half brother? I didn't know that.

"When Hélène Siccardi married Paul Fansten, little Renaud was only two years old. Paul Fansten's first wife died
in 1986, from cancer. The new Mrs. Fansten was always a
perfect mother to Renaud, just as she is to Virginie, but the
child is secretive, and the school director finds her abnor-
mally withdrawn. With me, she clams up, and I can't drag
a word out of her. That's why I'm visiting you now. It
seems to me that if this child has some secret to confide,
perhaps she would find it easier to turn to you. Has she provided you with any clue as to the possible identity of whoever might be behind these murders?"

No index finger.

"Has she claimed to have been present at one or more of
these?"

And what if they declared her insane? Will they take her
away from her parents? Put her with social services? What
if Virginie winds up in a foster home because of me? Shit,
I don't know what to do. No index finger.

"Think hard. No doubt you're the only person who's
able to help Virginie, and to help us."

Now, that one's the best! If they're counting on me, then
they're not out of the woods! I'm not moving a muscle.

"Very well. Thank you for your cooperation. If you'll

permit me, I'll be on my way. An additional visit to little Virginie would seem in order. I'll see you soon, miss. I wish you a swift recovery. . . ."

The door slams shut. Cretin! I'm not suffering from the flu! A swift recovery! Go recover yourself! Should I have told him more? Why was I silent? I'm stupid. And now it's too late.

THE HEAT IS STIFLING. TRULY THIS IS JULY. I'M SETTLED into my silastic gel cushion, beneath the bower, in the shade. Yvette put my hair into a ponytail—I loathe them—but she didn't ask my opinion. I've got the impression that I've become terribly thin. With my brown hair pulled back, my pallid face, and tired features, I must look more like a vampire than a top model.

Anyway, it doesn't seem to bother Paul. He came by to see me three or four times to bring fruit, a cake Hélène had made, and to drop off Virginie, whom Yvette had promised to take to the movies. . . . And yesterday he rested his hand on my shoulder and murmured, "I know what I'm about to say may seem cruel, but sometimes I envy your solitude; sometimes I, too, would like to be shut off from the world." Perfect! Super! Let's trade places! Unfortunately, nothing of the kind has happened. I remain nailed to my wheelchair, and he's standing, and before leaving he gave my shoulder a tight squeeze.

I'm thinking back to that as I sit and sweat beneath the bower. Yvette's busy making a cold fruit soup. We've been invited to a shish-kebab party, and she doesn't want to show up empty-handed.

Yes, that's how it is—I'm no longer banished from society; Hélène and Paul have introduced me to their friends—young couples from the housing development-swimming pool-tennis crowd—and everyone has adopted me. I'm the new mascot of the Boissy-les-Colombes new urban zone. I don't know why all these people are being so nice to me. Perhaps it makes them feel good and charitable to be tolerating me? The fact that I don't repulse them no doubt counts for a lot. I don't dribble, twist around in my seat, or roll my eyes. I'm rather like a Sleeping Beauty, dozing in her throne. Anyway, that's what I tell myself. Still, I have to be dragged everywhere, but people often speak to me. These minor sentences they just toss out, but which translate into more intimate concerns. I've learned to recognize their voices, identify them, and make mental representations of them—portraits.

Some of the Fanstens' closest acquaintances are Jean-Mi and Claude Mondini; he's an engineer and she's in charge of Catholic Aid. From her voice, I imagine her as a dynamic young woman, a little bit in a rut, who must be returning to her jogging. Jean-Mi has the enthusiastic tone of a guy who wants to come off as simple and nice. He has a beautiful voice, and sings in the choir. They have three well-raised children, two boys and a girl. Betty and Manu Quinson are very trendy: they're into all the heavy metal bands, use all the hip slang, take off weeks for seawater therapy and snowboarding, and follow a macrobiotic diet. Manu's an executive for Air France and Betty owns an upscale thrift shop in Versailles. It seems that Manu's a chubby little guy with a beard. I see Betty with a cat face, a curly mop of hair, and wide, flowing dresses. And, of course, there's Steph and Sophie Migoin. They're very friendly with the Fanstens. Stéphane's a businessman, and Sophie doesn't work. According to Hélène, their villa is one of the most luxurious in the whole neighborhood. Stéphane's deep voice is very impressive, and his booming laughter gives me quite a start. He's always knocking things over—a bottle of wine, glasses, plates. . . . He's the quintessential brute, the type of guy to whom you would say, "Steph, that's my foot you're standing on" or "Steph, would you mind playing commandos with the kids somewhere else besides under the table?" Sophie is more discreet. She has a pretentious voice, and I've given her an affected look—imitation Chanel suits and an angular face, impeccably made up. Even though I can't participate in their conversations, I'm not bored. I'm busy giving faces to these voices. With each new party, I change their eyes, their noses, their hair, as if drawing composite sketches.

For the past two weeks, Virginie has been at summer camp. She's due to return today. Hélène told me that Captain Yssart came by to question Virginie, but she was already on the bus for Auvergne. He said he'd see her when she got back. One would think it's not all that important. I don't know what to think anymore. All everyone else is thinking about is taking advantage of the summer and having a good time, despite all these events.

I think I'm also having a good time. After all these months of feeling so pessimistic, it finally feels like I'm alive again. I listen to everyone else talking and laughing, and in a small way it seems as if I were doing the same. Everyone's being very nice to "Rag Doll" Andrioli. Hélène told me that Sophie Migoin has been very jealous of me ever since her husband, Steph, declared to no one in particular that I was "the most stunning girl in this shithole of a town." Surely he was drunk, but I was glad to hear it all the same.

"You'll see! When you're cured, you'll be a big hit!" Hélène whispered to me the other day. Cured. Cured! I'm not sick, I'm out of service, and I haven't begun to see even the shadow of whatever improvements there may be. Index, index, and index again. A future filled with index fingers raised as far as the eye can see; I've had my fill. No negative thoughts, let's concentrate on the evening ahead.

A stream of sweat drips from my temples. Yvette is in the kitchen. I can't wipe it off; very unpleasant. If only she could come out for just a minute.

Ahh! Footsteps! Finally! I'm starting to suffocate out here.

But what the hell is she up to? You'd almost think she was creeping up softly.

The telephone rings, piercingly.

"Yes, hello? Yes, around seven o'clock, yes . . ."

Yvette has just answered the phone. Yvette . . . if Yvette has just picked up, then who's walking through the alleyway now?

Hélène? Paul? Is someone trying to surprise me?

Someone's tickling my neck with a leaf.

I absolutely hate games like these. I can feel someone's body heat next to me. An odor of sweat I don't recognize. Yvette's chatting away on the phone. I'm extremely agitated. I hate these little tricks, especially in my situation. It doesn't amuse me—it makes me nervous.

Something is touching my arm, something fine and pointy. Like a rod or . . . a needle?

What kind of bullshit is this?

Whatever it is, it's drawing something on my arm. It's . . . yes it's a letter. A *B*. It's a *B*. There's a pause, then another letter. An *I*. Yes, I'm sure it's an *I*. And now a *T*. *BIT* . . . Bitter? A *C* . . . *BITC* . . . oh, what's going on? Yvette! Yvette! I hear breathing. A whistling breath. I hate this! I hate this asshole game! And there it is, the *H*—my, how we're all laughing!

Ouch! He pricked me! The bastard pricked me! I felt the needle sink a good quarter inch into my flesh! I'm scared. I don't understand what's going on. I'm scared. Is he going to start all over? Oh, no! He's guiding the needle along my arm, my cheek . . . no, no! Aarrrgh!

He pricked my shoulder. That hurts! I don't want to do this. Stop it, you bastard. If I know who you are, I'd . . .

He's caressing my chest with his needle. Oh, my God, no! No, not the tip of my breast! Please! He stops, takes his time . . . I'd like to scream. He's bringing the needle down my dress and pressing it against my stomach, brushing my belly . . . he's sick! I'm falling victim to some maniac! Aarrrgh!

He's driven it into my thigh! Oh, it hurts, it hurts! Now he's pressing it against my genitals . . . no, please, no . . .

"We'll have to be leaving soon! They're expecting us around seven!"

Yvette! Yvette! Hurry!

No more odor of sweat, no more heat, only muffled footsteps as they fade in the distance. Yvette approaches humming "Madrid, Madrid." On the inside I'm crying tears of rage and terror. Yvette is right next to me.

"My God, have you been sweating! And red all over from it!"

She swipes at my face with her handkerchief. I'll never know if there were any tears.

"My, it's so hot today! Goodness! You've been bitten by mosquitoes!"

She pushes me toward the house. My heart is still beating a hundred miles an hour. I can feel the pinpricks slyly burning. It's not the pain, however, that's making my heart beat. It's the feeling of being abandoned, hands and feet bound, to the will, the caprice, of a stranger.

I just can't believe that someone would be so cruel as to get his kicks this way with a disabled person.

YVETTE'S GRUMBLING SOMETHING WHILE SHE changes my dress. She was also hot. She washed my body down with a damp washcloth, applied lotion on my "mosquito bites," went to change, and finally we were ready.

I felt very upset. It seemed as though I'd just had a nightmare. Was someone really there, right next to me, writing *BITCH* on my skin, getting off on frightening me?

Yvette pushed me outside and closed the door. We were on our way.

"Is everything okay?"

No index finger.

"I know what you mean. I'm also hot. It'll be better once we get there."

It's not the heat. But how am I to explain that to her? How can I be heard?

THE PARTY IS IN FULL SWING. THE SUN HAS GONE down and it's cooled off. Hélène told me they set up two big tables in the backyard, and that Paul is in charge of the barbecue.

I hear laughter blending, glasses clinking, and knives clanking on the plates. Hélène has placed me in a corner so that I'd have some peace. There must be twenty people here, and everyone seems to be having a good time. Betty, in a high-pitched voice, is telling me about the last time she and Manu went out on their catamaran in force-eight winds. Claude Mondini's explaining to someone or other how her new catechism class is a smashing success. And to say I was looking forward to this evening! All my enthusiasm is gone, and I can't stop wondering who among all these people would find it funny to prick a disabled woman with a needle. Kids are shouting and running about in every which way. Suddenly I remember that Virginie must be here!

This thought, far from reassuring me, makes my blood run cold. It could only mean more questions with no answers. And tonight, I really don't need that.

Right now I can hear her cold little voice: "Good evening, Elise. Are you all right?"

I raise my index finger but it's a lie. I'm not all right.

"I got to ride a pony in camp! It was terrific! I wish I could have stayed there all summer, but they didn't want me to. It's better there. It's calm."

I can hear Paul's voice: "Virginie, your cutlets are gonna get cold!"

"Coming!"

She leans closer and whispers "Be careful!" before disappearing.

I'm all alone. I'm not hungry. But I'm sorry I ever knew Virginie.

I feel a hand on my arm and jump—on the inside—thirty feet.

"Everything okay, Lise?"

It's Paul.

I don't raise my index finger. If anyone else asks me if I'm all right, I'm going to vomit.

"Too many people?"

No index finger. Still, this is much better than playing "Am I getting warm? Warmer? Hot?" That could take hours.

"Are you upset?"

Bull's-eye. I raise my index finger.

"Do you want to go home?"

No index finger. I especially don't want to go home.

"So, Paul, you're gonna show us those pictures?" Steph calls out from nearby, in his booming voice.

From Steph's eminently virile tone, I imagine a rugby player, endowed with a long blond mane, very blue eyes, and a big, fleshy mouth. Paul stands up again and lifts his hand from my arm, leaving a warm trace.

"See you later, Lise."

Paul has baptized me "Lise." He doesn't like my name. He claims that when he says "Elise," he always gets the feeling someone will start playing piano. Well, I don't like "Lise." It feels as if I were a hundred years old, wearing a little girl's cape from before the war.

Why did Virginie tell me to be careful? Her warning came at just the right time, that much is true. The music is deafening, some new band I'm unfamiliar with. People are screaming to be heard over the din. Ahh! They changed the disc. Bossa nova, much cooler.

"You know, Lise, Paul looked like he was trying to pick you up, but in fact he's very faithful."

It took my breath away. Who said that? Was it that pest Sophie? I didn't recognize her voice. As if . . . me and Paul . . . or Paul and me . . . in my condition? It seems to me, the only ones likely to have any interest in me are those stretcher-bearer types running around in Lourdes.

I'm starting to feel tired. They gave me avocado purée and Kiri. Yvette gave me some champagne to drink. She's radiant with joy, for her fruit soup was a smashing success. I can feel the chef gently rocking me. I don't get out much anymore, and sometimes Raybaud's medications plunge me into an irresistible slumber.

What time is it? My eyelids are so heavy. Everyone is drunk. Steph is singing bawdy songs at the top of his lungs. People are taking their leave, and I can hear car doors slamming. Yvette is chatting with Paul's mom, a retired postal worker in her sixties, who's vacationing with them for a few days. They're discussing tarot with great determination, oblivious to the din, and their somewhat high-pitched voices indicate they're a bit tipsy.

"Bye-bye, Lise!"

"See you soon!"

They wish me good night and casually pat me on the shoulder. But what do they really think of my silent, unmoving presence? I yawn, lifting my jaw, or at least that's how it feels.

"Mom! Yvette! Can you come help us put the tables away?"

"Coming!"

They go to work, still chattering and chuckling like schoolgirls. It must be very late. I'm really falling asleep.

I AWAKEN WITH A START. WHERE AM I? IN THE dark, of course, but where? There's no noise. I'm lying down, but this isn't my bed. It's made of leather. Is it a sofa? Maybe. There's an appliance making sputtering sounds. A refrigerator? Did we stay over at the Fanstens'? It's unbearable to be unable to open my eyes and look around. Be calm, Elise, be calm, relax, take a deep breath. I must be at Paul and Hélène's place. Perhaps Yvette was too tired to take us home.

Footsteps. I hear footsteps. The light touch of bare feet. No, not again, I—

"Elise! Are you sleeping?"

It's Virginie. What a relief. Like a machine, I raise my index finger.

"You're lying! If you were sleeping, how could you hear me?"

No index finger. I'm waiting.

"Yvette twisted her ankle when she went to the bathroom, so Daddy said you've got to stay here tonight, because she hurt herself badly. She was all swollen. Daddy put ice cubes in a bag and told her to lie back with ice around her ankle in Gramma's room, and we put you on the couch in the living room. You were sleeping like a baby. I just woke up, and thought you might have woken up all alone in the dark, so I came to see you. It happens to me all the time, waking up all alone in the dark, so I know how it can make you afraid."

Good little girl. So it looks like Yvette's busted her ankle. I hope it's not serious, because if it is . . . I can't see being with a new nurse, a stranger. Obviously, it would have to happen now. Virginie lowers her voice again, her barely audible words merely a breath in my ear: "You know what? I think Death from the Woods is gonna do it again. Death can't stay out of work for long. I think Death's jealous because I'm talking to you. It wants my undivided attention. But I like you. Every day I pray Death won't touch you. I even left a little note with a lot of kids' names on it so there'll be something else to think about."

I feel frozen over. I *am* frozen over. From head to toe. My thoughts are swirling about, at a hundred miles per hour. Either this child is completely bonkers or there's some dangerous madman on the loose in the area. Ladies and gentlemen, following Robin Hood, who stole from the rich to fill the pockets of the poor, I give you Death from the Woods, who spirits away the living to fill Heaven. I'm swimming in pure excitement! Not to mention feeling frozen. Virginie couldn't have invented the date and location of the crime involving little Michael and . . .

"I've got to get back, or else it could get dangerous!"

Hey! Hey, wait! I hear her rapid little footsteps on the stairs. Dangerous? Why "dangerous"? Is someone observing us? Have they at least remembered to lock the door? Virginie, don't leave me all alone! Come back! Come back! It's scary how I can scream in silence, even though I never was such a noisy person.

I'm listening. The refrigerator is humming. A clock is counting off ticktocks. It's windy outside; I can hear the noises of leaves rustling and papers flying. And my heart beating. No. If someone were here, Virginie would not have left me alone.

What's certain is that this child has a serious problem. One might even think that, to a certain degree, she has taken the murderer's side.

I'm an idiot. If Virginie knew the date and location of Michael's death, then it's simply because she came across the cadaver. That, plus the murder of her brother . . . she tuned out and invented the rest, Death from the Woods, et cetera.

Then who got his kicks pricking me with a needle?

I don't want to think about that. I . . .

Someone's here.

Above me.

Someone's breathing.

My stomach hurts. I've got a horrible feeling I might pee all over myself. Someone's touching me. A hand—a hand is touching me. Brushing my neck, shoulders, and the top of my chest. Not brutally, no, but rather gently. It's a large hand, a man's hand. Opening the buttons on my dress. Am I dreaming? What could this mean? What, ohh . . .

He's caressing me. I can feel his hands going up and down over my chest. Is this the same guy who got off on torturing me this afternoon? I don't know. This one's sweet. His breathing is fast and heavy. Am I about to be raped by a stranger on this goddamn sofa? What if it's Paul?

Paul's hand? I don't know. In spite of myself, I'm troubled by his caresses. I want him to stop. That's enough, I'm not a doll.

He's become very indecent.

It's nice, but I don't want it. I raise my index finger. A hand closes around mine and gives it a squeeze. A mouth comes crashing down over mine. Crashing down over my breasts. His hand is still gripping mine. My heart is beating so hard it might break. A pervert armed with needles and a mute rapist—it's all a bit much for one day. The man is heavy; I can feel the rough contact of his jeans against my bare thighs; is he going to . . . ?

Suddenly he gets back up. He's panting. He hastily rebuttons my dress and goes away as silently as he came.

Well, that's all for the sex episode.

I'm swimming in pure excitement. My body's on fire. Thank you, Mr. Stranger, for reminding me that I'm still a woman, but it's rather painful to know you've been sentenced to solitary confinement.

Paul? Is it possible?

Who'd have ever thought a vegetable's life could be so thrilling?

STARTLED AWAKE FROM THE SOUND OF A CARTOON show. Bambi's arguing with Panpan. Suddenly, from up close, Hélène's calm voice resounds, "Elise, are you up?"

Index finger.

"Do you want any orange juice?"

Index finger.

She's gone. I can hear Virginie as she breaks out laughing in front of the TV screen. Then Yvette's and Gramma's voices, probably coming from the kitchen. Yvette, no doubt speaking to Hélène, asks, "Is she up?"

"Yes. She wants orange juice. . . . No, that's okay, I'll get if for her. What does she usually have in the morning?"

"Oatmeal."

Uncomfortable silence.

"Ahh! Well, uh . . . I have cornflakes. I'll break some up in milk. That should work, shouldn't it?"

"That's all right. I'm really embarrassed to put upon you this way . . . if only I hadn't tripped on that step . . . I'm really just an old fool. . . . Luckily, it turned out better this way, because I don't know what I would have done with Miss Elise . . . could you imagine if I had to go to the hospital? . . ."

"Don't worry. Everything will be all right."

Hélène comes back. I feel a cool glass making contact with my lips. I swallow. The orange juice is good and cold.

"You must be wondering what's going on! Yvette twisted her ankle last night, just as she was leaving, and since you were asleep, we thought the simplest thing would be to have you stay over. I hope you weren't completely lost. . . ."

No, not at all, everything's perfect in the powerful emotion department. What's next on the program?

"The swelling on her ankle's gone down. I think everything'll be okay. We're gonna take you home, and if there's the slightest problem, Yvette will call us so that Mother can come by and give her a hand."

I can't even thank her.

"These are cornflakes, I hope you'll like them."

A spoonful of soggy, sugary cornflakes. I hate cereal. Why hasn't Yvette ever thought of yogurt? I love yogurt in the morning. Conscientiously, I swallow the cornflakes.

Someone's running past.

"Where are you going, Virginie?"

"Out to the backyard! Hi, Elise!"

"Don't go too far, you hear me?"

"No, no!"

The door slams shut. Why isn't Paul around? As if hearing my question, Hélène continues, "Paul went jogging with Steph."

Good old Paul. He's got to stay in shape so that he can assault all the quadriplegics in the neighborhood.

What if it wasn't him?

Hélène suddenly realizes that I must feel like going to the toilet. Whispering between women. Yvette finally suggests that she use a plastic basin, which she does. Everyone pretends to think it's normal, but for me it's routine. It was hard at first at the hospital, but you get used to it. Once the bladder operation is over, Hélène runs a washcloth over my face and fixes my hair.

The door opens and Steph's deep voice rings out, "Good morning, good ladies! So, how's that ankle of yours? Better? You shouldn't drink so much when you can't hold the road!"

Then he bursts out in a manly laugh. Indignantly Yvette protests, "But I hardly had anything to drink. My ankle just slipped!"

Yada, yada, yada . . . I'm stuck on the sofa, doing my sack-of-potatoes imitation, listening to this avalanche of witticisms. Finally, it's decided that Paul will give Yvette a lift back to the house so as not to put any undue strain on her ankle, while Steph will lead me back on foot. Could it be that Paul is avoiding me?

Two pairs of men's hands lift me up and set me down in

my wheelchair. I try to make out which hands are touching me, but it's impossible.

It's hot outside, and the air is heavy and unmoving. Steph is pushing my wheelchair, whistling *La Mer.* I don't feel the sun on my skin, so it must be overcast. A strong smell of grass. A bird frantically trills at the top of its lungs. Steph stops whistling.

"It's weird to think you've never seen me."

What I find weird is this friendship that ties one as delicate as Paul with this big brute.

"How do you picture me? For example, do you see me as kind of puny or big?"

Stupid question. How am I supposed to answer? He realizes that.

"Okay. Let's say . . . big?"

Index finger. I'm not going to let you down, old chum.

"You win! I'm ninety kilos, at one-point-eight meters."

What is this, he's going to detail his measurements for me?

"Virginie likes you a lot."

This guy sure knows how to change the subject, 180 degrees.

"She was very disturbed by her brother's death. Or should I say her half brother. And then there's these other kids who got murdered. . . . I don't understand why Paul didn't ask to be transferred. It must be terrible for Hélène. They moved, of course, but only ten miles away. . . . I find you ravishing.

Three hundred sixty degrees.

"The thought of meeting you had me really uptight—handicapped people make me uneasy. But then, I dunno . . . we're hitting it off, aren't we?"

Speak for yourself!

"To the point where Sophie made a scene, could you imagine? Maybe you've awakened that old fantasy about the Sioux coming up on a white woman who's fainted."

So here I am, being carted around in the foothills of the Sierra Nevada by King Kong here in a jogging suit!

"I'm very jealous of Paul. I can't stand it that he touches you."

He's a madman. Another madman. In the time it takes to cook a microwave pizza, the thought crosses my mind that it could be . . . the needle . . . could it be him? The wheelchair comes to a sudden stop, tearing me away from my calculations. Behind me, I hear a dull thud, as if something were falling. What the hell is he up to?

Silence. A bird nearby whistles gleefully as it flies off. Steph? Something wet has fallen on my forearm. I can feel my skin crawling. Another drop. It's giving me goose bumps. In the distance is the sound of thunder. I take a deep breath; it's only a storm. But what about Steph? Did he go take a piss in a copse of trees? Why didn't he say anything? More and more drops are coming down; this is going to be a real deluge. I feel uneasy. I don't know where we are. I guess we've been crossing the Vidal Woods, a green space groomed for pedestrians, the shortest way to my house.

Steph's silence is making me nervous.

Oh, good, I can feel the wheelchair shaking; we must be back on our way. All the same, he could explain what's going on. I raise my index finger as a way of making him understand that I wouldn't mind having a chat. But it's a wasted effort. But what's gotten into him? He's pushing me faster and faster. The wheelchair jumps with every bump, and I'm jiggling like a Jell-O mold. This guy's really sick.

I don't like this. No, I don't like this one bit. The wheelchair is picking up speed. I can feel the wind whistling in my ears. It's raining now. Great big drops splashing my face. Oh, of course! I'm so stupid! He's running to get out of the rain! He doesn't feel like getting soaked. Still, he could say something. He takes a right going full speed, like a Monte Carlo race car. Now we're going downhill, and I think I'm going to be thrown forward.

But there's no hill on the way to my house.

Hey! This guy's nuts! The wheelchair has just banged against some obstacle and I almost fell over. I'm raising my index finger at regular intervals, but he keeps charging ahead. Now I know what it must have felt like in the landau in *The Battleship Potemkin*. As soon as we get back to the house, I'm . . . well . . . the first chance I get . . . if someone were to ask . . . oh, shit! I couldn't even complain about him, I can't complain about anything, damn it!

Still going downhill. As far as I can remember, the only slope in this park is on the path leading to the pond. And I can't see why . . .

Aarrgh! I'm falling down! I knew this would happen! I'm going to get hurt, I'm—*water*—this is water! Well, this asshole has managed to make me fall into the pond, into the water, but my feet can't touch the bottom; I feel myself sinking, but what the hell's he doing? Steph. Steph, I'm going down, I'm going down, sinking beneath the water. I want to breathe, to breathe, oh, no, *no!*

AM I DEAD? MY CHEST HURTS—IT'S BURNING. OHHH!
Someone's just pressed down on it, right over my heart.
Water shoots out of my mouth, and I hear myself cough. I
feel like vomiting, like—

"Do you hear me? Hey, do you hear me? Shit, I gotta
turn her head. Looks like she's gonna vomit . . ."

And he does. I breathe in, a great, painful, delicious in-
take of breath that burns me from top to bottom. Water is
streaming down my face. We're in a torrential rain.

"Don't move. It's gonna be all right."

I'll have no trouble obeying that order. Hands lift me up
and sit me down.

"You're lucky I came by to get my tackle box, 'cause
nobody was out in the park today, what with this rain."

It's a man's voice, sort of gruff; I'd place him in his
fifties.

"You're also lucky I took a course in first aid. You swallowed enough water to douse a candle. Don't worry about
your wheelchair. It got caught in some roots by the bank.
Can you hear me at least?"

I realize I must be looking at him through hollow eyes, for I've lost my sunglasses. I raise my index finger.

"You can't speak?"

Index finger.

"Fine, listen . . . I'm gonna carry you over to my car there, and then we'll call the police, okay?"

Index finger.

He lifts me, and I make out the smell of wet wool. I feel an oilskin touching me as he takes tiresome steps over soaking ground. The rain comes down in copious slaps.

"Here we are!"

With one hand he opens the door, and I almost slip and fall to the ground, but he holds on to me for all he's worth. So here I am, set down on the cushion, which must be the backseat, since I'm lying down.

"I'll be back."

I feel like shouting, "Don't leave me alone." I've got an awful headache, and I'm cold and shivering. The nervous reaction, I suppose. But what the hell happened? Where is Steph? Provided this courageous guy will be back soon . . . why hasn't he got a phone in his car? To think I owe my life to a tackle box. The pattering of the rain on the roof of the car is drowning out all other sounds out there, and I'm alone, out of time, enclosed in a bubble, and I have no idea what's happening to me. It looks like everything's unfolding in overdrive.

IN MY LIVING ROOM, I'M NICE AND WARM, BUNDLED up in a quilt and wearing warm socks. My rescuer is having coffee with Yvette, while I'm conferring with Yssart, a.k.a. Bonzo. When the cops came around, they took us to the hospital. And there, by some stroke of luck, we ran into Raybaud. A stroke of luck, indeed, because without him, we would have had to wait there for some insane length of time before they could establish my identity. To make a long story short, dear old Raybaud examined me, decreed that everything was all right, that I was a drowning victim in fine form, and that it was okay to take me home. I don't know who tipped off Yssart, but he showed up an hour later.

The man who rescued me—his name is Jean Guillaume, and he's a plumber—insisted on going with me. Yvette tripped over herself saying thank you, told him of her ank-lesque sufferings, and now they're sitting together in the kitchen, enmeshed in conversation. Yssart must be sitting on the couch, staring at me through what I imagine to be his piglike eyes. I'm tired and would like to be left alone. To sleep. I've had enough of this. His courteous little voice follows me like a tiny but insistent bite.

"And yet you cannot explain what turn of fate had you in that pond, in the only spot where the waters reach depths of nearly six feet?"

No, I cannot—no index finger. He sighs an Yssartian sigh.

"It was Stéphane Migoin pushing your wheelchair, wasn't it?"

Index finger.

"He was knocked out with a blunt object that almost broke his occipital bone. He was found in a ditch, passed out and covered with blood. He claims to remember nothing."

Steph!? Knocked out!? So then this was no accident. . . . This was . . .

"A murder attempt. That's how I would categorize the at-tack to which you've been victim, Miss Andrioli. A very as-tonishing murder attempt, on one who is handicapped and has not taken out life insurance on herself and who would be quite incapable of revealing whatever it may be regard-ing whomever it may be. You can appreciate why I'm so confused."

What about me? What does that make me? They've stolen my arms, my legs, my sight, and my voice, and now they want to kill me? What am I supposed to say, I who cannot even scream, who can only sit back and take it, over and over, like a punching bag? I hate you, Captain Yssart. I hate your polite, honeyed voice, your sickly sweet man-ners, and your insistence on taking yourself for Hercule

Poirot. Get lost, will you! Leave me alone! All of you, just leave me alone!

"I suppose you are exhausted and wish to rest. I must seem quite bothersome to you. But you must believe that I'm being bothersome to you only in your own personal interest. I wasn't the one whom someone tried to kill this morning. And it won't be me they'll try to snuff out tomorrow. Do you understand me?"

Index finger. Dirty bastard. I've already got the creeps. You don't have to give me any more.

"I can tell you, Miss Andrioli, that most often the facts are like pieces of a puzzle, and they've got to fit together. When they don't, it's because a piece has been bent out of shape or rigged. An absence of logic is frightfully rare in the human system. Yet I can see no logic in what's been happening to you. Unless we were to link this incident with your friendship with little Virginie, who if I'm not mistaken came home from summer camp only yesterday."

You snake! You never stopped spying on us.

"It would lead me to believe that Virginie, perhaps without knowing it, has confided to you some information that represents a potential danger for a third person; a danger so great that it might be better to resolve to do away with you than incur the risk that this bit of information might be divulged. Have you any knowledge of information of this sort, Miss Andrioli?"

That doesn't seem to hold water. If I understand correctly, Yssart is supposing that the guy who attacked me is the one who murdered the children, and that he would have gone mad because Virginie had confided to me something about him. Objection, Your Honor, but if he feared Virginie might tell me something, then why wouldn't he do away with her, pure and simple, instead of attacking me, who can't reveal anything?

"May I remind you that I have asked you a question?"

Oh, yes, you did.

"Has Virginie confided to you any information of capital importance about the man who murdered Michael?"

No index finger. I'm not lying. She has confided nothing

to me that would even begin to identify him. In fact, all she
has said is that she was present at the murders of Michael
and Renaud, her brother. Yet it is certain that if Yssart knew
this, he could question her and tear her secret from her. To
do that, he would have to ask me the right question. He
must have the gift of double vision, because that's exactly
what he did.

"Miss Andrioli, during our last discussion, I asked you,
without receiving any answer, if Virginie had confirmed
that she had been present at one or more of these murders.
I would like to reiterate my question. Has she said something to this effect?"

I can't hesitate anymore. I raise my index finger.

"Which children were involved?"

He counts off the list of victims. I raise my finger when
I hear the names Renaud and Michael.

"Very well. It's funny how our memory can play tricks
on us, isn't it. In any case, I'm pleased that you've recovered yours. Unfortunately, it can't be of much help to us
now. You see, Virginie lied to you. She couldn't have been
there for her brother's murder. When that occurred, she
was with her mother, making jam. Hélène Fansten is pos-
itive about this: Virginie didn't leave the house that morning. She was down with the flu and it was raining. And
again, regarding Michael, Virginie was lying to you: she
was out riding her bicycle with him, but Hélène Fansten
forbade her to leave the housing estate—you'll understand how, since what happened to Renaud, she'd be
more cautious—and Virginie came back and played in
their backyard; she didn't accompany Michael into the
woods. Do you understand what I'm saying to you? She
lied to you."

This isn't possible. How could she know where
Michael's body was? And how could she know that he was
dead when they hadn't yet discovered him? She must have
escaped her mother's sight; that's the only explanation.

"On the morning of May twenty-eighth, after Hélène
Fansten had forbidden Virginie to accompany Michael, she
made her do her piano exercises, and then they cleaned up

the backyard. She couldn't have slipped away from Mrs. Fansten, who did not leave her for one minute."

Hélène must be mistaken. All it took was a quarter of an hour with her head turned . . .

"I'm not telling you all this for the pleasure of chatting with you, but so that you'll be aware of the serious problems Virginie must be suffering from. Problems that, in my opinion, can only be explained by one very simple reason: she was not present at these murders, but she thinks she knows the murderer's identity."

Wrong, Yssart. If she "thinks she knows the murderer's identity," then why would the murderer want to kill me? She *knows* the murderer's identity, and he is afraid she might reveal it to me. And he can't kill Virginie, because every cop in the area is keeping an eye on her.

"Whatever the case may be, I am going to ask you to please be extremely wary of what Virginie might tell you. We'll be able to settle this difficult business only when we all cooperate. Children have been murdered and horribly mutilated, Miss Andrioli. Someone tried to kill you. Someone attacked your friend Stéphane Migoin. This isn't a game. It's a matter of life and death. Can I count on you?"

Index finger. Well, obviously, you can't say no to a guy who puts on a big act about good and evil. What's more, I'm not unhappy that Captain Yssart is here to watch over me, given that I now feel that the situation is getting a wee bit out of hand. Suddenly I become aware of the words he pronounced: "horribly mutilated." No one said anything about mutilations! If only I could speak, ask questions! I can't stand this silence in my throat anymore! I raise my index finger.

"Is there something you would like to know?"

Index finger.

"Then I'll have to guess. Let's see . . . does it have anything to do with what I've just said?"

Index finger. Say what you will, but there's something good about order and method.

"The mutilations?"

Goddamn it, this guy is a medium! He's not a cop, he's

a psychic! He could make a fortune at the King's Fair! I rush to raise my index finger.

"We didn't mention that to the media. And I'm only revealing this to you because I know you won't say a thing."

And with good reason!

"The victims were not only strangled"—he lowers his voice and comes closer—"but they were also mutilated with a sharp instrument, a knife with a thin blade. There were quite a few different types of wounds, from the hands being amputated, as was the case with Michael Massenet, to enucleation, which was the case for Charles-Eric Galliano."

Enucleation. The word slowly works its way to my brain until finally I understand what it means. His eyes were taken out. A small, distorted face with empty eye sockets. And just behind that creeps "hands amputated," which isn't so bad, either. Suddenly I'm sorry that Yssart decided to tell me everything!

"With Renaud Fansten, what shocked us at the time was that he was scalped. It's incomprehensible."

I'm hanging on to the tone of Yssart's voice, to my own deductions, to any deductions; this logic is logical, reassuring, pushing away enucleations in the dark, sweltering heat of things that never happen. But if the victims suffered mutilations, then the cops should have known by the second murder that they were dealing with a maniac!

"I know what you might be saying to me: Why weren't the first few murders treated as the work of one single killer? With the first case, that of Victor Legendre, it was only a simple strangulation. Now I think the murderer must have been interrupted in the middle of his work. In the second case, Charles-Eric Galliano was strangled, and his eyes . . . uh . . . disappeared. It was when Renaud Fansten was murdered that we started to see a link. He was strangled and scalped, but he wasn't raped. The association of strangulation with mutilation but with no sexual assault rang a bell. We didn't want to divulge any information that might reveal something of capital importance during cross-examination. The case of the Massenet boy, which

also showed these three characteristics, obviously rein-
forced our belief that this was a maniac. We still don't
know who we're looking for, but we know *what* we're looking for: an individual suffering from structural personality
problems who may or may not be aware of what he's doing. Very well. I hope I haven't bored you with all these details, but I must take my leave. Demands of the service. I'll
see you soon, and thank you for your help."

Clicks of heels on the wooden floor, the door slamming
shut, and here I am, by myself, dumbfounded by this avalanche of information. Without a doubt, my role as the favorite confidante is confirmed. How long will it be before
the maniac comes here himself to pour his heart out in my
cute little ear and then cut it off and take it home to speak
to it all night? If Yvette were informed about these mutilations, I could imagine her indignation.

But why would anyone do such things? Stupid question,
Elise: the "butcher of Milwaukee," who has just died, murdered in prison, kept the skulls of his victims in his cupboard
after boiling and lovingly painting them. You see the point,
don't you? Well, he did. He was sentenced for murder, and
for having sexual relations with some of those severed
heads. Just try to imagine that guy while he's doing that, really doing it . . . you can't believe it. And yet it exists.

Laughter in the kitchen. The noise of saucepans, and a
bottle as it's uncorked. I've got a feeling that Mr. Jean Guillaume will be asked to stay for dinner. After all, Yvette has
been a widow for ten years, and it's about time she found
someone new. Honestly, Yvette's love life is not the problem of the moment. It's rather the fact that there's a murderer prowling around, that Virginie has lied, that she's
definitely in danger, and that I really don't know what to do.
That there's really nothing I can do. Aside from trying to
understand.

Why did Virginie claim to have been present at these
murders? I'm thinking more and more that she came across
the bodies by chance, and I agree with Yssart: she suspects
someone, and it has disturbed her to the point of making up
the rest.

Why did someone find it funny to frighten me with a needle?

Why did someone (no doubt the same person) attack Stéphane in order to push me into the pond? Who wanted to kill me, and why?

Who came to caress me in the middle of the night?

As Yssart said, everything must fit together. It's a question of simply going through the facts over and over until they stack up.

Was the man who found it so funny to frighten me the same one who came during the night to feel me up—let's not be afraid of that expression—and who tried to kill me? I don't think so. The man who touched me had no hatred, no anger. He was a bit uneasy, a little scared—yes, I sensed fear and agitation. He was acting on an impulse he could not resist, one he was ashamed of, but he was neither brutal nor cruel. So there are two men. One who is sadistic, who knows how to handle a needle, with a good chance of being the same one who threw me into the pond, and then there's someone who is sexually obsessed and in love with me.

As far as conquests go, I could do better. . . .

Little by little, it's dawning on me that someone tried to kill me. At this very moment, I should be *dead*. Brrr. What about Stéphane? If I had died, would he be accused? Fortunately for him he was assaulted. Yes, very fortunate, because without any witnesses, he would make a very likely suspect. Stéphane . . . his behavior is a bit strange. Could he have hit himself with a stick? And fake being unconscious? Why not? The scalp can bleed quite easily, and these big jocks hardly ever fear pain. If I were to acknowledge that he was the one who pushed me into the pond, that he wanted to murder me, then I would also acknowledge that he was the one who came and had fun with his needle. And there's a strong chance that the man who has done these two things is the same one who has murdered the children. Stéphane? It's true that Virginie knows him well and likes him very much. Oh, my, my head feels like a melon. I wish Yvette would put me in bed. My throat hurts. And I'm afraid. If only I understood why someone was trying to kill me. It's already frightening enough to think that someone wishes you dead, but if you can't defend yourself, then it becomes terrifying. Will he try again?

"Is everything all right? You're not cold? I hope you haven't caught cold. Who'd ever believe that Mr. Stéphane would be attacked like that in the park? And then your wheelchair starting to tumble down the hill. Things like that don't happen by chance. Let me see your hands. No, that's okay, they're good and warm."

My throat hurts something terrible, and if my hands are warm, then it's because I've picked up a bad cold.

"Are you thirsty? Hungry?"

No index finger.

"Come on, you've got to eat something. Mr. Guillaume will be staying for dinner. He's been so nice. Imagine if he hadn't been there . . ."

I know. I'd be food for the tadpoles.

"I've made a stew, with ravioli. I think you'll be able to eat ravioli."

The problem when it comes to feeding me stems from the fact that I have trouble coordinating my jaws, which are vital to chewing. That's why I'm fed oatmeal, purées, liquids, or anything that can be swallowed right away. What I like is meat—red, bloody meat—pastas, pizzas. Chorizo. A slice of chorizo and green olives with an icy cold beer.

Yvette is already off. I can hear her dashing about. Jean Guillaume comes closer.

"So, are you feeling better?"

Index finger.

"Let's celebrate, then. I'll go buy champagne!"

"Oh, come on, no! We really shouldn't," Yvette protests.

"Yes, we should! It's not every day you escape the jaws of death!"

Let's just say that as far as I'm concerned, it's not the first time. The first time was in Belfast. Benoît . . . I can feel a kick from my spleen. I don't want to think about Benoît, but it's stronger than I am. I'm bombarded with a wave of images unfurling in my mind. I can see the two of us together again, getting ready for our trip, lying on his bed with travel brochures spread out before us on crisp sheets. . . . In a sense, I'm happy that Benoît's mother didn't sell the apartment. There's still one place in the universe where some tangible traces of Benoît have been left behind. Yvette told me that his mother did not touch a thing. She simply had the shutters closed. Benoît's mother is aging and infirm. She lives in a retirement home in Bourges. The death of her only son has taken away her will to live. And my raison d'être. Not true, Elise, because he died, and you didn't, and you have no plans to kill yourself.

The door closes again. Yvette sets the table; I can hear her quick, precise movements.

"This man's very kind, in a funny sort of way."

Who is she talking about? Oh, yes! Guillaume.

"And with such manners! These days, people are so crude. It's such a pleasure to meet a man who knows how to behave. He's not that big, but solid. He showed me his abdominal muscles. You'd think they were made of concrete."

Well, you don't say, Yvette. You seem to be having a good time as far as I can tell. I suppose feeling the abs of some stranger in my kitchen isn't indecent exposure, is it? It seems everyone has gone nuts this month.

"What did that captain want from you anyway?" she continues. "There's one who hasn't been spoiled by nature. And so arrogant! He'd do well to find out who's been killing those kids instead of weaseling around for hours."

I'm in perfect agreement with you, Yvette, but I've got this unpleasant feeling that the one who's been killing those kids has some connection with me.

Dinner goes well. Yvette has me eat first, then places me nearby as they finish dining. Mr. Guillaume is telling jokes. He tells them well. Yvette bursts out in laughter and I realize that I've rarely heard her laugh. He speaks to her of his wife. She left him five years ago for his best friend, who operates a metal turner and milling machine for Renault. Yvette speaks of her husband. He left her ten years ago for a better world, after thirty years of good, loyal service to the SNCF. A Polish man named Holzinski who gave her three sons: one lives in Montreal, another in Paris, and the third in Ardèche. Guillaume has no children, for his wife was sterile. I listen, thinking of everything that has just happened, upsetting my "sick person" routine and tearing apart this shroud of boredom under which I was starting to choke.

The telephone rings.

"Goodness, that telephone! It'll never let me be!" Yvette grumbles as she gets up. "Hello? Yes . . . it's for you, Elise."

For me? This must be the first time in ten months that someone is calling me. I'm rolled over to the phone, and Yvette sets the receiver against my ear.

"Hello, Elise?"

"Go ahead, she can hear you!" Yvette screams over my head.

"Elise, it's Stéphane."

I don't know why, but my heart is jumping all over my chest. His voice is small, far different from his usual rasping voice.

"Elise, I wanted to tell you I'm sorry about what happened. I don't know what happened; I was walking, and then, suddenly, bam! I was really seeing stars! Then there was nothing else, just a total blackout. When they told me what happened to you . . ."

In the background I hear footsteps, and then a whining woman's voice: "What are you doing, Steph? It's getting cold!"

Quickly, he continues, "I hope you're okay now. I'll come by and see you tomorrow. Bye-bye. Love you."

Then he hangs up. Yvette puts the receiver down for me.

"Is everything all right?"

Index finger.

"Poor guy. He's really so nice. Pity his wife's such a shrew. I'm talking about the young man who was with Elise this morning. Stéphane Migoin."

I understand that she is speaking to Jean Guillaume, and again descend into my thoughts. Do I really feel like seeing Stéphane tomorrow? Or Paul and Hélène? Why haven't they called? They could at least come by and see how I'm doing. I ruminate over this until dessert, tirelessly turning these latest events over in my mind, when Guillaume pops the cork on a bottle of champagne. Yvette chuckles and the champagne bubbles in the glasses. I'm entitled to one, and it's good and cool. Someone's ringing the doorbell.

Yvette's going to open it while Guillaume takes more fruit salad.

Surprise! Who could it be but the whole Fansten family! Virginie crosses the room running and kisses me on both cheeks. Yvette introduces Jean Guillaume to everyone, congratulations go back and forth, "you must have something to drink," which is exactly why Paul, too, had brought champagne, et cetera, et cetera, and I understand that the whole thing was premeditated. They had told Yvette ahead of time that they would be coming for dessert, and Yvette did not tell me, to leave it as a surprise. Hélène gently kisses me and asks me if I'm all right. Paul's mother kisses Yvette and asks me if I'm all right. Paul hasn't kissed me but asks me if I'm all right. Thankfully, Guillaume has handed out glasses of champagne to them all, and after toasting my health, everyone quiets down to drink.

It's good to return from the dead. People are interested in you.

The two bottles are empty, so Yvette serves coffee. Paul is sitting next to me.

"I went to see Steph. He's got a bandage all around his head. Kind of makes him look funny. Poor guy. He's still wondering what happened."

"I don't see how a young man as strong as him could let himself be attacked like that!" Hélène breaks in. "Without hearing a thing, or seeing anything coming! Now, he's the last person I could see being assaulted."

Me, too.

Paul continues, "What about you, Mr. Guillaume? You didn't see the suspect at all?"

"Like I was telling the cop, Inspector What's-his-name, it was raining cats and dogs. I had my hood over my face, and I was running with my head down so . . . even if I did come across somebody, with the wet grass muffling the sounds. . . . All I know is I saw the wheelchair knocked over and the young lady was underwater. Only her feet were sticking out, and there were bubbles. I jumped in and caught her by the ankles. Luckily, she doesn't weigh that much!"

"You really must have missed the attacker by just a few minutes," Paul points out.

"He could have hidden in the grove and waited for me to get going before fleeing quietly."

"Could we talk about something else?" Hélène suggests: "Perhaps Elise doesn't care to hear us going over this again. Everyone asked about you, Elise, and I reassured them as best I could. Claude will come by to see you tomorrow."

"Who wants fruit salad?" says Yvette.

A little hand rests upon mine, and in the din of voices following Hélène's remark, I hear a little voice murmuring in my ear: "I told you to be careful. Death noticed you, and it's mad at you. So you know I think another kid's gonna be punished now."

Punished?

"Mathieu Golbert, a CM1 who's always making up stories. Death thinks he's very pretty. It's a bad sign. When Death tells me *I'm* pretty, I hide because I know what that means. I'm waiting for it to be over, you know what I mean? I want fruit salad, too!"

No, wait. Wait, Virginie! What name did she say? Mathieu, Mathieu Golbert, yes, I know him, his mother has a hair salon, they used to come to the movie theater often. He's a pretty little boy, with great big blue eyes. What to do? I've got to warn Yssart. If ever Virginie's telling the truth . . . oh, I don't know what to think anymore. This girl is really so strange!

There's a hand on my shoulder, and on the inside I flinch. A large, firm hand. It's Paul. He doesn't say anything. He's satisfied to give my shoulder a squeeze. His thumb is lightly brushing the nape of my neck. It lasts a few seconds and then he pulls his hand away. I have the feeling that I was just blushing. But everyone goes on speaking as though nothing were wrong. So it was him that night. That night! It feels as if it were week back. I've lived more in twenty-four hours than in ten months.

EVERYONE HAS GONE. I'M IN BED. I THINK I'LL BE falling asleep quickly. Images of Virginie, Paul, Stéphane, Hélène, and Jean Guillaume are swirling in my head. . . . These are all people I can only imagine—composite sketches in color. If one day I recover my sense of sight, I'll certainly be dumbfounded to see their true faces. Mathieu Golbert . . . I've got to do something for him.

FIVE

IT WON'T STOP RAINING—A SUMMER RAIN, WITH all the violence, joy, and turbulence of a little pup. Yvette normally hates the rain, but she's quite busy at the moment. She's thinking about what she'll do tomorrow night in honor of Mr. Jean Guillaume, who is invited once again.

After yesterday and its explosion of violence, everything is calm again—an insidious, unsettling calm. I feel as if I were sitting in the eye of the storm. I awoke thinking about Mathieu Golbert. And the whole time Yvette spent tending to my morning necessities, I couldn't stop thinking about what I might do, but didn't come up with a thing. Someone's ringing the bell. I feel like a comedic actress stuck in a play where characters constantly enter and exit. I hear Yvette's voice, exclaiming, "Oh, my God! You look like a mess! Does it hurt?"

Stéphane: "No, it's okay. . . . Is Elise home?"

"No, she went to her dance class," I say to myself in my chest.

"It's Mr. Migoin."

He walks toward me with heavy steps. I'm in a bathrobe, with my hair up and my sunglasses on. He comes to a stop. I hear him breathing. Yvette has gone back out. We're alone with the rain.

"Elise . . ."

His voice is funny—slightly broken, childlike.

"I'm really sorry. If only I'd heard the guy coming . . . you must have been so afraid. . . ."

He takes my hand and squeezes it between his great big paws, which I imagine are red and hairy. My stomach contracts as I think these could be the hands that killed four children.

"You must be thinking that I'm a bit crazy . . ."

Index finger.

"I don't know what's happening to me. I . . . since I met you, I can't think of anyone but you."

This guy doesn't even know me. He doesn't know the sound of my voice, the ideas I might have. Is he in love with a rag doll or what?

"You look so sweet."

Me? I'm a bitch. I'm belligerent and ill tempered—a screeching harpie. Benoît always used to say I had the worst personality in the Northern Hemisphere.

"I love your face, Elise, the shape of your lips, the nape of your neck, your shoulders . . . I'm very unhappy. It feels like I'm living in a nightmare. I don't understand what's happening to me."

He goes back to his breathing.

"I can't hope that you would feel the same . . ."

No index finger. He might as well be talking like a book. No index finger.

". . . but I want you to know that I'm your friend. Truly your friend. I won't let anyone hurt you."

Go on. And I suppose last night was no different. . . .

"Catherine's here!" Yvette breaks in, prosaically.

Stéphane abruptly gets to his feet.

"See you soon, Elise. Don't forget what I told you. Oh, hi, Cathy!"

"Steph! Well, what do you know! Hey, you look really messed up . . ."

"No, it's nothing. I'm okay."

"Are you still gonna be in the match on Sunday?"

"Sure am. I've gotta go. I'm late. See you."

Match? Oh, yes, he plays tennis. I never knew that he and the Great Catherine knew each other. She sets my wheelchair into the lying position and starts kneading my knees.

"I didn't know that Migoin was a friend of Elise," she calls toward the kitchen.

"We met him through Paul and Hélène Fansten. He's really quite a brave young man."

"What happened to him?"

"What? You didn't hear?"

There's a secret consultation going on, in which Catherine is briefed on the adventure from yesterday. It makes her forget to unscrew my kneecaps, and so I can reflect in peace.

For example, how is it that when Virginie was away, nothing happened? No, no, I'm not lending demonic qualities to this child, but what links could tie her to "Death from the Woods"? Would a child have the strength to kill another child? Stop. I'm starting off in the wrong direction. There's no other example of a seven-year-old serial killer. So what's up with Virginie? Because I can tell that there's something not quite right with her. She isn't clean. She's too stiff, too wise; her voice is too calm. You're going to tell me that with everything she's seen . . . or hasn't seen, I don't know anymore. *Ouch!* That big asshole Catherine is putting my left shoulder out of joint. Somehow I've got to be able to attract Yvette's attention and let her know that I've got something to say to Yssart. As soon as Catherine is gone, I'll give it a try.

CATHERINE HAS LEFT, BUT OBVIOUSLY YVETTE'S NOT worrying about me: she's dusting the house in honor of Mr. Guillaume, as if we were receiving the president of the Republic. From time to time I raise my index finger when I hear her pass next to me, but it's a pure waste of time—she must have her nose glued to the dust. But worst of all, she's put on a books-on-tape cassette that Hélène took out from the public library—no, excuse me, the public media center—and I'm listening to some enthusiastic voice reciting Balzac. The thought was nice but, for one, I hate having books read to me, and, two, I know the book by heart, having read it several times. Well . . . I can't spend my life complaining.

Ah! The first side is over. Yvette will come and turn the cassette over. I can hear her footsteps. Quick—index, index, index.

"Yes, yes, I know, I'm coming."

No, Yvette, no. Index, index, index.

"My goodness, one minute, will you. How impatient you are. You're really getting terrible!"

Oh, shit!

Balzac is at it again, booming out from the box. I'd be able to hear it even at the back of the garden. Yvette, too, is at it again, muttering something. All that's left is to wait for a favorable moment.

I awake with a start. I dozed off, cradled by the enthusiastic voice. Where is Yvette? I listen, trying to locate her. Oh, outside. She's talking to someone. I recognize Hélène's voice saying, "Bye-bye." Yvette's coming back inside.

"You're lucky. Hélène's brought you some more cassettes."

Super. I hope it's his complete works in 366 volumes.

"Do you want to listen to one now?"

No index finger.

"Fine. Whatever you want. Do you want something else?"

Index finger.

"Are you thirsty?"

No index finger.

"Hungry?"

No index finger.

"Do you have to pee?"

No index ringer.

"Did you want to see Hélène?"

No index finger. I feel Yvette growing impatient.

"Someone else?"

Index finger.

"Virginie?"

No index finger.

"Is it in relation to the accident yesterday?"

Index finger.

"The police, then?"

Index finger. Marvelous Yvette. Once I'm recovered, I'll give you a raise, I'll make you my heir, I'll . . .

"You want me to call up that picayune captain?"

Index finger.

"Fine. If that'll make you happy."

She's heading for the telephone. Good. Everything is going well. I'm controlling the situation.

"The captain is in Paris. He won't be back until Monday. Oh, I forgot to take my rabbit off the stove!"

She's off in a wild stampede toward the kitchen. I've got no choice but to hope that Yssart will be back before it's too late, or that Virginie has just told me any old tale.

Someone's ringing at the door. I ought to hire a maid for the sole purpose of opening the door and sounding the three knocks.

This time it was Claude Mondini. No sooner than entering does she kiss me on both cheeks. She smells of honeysuckle eau de toilette.

"Poor Elise! Fortunately, everything turned out all right! I've always said that these woods were dangerous. I forbid the kids to play in them. Jean-Mi also sends his love. Hmmm, it smells good here. Yvette, what are you concocting for us?"

"Rabbit in mustard sauce."

"That sounds delicious! So, my poor little Elise, are you okay?"

Index finger.

"I can't stay long. I've got to arrange for a canoeing trip on Sunday with the kids from La Tourbière. I know your life isn't easy, Elise, but if only you could see these poor kids. Their environment at home is heartbreaking. Well,

I'll give you a kiss good-bye and then I've got to run. Yvette, if you need something, anything, you'll give us a call, won't you?"

"Yes, yes. Thanks again."

"Bye-bye, Elise. See you soon!"

Off she goes, leaving springtime fragrances floating in the air. I'm a bit confused about something: did she stay three minutes or four? But above all I'm relieved, as I was secretly in terror that she might persuade Yvette to roll me to Mass on Sunday morning, "so that I could still reach a spiritual dimension."

On Sunday morning, Benoît and I would stay in bed until eleven, talking about everything and nothing at all . . .

I miss you, Benoît.

IT'S BEEN CALM FOR FIVE DAYS. IT'S MAGNIFICENT. NO one to feel me up, hurt me, or try to kill me. Two hours a day of Balzac, lovely weather, succulent strawberries, and Raybaud, who's paid me a few compliments. It seems that they can sense my whole left hand trembling under the lead of the index finger. Oh, my God, if only this could be true! If it could start to move once again, then I would learn to write left-handed. I could say hello and good-bye and make a whole slew of signs—V for victory, the pointed zero, the thumbs-down, or the thumbs-up to say okay. I could give the obscene middle finger, the bad luck sign, cross my fingers to protect against bad luck, or do anything else I possibly could do with a hand! I'm exercising non-stop, like a madwoman. I'm going to move this fucking hand, and not only that, I will recover use of my body, bit by bit, I swear it, until I can get up and turn off this lousy radio—cassette player!

God must have heard me because it has become silent. Oh, yes, it's one o'clock. Yvette wants to listen to the news. Yada-yada-yada foreign policy . . . plan for an antiterrorist campaign . . . the farmers are outraged . . . The prime minister . . . wars here, wars there . . . flooding in the southeast . . . well, that should be a change from the drought they've been having . . . a clue in the murder of little Michael Massenet, the police are looking for a witness . . . What?!

"Did you hear that, Elise?" Yvette exclaims, suddenly excited.

Index finger.

"I'm going to call Hélène. Maybe she knows something."

I listen with my ears open wide, but they say no more. The weather: this sunshine won't last, autumn will be rough, and winter is coming early; when they're done laughing, they say it's almost time for the kids to go back to school. Yvette comes back.

"She heard, too, but she doesn't know anything, either. She seemed a bit shaken. Anyway, the captain should have spoken to her about it. It does concern her, after all. Especially with her part-time job, she can't always be looking after Virginie."

A clue . . . I need to see Yssart soon. Poor Hélène! She's so discreet that people often forget the drama they've lived through. Neither she nor Paul ever talk about Renaud, and Yvette told me they gave all his things away to Catholic Aid. It seems they have a photo of him in their dining room. A pretty little boy with brown hair and blue eyes, with ears that stick out (according to Yvette) and reddish highlights. He doesn't resemble Virginie in the least; she has straight blond hair and brown eyes. Yvette says she's ravishing—"a real doll"—but I suspect she's partial.

Yvette clears the table, still grousing about murderers, the coming weather, taxes, the difficulty of life, and God's shameful indifference. She comes back and announces that it's far too nice outside to stay all cooped up. She called Hélène, and told her she would be taking Virginie and me for a walk. Hélène doesn't mind, and Yvette even got the impression that it might do her some good to be alone awhile.

VIRGINIE IS SCAMPERING BY MY SIDE. YVETTE PRE-ferred to avoid the Vidal Woods, so we're strolling along the esplanade next to the shopping center. I remember benches and sandwich vendors, rolling skates and skate-boarders crisscrossing the esplanade at high speeds. A ball in the distance makes an insistent tap, tap, tap, and overexcited children go tweet, tweet, tweet. At the center of the plaza, I remember there being a great square wading pool surrounded by a fountain of twisted metal, where kids threw detritus that more or less floated on the surface.

The fountain is in action. I can hear the water jets churning. We stop. Yvette sighs an easy sigh. I suppose she has sat down.

"Virginie, don't go too far!"

"No, no. I'm playing in the pool."

For the time being we are both sitting and taking it easy; I'm listening to the sounds of the living, while Yvette dreams of who knows what. Virginie's small voice tears me from my torpor: "Can I buy some Malabars?"

"Bonbons aren't good for your teeth."

"They're not bonbons. It's chewing gum."

"It's the same thing. And what's your name, young man? Has the cat got your tongue?"

"Mom always buys me some. His name's Mathieu."

I can't believe it!

"Look, here's five francs. Don't lose it. Where's your mommy, Mathieu?" asks Yvette.

"She's at the salon, over there."

"His mom's a hairdresser. He came with his big brother," Virginie explains.

"Ah! Well, go ahead, but come back right away, and don't talk to anybody!"

That's him. That's Mathieu Golbert. What the hell is Virginie doing with him? Oh, my God! Is she acting as the . . . procurer for the murderer? No, I mustn't have such thoughts. Is Yvette keeping an eye on them at least? Is it normal for them to take so much time? I hear paper rustling, and deduce that Yvette is reading her newspaper. Yvette, this is no time to be reading!

"I can't understand why such a seductive young man like Prince Albert isn't married yet . . ."

Yvette! Forget about Albert! Keep an eye on the kids!

"The way they bore us with their sports. I can't believe this. You can't read a newspaper without getting all these sports. Pages and pages of sports . . ."

Yvette, dear Yvette, will you take your eyes off the paper and please have a look around?

"I had five!"

Virginie! Oofah!

"You'll see. You'll have plenty of cavities if you go on eating candy like that."

"The dentist's very nice."

"That's no reason. It costs a lot of money to go to the dentist. Where's your little friend?"

"He went back with his brother. He had to go home."

"Oh? So, do you want to sit down? I'll give you the funnies if you'd like."

"Yes, I would."

I can't help but feel a dull sort of anguish. Mathieu's presence seems rather a strange coincidence, his sudden absence even more so.

"Is anyone sitting here?" a woman with a northern accent politely asks.

"No, not at all. Have a seat. Slide over a little, Virj."

Virginie is right against my wheelchair now. Yvette and the woman from the north have started to exchange gossip.

"Elise, do you hear me?" Virginie suddenly whispers.

Index finger.

"I'm afraid for Mathieu."

So am I.

"I think he's gonna be dead."

Oh, no! No! If only I could grab this little brat and shake her, tear her secrets from her . . .

"I saw Death. Over there, near the parking lot."

A strange sensation comes over me. It's as though someone were pouring lead into my stomach. This idiotic face of mine can't express anything! And this idiotic mouth that can't cry out. It all must look rather funny, because Yvette interrupts her conversation to say, "You look rather bemused. Is something the matter?"

Index finger. Yes, something is the matter.

"Do you want to go home?"

No index finger.

"Do you want to go walking a bit?"

Yes, that's it, let's walk a bit. Perhaps Mathieu will turn up. I raise my index finger.

"All right," Yvette sighs, with resignation in her voice, "let's go. Bye-bye," she calls out to the lady from the north, whose eyes, I imagine, are riveted on me.

We set off. Virginie is singing to herself. In an instant it occurs to me that it's *Once There Was a Little Ship*. She's gotten to the passage where the foam gets eaten up, and this to me does not seem a good sign.

We proceed this way for a little while, and I can tell from Yvette's rough, jerky way of pushing the wheelchair that she's in a bad mood. Some kids are coming to speak with Virginie, so we must be right near the fountain, because the sound of the water is much louder. I'm starting to tell myself that I suffer from an overactive imagination. Suddenly Yvette calls out, "Virginie! Come here!"

"What?"

"Who's that boy who was just talking to you? The tall one, wearing the red helmet?"

"Which tall one?"

"Hey, young man! Young man!" Yvette shouts. "Yes, you! With the red helmet!"

She leans toward me and whispers in my ear, "You never know if he's one of those dealers."

Under different circumstances, I'd feel like laughing.

"Yeah?"

"Did you want something?"

"I just wanted to know if Virj had seen my little brother Mathieu."

I sense catastrophe bearing down on us.

"But he was with you!" Yvette says in astonishment.

"No, he went to buy Malabars with her, and it started to take a while. I dunno what the hell that little asshole's up to, but—"

"Listen, I don't mean to alarm you, but he told Virginie he was going back to you."

"That's what he told you, Virj?"

"Yes. He said he didn't want you to yell at him."

"Shit . . . Goddamn it, if I find him . . ."

"Officer!" Yvette shrieks. "Officer!"

"No, don't bother. He's probably off somewhere acting like an asshole!"

"What's going on?" a voice with a pronounced Parisian accent asks.

A terrifying scream behind us. It's enough to pierce my eardrums.

"What is it?" Yvette cries, dumbfounded.

My heart's pounding in my chest. A second scream. It's a woman. The shrill blowing of a whistle, followed by the sound of sudden running.

"Stay here, Virginie!"

Movements of the crowd, astonished exclamations.

"No! You stay here, and give me your hand!" Yvette thunders.

With all these voices around us, I feel caught in a whirlpool, keeling over in an ocean of rumbling. Whistles shriek, ambulance and police sirens blare, and my heart is pounding in my temples.

"Clear it out! All right, let us through, will you."

"What is it?"

"I don't know anything more than you. Push aside."

Chilling chatter: "It seems they found a dead body." "In the parking lot over there." "A woman found him." "It's a dead body. A kid."

"Excuse me, sir, do you know what's going on?" Yvette asks, panicking.

"A child has been found dead in the parking lot."

"Oh, my God! Do you know . . . does anyone know who it is?"

"No, I don't think so."

A piercing wail rises above the crowd. Everyone goes silent at the voice of a terror-stricken adolescent: "Mathieu! No! Mathieu! No, damn it!"

I hear an odd watery little sound and understand that Virginie has begun to cry.

"There, there, don't cry, sweetie! Oh, my God, this is horrible! Oh, Elise, have you heard?"

Index finger. I've heard so well, I think I might puke my guts up. This just can't be true. It's a dream, a hallucination. Mathieu can't be dead.

"They're putting his brother into the police car," Yvette calls to me. "The poor boy . . . the poor boy . . ."

A man's voice, sounding irritated, screams, "Get out of the way, for God's sake, there's nothing to see here, just like I said. Let us through."

With all this hubbub and turmoil, someone might almost think it was a fairground. I imagine a small body thrown onto a stretcher—a small body hacked to pieces. Virginie is still crying quietly.

"You have to tell them what you know," Yvette says, decisively.

We're en route. As we bump into people, Yvette apologizes over and over, and Virginie sobs. Yvette obstinately proceeds, pushing my wheelchair and tugging Virginie, still crying, imperturbable amid the insults and jeers.

"Officer! Officer!"

"What? I'm busy."

"The little girl played with him just a little while ago."

"What him?"

"Uh, well, the . . . the victim!"

"How do you know what all this is about?"

"I'm telling you, we know him. His name is Mathieu. His big brother is in the car."

"Come with me. Step aside, will you, let the lady pass. No, sir, no, it's okay like that, step back now."

We move ahead.

"This lady says the little girl played with the victim just a little while ago."

A virile young voice says, "She did? Well, come this way. So, little girl, what's your name?"

"Vir . . . gi . . . nie."

"And why are you crying?"

"Mommy," she stammers.

"It must be the shock," Yvette interrupts.

"Were you just playing with Mathieu?"

"They went to buy candy together, and she came back by herself. And his brother hasn't seen him since, nor have we," Yvette answers for Virginie.

"You went to buy candy?"

"No, Malabars . . ." Virginie hiccups.

"And where did Mathieu go then? Did he talk to someone?"

"I don't know. He said he was going to see his big brother."

"You didn't see anyone talking to him? A grown-up, I mean."

"No."

Dirty little liar. You saw the murderer. You told me yourself. You saw him, but now you're clamming up. Why? Why?!

"Well, listen . . . If you remember anything, you'll tell Gramma."

"She's not Gramma. She's Elise's maid."

"I'm Miss Andrioli's caretaker," Yvette says, correcting her, sounding offended.

"Miss Andrioli? Is that you?" the captain asks.

"She can't answer. She's been the victim of a very serious accident."

"I see. Excuse me. Well, let me know where I can get in touch with you."

"Yvette Holzinski, two chemin des Carmes, in Boissy. Miss Andrioli, Elise, lives in the same place. The little girl's name is Virginie Fansten, of fourteen avenue Charles-de-Gaulle, in the Merisiers development."

"Okay, here's my card. I'm Inspector Gassin. Florent Gassin. You'll have to come by to give a deposition."

"We know Captain Yssart."

"You do? He's in Paris. Excuse me, but I've got to go. So do you understand, Virginie? If you remember anything, give me a call. It's very important . . ."

Virginie snuffles without answering. Inspector Gassin takes his leave. Yvette starts off and whispers, "They've taken his body away on a stretcher, in a plastic bag, like on TV. It was awful. I hope Virginie didn't see him."

Our ride home is somber. We proceed in silence. I feel sad—terribly sad—and completely stunned. To say that Mathieu might have been saved if only Virginie had agreed to talk . . . The way she was crying! The poor kid must feel completely lost. Just a little while ago, I was terribly angry with her. Now I don't know anymore, I just feel sorry for her. Mathieu murdered. Just as she told me. What if she simply had a gift for clairvoyance?

IT'S COLD IN THE LIVING ROOM. AS NIGHT FALLS, THE air has cooled off. Yvette took Virginie home, then began to iron while making conversation with me: "Those poor Fanstens. It's been quite a shock for them. They must be thinking the man who murdered Renaud is in the vicinity. And then Virginie—she couldn't stop crying! It was all so sinister! I wish Paul could have been there, but he had to see a client or who knows what. On my way home I came across Stéphane Migoin. He's not wearing a bandage anymore. He says hi. He was in a hurry, he had to be at some construction site."

That's true, he does have a construction firm. As far as I can recall, he knew Paul through the bank. Yes, that's it, he is a customer at the bank, and Paul, as vice-chairman, personally tended to his account. They discovered they had the same passion for running. Their secret dream was to run the New York Marathon. They work out like crazy. Personally, I never cared for running, especially not on asphalt. Oh, the news is on . . . always the same thing. Ah, here it is.

> "Another chilling murder in the greater Paris region. Nine-year-old Mathieu Golbert was found murdered this afternoon in the parking lot of a shopping center. This savage murder may be the work of the same madman who strangled eight-year-old Michael Massenet already two months

ago. Terror reigns today in Boissy-les-Colombes. Michel Falcon, our special correspondent, is on the scene. Michel?"

"This is Michel Falcon. Tonight, the residents of Boissy-les-Colombes and Yvelines are gripped with dismay, for in less than three months two children have been murdered here. The assumption they're going by, which today seems to have been confirmed, which ties these two murders to other cases going back five years, is not one that will reassure the residents of this peaceful community. In Boissy-les-Colombes tonight, people are close to panic, and some are already talking about forming neighborhood watches. At the moment, Captain Yssart, heading up the investigation in this district, refuses to release any statement, but has confirmed that they are definitely piecing together many of the clues."

Now they're briefly going over the other murders, most likely accompanied by the kids' photos. Interviews with a retired person, a housewife, and an auto mechanic. Wails, tears, a door slamming shut, and a man shouting, "Leave us alone!" It is Mathieu's family, *"who, still shocked by today's events, seems in no condition to welcome our news team."*

The telephone rings. Yvette gets up, grumbling. The announcer moves on to a sailboat race going on in the Mediterranean.

"Hello? Oh, it's you, Jean. Good evening . . . Yes, it's terrible, isn't it? We're very disturbed by it. Oh, no, don't bother. That's nice of you, thanks. . . . Tomorrow, yes, we're still on. The worst thing is that we were there, at the shopping center. . . . Yes, Virginie was playing with the little boy just before he disappeared, can you imagine? Like you say . . ."

It's hard to follow Yvette's conversation with Jean Guillaume and the news at the same time. Something else is ringing. This time it's the front door. Things are definitely bustling. Yvette excuses herself, hangs up, and runs to open up.

"Is Miss Andrioli here?"

Yssart! He must have come right back from Paris.

"This way. We were in the middle of dinner."

"I'm sorry. *Bon appétit*. Good evening, Miss Andrioli."

Index finger.

"I came back as soon as I found out what happened. If you don't mind, I would like to have a word with Miss Andrioli in particular."

He zips me into the vestibule—I can smell the furniture polish Yvette was using this morning—and then takes off like a shot. "Strange coincidence, isn't it? Both you and Virginie being present at the scene of the murder. You know, I'm beginning to find this chain of coincidences particularly unpleasant. With Mathieu Golbert, the murderer made an incision in his thorax and pulled out his heart. After he was dead, of course."

Of course. Am I going to vomit?

"The body was lying between two cars. The murderer must have been out of his mind, operating this way in broad daylight in a busy parking lot, but it's true that if he were crouched between vehicles, he would be invisible to surveillance cameras. I've tried it. It's hard to imagine that the murderer fled with his victim's heart in his pocket. Do you know what I would tend to believe? That he came by car and left the same way. The problem with these automatic parking lots is that employees generally aren't paying attention to passing vehicles, but you never know. You see, I'm playing fair with you. Does Virginie know something?"

This guy blows me away. He speaks a mile a minute and throws out fifty bits of information all at once. Does Virginie know something? I don't know a thing about it. I raise my index finger just in case.

"Did she see Mathieu leave with someone?"

Half an index finger. That is, I raise it, but it's folded like a hook.

"Did she see someone she knew?"

Index finger.

"Who? Do you know?"

No index finger. He sighs.

"Every murderer has a motive. I don't mean to say a motive that to us would seem worthwhile. But rather a motive that has a personal meaning for him. For example, a murderer may have decided to start an ear collection. Or to rub out anyone who stands five feet eleven and a half, wearing yellow moccasins. Or to strangle his lovers while they were asleep and keep their body next to him, to watch TV, like that English killer. You see what I mean? If you try to pin down a maniac by thinking up a 'reasonable' motive, then you're barking up the wrong tree. But if you think his acts are random, for the simple pleasure of killing, then you're barking up the wrong tree again. If he were being irrational, then his victims would be varied. But that's quite rare. In ninety-nine percent of all cases, the psychopathic killer always latches on to the same kind of victim. He obstinately pursues a goal, and feels gratified only when killing certain people in a certain way. But I must be boring you with my speech. I was on my way over to the Fanstens and stopped at your house on the off chance. It's always nice to speak with you. Well, I'll be leaving you now, Miss Andrioli. And don't overexert yourself. Your life seems rather shaken up these days."

Son of a bitch! He leads me back into the living room and takes off before Yvette even has the chance to say good-bye. This guy's impossible. Some killer is traipsing around under our nose, and all the while, some clown-faced captain is giving me a class on the psychology of murderers. Yvette piles up the plates, grumbling.

I think about Mathieu again. Poor little kid. It makes me shudder. At the hospital, when I understood that Benoît was dead, I wanted to howl like a wolf. And for days and days I couldn't quite believe he would never again talk to me, he would never again be next to me, would never again make me laugh. Tonight, Mathieu's mother must feel like screaming. And Hélène—cool, smiling Hélène—must be so afraid for Virginie! Even though Virginie is a girl. Because, honestly, when you think about it, all the victims are male. Perhaps the killer is particularly attracted to little boys. "Always the same kind of victim," just as Bonzo the Clown says. I'd like to get all that out of my head. But I can't; I can't simply tell myself, "Let's not think about it anymore." If only I had not heard Mathieu's voice; if only it were the name of a stranger on TV. I was so happy to meet the Fanstens, but now it's just one great big mess.

SIX

MATHIEU GOLBERT'S BURIAL WILL BE HELD THIS morning. Everyone is going: the Mondinis, the Quinsons, and the Migoins. Yvette left with Paul a half hour ago. Hélène refused to attend. I hear her nervously turning the pages of a magazine, as if she were in a doctor's waiting room. When Yvette heard that Hélène did not want to go, she had the bright idea to suggest that she come keep me company while she herself attended the burial. "That'll keep her from sitting at home, down in the dumps," she explained. Virginie is playing outside with her dolls. One of them is getting a forceful spanking: "Now, see here, naughty little girl, this is for your own good," and then pow, pow, pow. I don't know what score she's settling, but she's going about it wholeheartedly.

It seems to be a very beautiful day—a pure blue sky, without a hint of wind. I can imagine the solemn funeral cortege proceeding beneath the sun, past yellowing fields. And to think Benoît is at rest in this cemetery. They created it in 1976, as I recall, so as far as cemeteries go, it's practically brand new, on a grassy spot. I can't even go to meditate by Benoît's grave. Yvette told me that Renaud, too, is buried there. I can understand how it must be too much for Hélène to attend the funeral service for a little boy buried near her husband's child. Did the murderer go to the burial? It happens a lot in the movies.

Hélène is barely speaking to me, aside from a few words about the weather. She's just struck a match, and the smell of smoke spreads through the room. Pages rustle as they are hastily turned. She's breathing rapidly. Too rapidly.

"What's worst is knowing that he's lying in that little box. That your child is in a box. Like . . . like a package. Not much bigger than . . . than a case of wine, for example. Funny, isn't it?"

She is not well. With difficulty, I swallow saliva. Her voice is trembling. Provided that she doesn't start crying. I never know what to do when people cry.

"Paul wanted to go to the burial. I don't see why, we don't even know these people, but he wanted to go, out of solidarity. That's a pretty big word. It won't bring their son back. I didn't want him to go, but when he decides to do something . . . I didn't want to be alone, not on a day like today. You'll have to excuse me, Elise, I must be talking your ear off."

No, not at all, Hélène, but how am I to tell you this? How am I to tell you that I understand your pain? This piece of junk for a body I've got that refuses me any service. Damn, here's Virginie.

"Can I have some water? Mommy? What's the matter, Mommy?"

"Nothing, darling, nothing. Go get some water in the kitchen."

"Are you sad because of Mathieu?"

"Yes, a little."

"It's not so bad. Mathieu must be happy now that he's going to heaven."

"I'm sure he is. Now go get something to drink."

Little steps running.

"I get so edgy when I'm this way. It's ridiculous. It's a good thing Paul's not here to see me. He can't stand it when I have these attacks."

Good old Paul definitely seems to be the model of patience. I understand better why Hélène always seems so sad and detached. Virginie sweeps through like a whirlwind and goes out into the garden screaming. She seems absolutely untouched by her friend's death. It's strange when I think how much she cried the other day. She must have put it all away in a corner of her head, and refuses to think about it.

What time is it anyway? Hélène has gone back to pretending to read. In this morbid atmosphere, I feel as tense as a violin string.

"I never should have allowed Renaud to play outside that day. It was bound to happen. Bound to happen."

She's going to work herself up to the point of hysteria, I can feel it, and what will I be able to do about it? I raise my index finger just in case.

"No, I know it isn't my fault, I know, Elise; you can't tell me otherwise."

Index finger.

"I knew it was going to happen, I knew it, I could feel it, and I did nothing—not a thing. Virginie was the one who found him. She called me. He was facedown, and all that blood! I took Virginie in my arms and ran to the house to call the paramedics. I didn't want Virginie to see him. I went back with a bath towel and threw it on top of him, and it turned all red. I hate red. I never wear it."

Her voice is getting dangerously high. Someone's ringing at the door. Oo-fah!

"Hello, Virginie, my sweetheart. How are you?"

Yvette. She's come home.

"Everything was okay, Hélène? We weren't too long? Paul's waiting for you in the car. He's in a hurry. Hélène?"

"I'm coming. I was just looking for a handkerchief in my bag. I've got one of those colds again."

"A cold? It must be hay fever. It's so hot."

"Of course. Well, I've gotta go. Bye-bye, Elise, bye, Yvette, see you soon. Virginie, let's go!"

"Bye-bye."

"Bye-bye, my little pet!"

The door slams shut.

"Oh, my, it was dreadful," Yvette exclaims as she starts to set the table. If only you could see it! They had to hold his mother back. She wanted to throw herself upon the casket. Paul was ghostly pale. Claude Mondini burst into tears, and her husband nearly did the same. And then there were the Quinsons—those people always make a point of being noticed. Betty was wearing a veil, looking completely ridiculous, and Manuel was in a white suit. What do they think this is, China? Coming to a burial in white! Captain Yssart wasn't there, but there was this young inspector, Florent Gassin, a nice boy, though he seems so serious. He looks a little like Patrick Bruel, you know?"

Yet another cute guy from my old crowd. Cut it out! I don't know what I'm supposed to do with that!

"Stéphane was also there, with his wife. So full of herself, that one! Half his face is all blue and swollen. Where did I put that butter dish? Oh, there it is! All that, plus the sweltering heat. Everyone was melting. And the priest, some young guy with an accent from the south, or from somewhere, I don't know—no one could understand any of it. He was laying it on a bit thick with his words of consolation. I would've given anything to be somewhere else. As soon as it was over, Paul gave me the signal, and we left."

I can only imagine too well the horror of this burial. Did Paul pass before his own son's tomb? Yvette is running water in the kitchen. Her voice reaches me from a distance: "Jean didn't want to come. He finds it all morbid."

Jean? Oh, yes, Jean Guillaume. So, already, we're on a first-name basis. . . . Morbid, that's for sure. A burial . . . the ideal thing would be burials without death, but, don't you know, those are rare.

"Here it is! Ready!"

She rolls my wheelchair up to the table. I can make out the smell of . . . let's see . . . corn? Right on the nose. My perceptions are getting better. I'm chewing as best I can. A hand rests on my wrist. I freeze.

"I hope the police catch this monster soon. It's really just too horrible. Look, I'm not even hungry."

My swallowing is a bit more painful than usual. I'm hungry. Maybe it's monstrous, but I'm hungry. Well, that's too bad, because Yvette is angrily clearing the table. Dessert maybe? No, no dessert. I hear her serving coffee. The smell of coffee tickles my nostrils. A good, strong coffee you can stick your spoon in . . . but obviously I'm not entitled to any. So I sit like a lump in my chair with a churning stomach. The rest of the day unwinds in this bleak setting, with Yvette and all her turmoil as company. In my head, I'm replaying the film of events nonstop:

1. I meet Virginie, who tells me she knows some things about a murderer of children.
2. Her story is confirmed with the discovery of little Michael Massenet.
3. I'm introduced to her parents, Paul and Hélène Fansten, and their friends: Stéphane and Sophie Migoin, Manuel and Betty Quinson, and Jean-Mi and Claude Mondine.
4. Someone tries to kill me—*me!*
5. Virginie predicts for me the death of Mathieu.
6. Mathieu is murdered.

What's the conclusion?
Virginie is at the heart of this whole affair. But what is my part in this?
·How can I even play a part in this sinister farce, handicapped as I am?
I guess the weather's turned rainy. The sky is like me—indecisive, grumpy, and tormented.

IT'S THE AFTERNOON. I'M SITTING IN THE LIVING room, listening to *Mr. Seguin's Goat*. No, I haven't regressed to childhood, but Virginie's here, and she's brought some cassettes.

"In *Jurassic Park,* they also use a goat for bait," she suddenly informs me.

And in Boissy-les-Colombes, *I'm* the one they use as a goat, I feel like answering.

"It's not the wolves' fault if they kill lambs. They have to eat."

Exactly. I feel you coming closer. Go on.

"And sometimes with people it's similar. They do things because they have to. Even if it's bad."

Virginie, my little angel, you've just brought up the problem of free will, and unfortunately I can't help you solve it, because, for one, I'm mute, and also I have no answer.

"Yes, she does hear."

What? I don't quite understand what she just said. "Yes, she does hear"? Whom is she talking to? Yvette? But Yvette has taken advantage of Virginie's being here so that she could run out to the drugstore.

"No. I said she hears, but she doesn't speak!"

What is she up to? *Mr. Seguin's Goat* stops. Virginie must be putting in another cassette because I can hear the machine being handled. Ah, *Peter and the Wolf* by Prokofiev. The music spills out into and the living room, and I cock my ear to hear over it.

"She's very nice. You mustn't hurt her!"

Virginie? Virginie, precious, what are you talking about? I raise my index finger.

"Don't worry, Elise, I explained it all."

Explained what? To whom? I'm starting to feel mildly tense. What if she wasn't kidding? What if she really was talking to someone?

"He thinks you're very pretty."

Oh, no! I try with all my strength to listen, to make out the slightest breath, the slightest movement, but this damn music drowns out everything.

"He comes to see me often. He's afraid, you understand?"

Who? Who, for God's sake?!

"Stop it! I told you not to touch her!"

She's not pretending. The little girl's not playing around. She's talking to someone now. Someone who is in my living room, looking at me. Someone who does not say anything. Who thinks I'm pretty. Who wants to touch me. Stop! I feel icy sweat dripping down my sides. Is she there with "him," the killer? I'm so edgy, I feel I might fly to pieces. Say something, you son of a bitch, speak!

"Mommy doesn't want me to talk to him. She says he's bad."

What? Hélène knows him, too? A creak on my right . . . what is it? Is someone moving toward me?

"But I know he's scared, all alone in the dark. So I'll let him come over."

Did I hear a sigh? Did I just hear a sigh next to me? Stop it, Virginie, I'm begging you. Take this guy outside—outside! I raise my index finger several times in a row.

"You don't believe me, either? No one believes me, but it's true. Renaud's over there. He's coming to see me."

Renaud? I don't understand. Renaud? Does she . . . my God, does she believe her brother's here?

"He's scared in his coffin, so he comes to see me when I'm all alone. And with you, it's like I was all alone, because you can't see anything."

She believes her dead brother is coming to visit her. Yssart is right, she's completely disturbed. Poor kid. I'd like to take her in my arms and . . . and above all, I'm relieved, though in a terrible way. Okay, it's disgusting to be happy to know that Virginie is sick, but frankly I prefer that to the presence of a killer in my living room. I feel all soft—my reaction.

"He says he wouldn't have let himself be dead if he had known it would be like this."

Such a calm little voice. I wonder how she sees her brother. Like a zombie in a film? An unpleasant image I wish I hadn't brought to mind—I've seen enough horror films to "see" him, too, half-decomposed and standing next to my wheelchair with a smile so steady and wide, you'd think someone had sewn the ends of his mouth to each ear. . . .

"Virginie! Lower the music, will you! You're going to go deaf. It took me a while. There was such a crowd!"

Ah! If I could leap, I would have bumped my head on the ceiling. Yvette! My appointed savior! Her footsteps cross the floor.

"I've told you not to open the door."

Why would she make a remark like that? No one opened the door.

"Virginie, put that book down and answer me," Yvette continues. "Why did you open the door?"

"I forgot Bilou in the backyard."

Bilou is her doll. The problem is, I don't remember hearing her go out. She only left to go pee. Did she take that occasion to go into the backyard? And let someone in? No, phantoms don't enter through doors. Unless this is not a phantom. What am I saying? I'm losing it. Unless this was a creature of flesh and bones, whom she let in . . . oh, my, we've got trouble here, guys! Elise Andrioli's brain is about to explode. Hello, Dr. Raybaud, you'd better check your patient (with unfailing patience) into a care facility immediately—one that is very peaceful and, above all, very far from Boissy-les-Colombes.

"Come have a sip. I'll make you a cup of herb tea, Elise."

Virginie gets up and docilely follows Yvette. But just before leaving, she whispers, "I had to let him in. He doesn't know how to pass through walls yet. It's too hard, you know."

Obviously, if he doesn't know how to pass through walls yet. . . . She goes off. So here I stay, with a squirrel turning around in my head—*squeak, squeak*—what is this shit?—*squeak, squeak*—trying to understand.

The herbal tea is too hot—lime-flavored, the kind that makes me sick to my stomach. I don't want herbal tea, I want calvados, a calvados that's just right, that burns a hole in your stomach. Herbal tea makes me puke. I swallow it slowly, and in small sips. Virginie is coloring something— I don't know what—I can hear her crayons as they run over the paper.

"What are you drawing, darling? A scarecrow?"

Yvette's voice is full of concern, yet confused.

"No! It's a little boy!"

"That's an odd little boy you have. He's all stiff, with his arms spread wide, and he's green all over . . ."

"That's what he's like!"

"Goodness, it's not worth getting angry over! Whatever I'm saying is only for you. I'm just kidding, after all . . . Would you like some more herbal tea?"

No index finger.

"Too bad. You want to help me with the dishes, Virginie?"

"Okay!"

What I would give to see that drawing: a stiff, green little boy! I greatly fear that Virginie has tipped over into another universe. Between the death of her brother and these recent events . . . And Yssart's doing nothing about it!

Doorbell.

It's Florent Gassin, the young inspector. He smells of leather, tobacco, and eau de toilette. I imagine he's wearing an RAF-style bomber jacket and faded jeans.

"I hope I'm not disturbing you . . . but, anyway, Captain Yssart asked me to stop by. I would like a few details on the circumstances of your attack the other day."

Index finger. He must be shifting back and forth, uneasily, from one foot to the other. The floor is creaking.

"Did anybody know you were going to go through the woods?"

No index finger. Why would he ask me that? Has he already asked Stéphane the same questions?

"Is this the routine you normally follow?"

Is that to say the routine my wheelchair-pushers follow, my sweet? Yes, generally. Therefore, index finger.

"Did you lose consciousness?"

Index finger.

"When you came to, was Jean Guillaume there?"

Index finger. God, this is monotonous!

"Was it raining when the accident took place?"

Index finger. What does the rain have to do with it?

"That's all. Thank you."

His notebook thuds shut. Yvette emerges: "Would you like something to drink?"

"Uhh . . . no, thanks, I'm in a hurry. By the way, is it true what they say? That Stéphane and his wife are getting a divorce?"

"Oh, that. I know nothing about it! I don't listen to gossip," Yvette replies, sounding very dignified. "Are you done?"

"Yes, I'll be leaving you. It appears his wife is fiercely jealous. Anyway, that's what they say. Well, then, goodbye, ladies."

If I understand correctly, they suspect this shrew Sophie of assaulting her husband and throwing me into the water out of jealousy. . . . Why not? At this point, all these theories carry equal weight.

"That inspector's as cute as they get," Yvette calls while putting away something or other. "Not like that nasty boss of his . . . but I don't know where he was going with all those questions. Well . . . Virginie, precious, it's time for you to go home. Get ready. Daddy's coming."

Doorbell. Daddy's here.

"Hello, Yvette, hello, Lise. It's funny how the weather's cooled off, isn't it? Ready, Virj?"

"Come in, Paul. Excuse me, I've got something on the stove." Yvette slips out.

"Daddy, do you want to see my drawing?"

"Yes, but show me quick. Is everything okay, Lise?"

Index finger. His voice sounds tired.

Virginie trots over.

"Look."

The sharp sound of a slap. What's going on?

"Don't ever start with that again. You hear me, Virginie? Never!"

His voice was low and subdued. He must really be furious. *Riiip,* goes the paper as it's torn. Virginie sniffles.

"Okay, we're going. Bye, Lise. Bye, Yvette."

It was all carried out with as much warmth as a three-star freezer. It knocked me on my ass. Paul is always so cool. Obviously, if Virginie shoved the drawing of Renaud as a zombie right under his nose . . . but anyway, it's not her fault if she's traumatized, poor thing. You'd think nobody in

the family realizes this. Soon they'll be smacking her because of the nightmares she'll have. In any case, I'm living
a nightmare of my own. As if I didn't already have enough
things to piss me off, as if I weren't already so unhappy . . .
no, mustn't wallow in self-pity. And to think I can't even
decide for myself whether I should get good and drunk to
forget it all.

THE INVESTIGATION IS AT A STANDSTILL. THE
weather is gloomy. So am I. It's cool, and it's drizzling.
Yvette has started to put away her summer things, and is
going through her winter clothes. The Great Catherine has
just left, after our daily session of chat/massage. She's confirmed for us that the Migoins are really splitting up.
Stéphane confided this to her on the tennis court. And it
looks like things aren't all they're cracked up to be between Paul and Hélène. Is it the change in seasons that has
willed this? Yesterday, when Hélène came to see me, I got
the impression she was crying. The only ones who seem to
be in good shape are Jean Guillaume and Yvette. They
went to the movies last night. That's why Hélène came
over. They went to see the latest Clint Eastwood film. I
loved the movies so much. Fuck it. Fuck this life, fuck
death, fuck the whole world.

SEVEN

WE'RE OUT ON A SUNDAY DRIVE. PAUL'S TAKEN US for a spin through the Essonne ("It's so beautiful at the end of the summer"). I'm sitting in front, strapped in by the safety belt. Hélène and Virginie are in the backseat. Yvette has taken advantage of the occasion to visit some sort of distant cousin, accompanied, of course, by Jean Guillaume. The window is half-open, and the country smell of damp grass is coming through. No one's talking. From time to time, Paul calls out, "Did you see that church? It's wonderful!" or for variety says, "Did you see that old farm? That's one hell of a building!" Hélène answers, "Yes, it's very nice." Virginie's reading her *Club Five,* not bothering with anyone.

"You're not cold, are you, Lise?" Paul inquires considerately.

No index finger. I'm dying from the heat. Yvette dressed me for an Arctic expedition.

"You think she's cold?" Paul asks Hélène.

"If she were cold, she would have answered," she replies.

I can feel a domestic spat looming on the horizon. We take a left turn and I tip over to the side.

"You could keep your eyes on the road, you know! You're driving like a maniac!" Hélène yells.

Bingo! Here we go!

"Oh, cut it out! Like that never happened to you! You didn't see how tight it was?"

"Obviously, you've always got a good excuse!"

Yoo hoo! I'm completely slumped over to the side.

"You can really be annoying when you want to!"

"And sometimes all you do is pretend. Anyway, I knew it would all turn out this way. You were already in a foul mood when we left!"

"What?! *You're* the one who was in a foul mood. You haven't spoken a single word all afternoon!"

"Well, what do you want me to say? Am I supposed to get ecstatic over every pile of rocks we pass? Excuse me, but there are more thrilling ways to spend our time than driving through the rain like a bunch of old farts."

"That's it! You always have to put down everything. Damn it!"

He slams on the brakes, and I tip forward. The door slams shut.

"Where's Daddy going?"

"To pee."

"I'm going, too!"

Another door slams shut.

"Dirty bastard," Hélène mutters behind me.

I'm completely over to the right, but no one realizes this. It's too bad, because if we go on driving this way, I'll wind up puking. The front door opens.

"So, has Mr. Fansten calmed down at all?"

"Listen, you're gonna stop this, okay? This is not the time, Hélène, it really isn't, all right?"

"And why not?"

"You know, you're lucky you're a woman. 'Cause there are times—"

"You didn't bring her along so much before, did you? That's when you needed me!"

"Why, you—"

Slap! Paul is definitely quick with his hands, at least for now.

"How dare you?! Are you out of your mind or what!"

The door slams shut. All sorts of screams abound.

"Mommy! Daddy! Stop it! Stop it!"

I'd love to be able to lift my head. I'd love to be somewhere else. I hate being in situations like these. Clack, clack, clack, everyone's back in the car. In deathly silence. Paul turns on the radio, and Beethoven floods the passenger compartment. We're off again, nervously. We're driving. I'm dangling like an old bag hung from a nail. Well, it's great to get out. What did she mean when she blurted, "That's when you needed me"? Oh, well, I guess it's none of my business, but it's true I know nothing about them. I'm even wondering why they're interested in me. After all, I'm really not such great company; I'm more like a potluck dinner—whatever you get out of me is what you've brought to me. Well . . . it seems Virginie is once again immersed in her book. If, on top of everything, her parents are arguing, it's not going to solve her problems. Now I understand why she pretends her brother is still "alive." Brrr.

Beethoven is interrupted to leave time for the news. Blah, blah, blah.

"There has been a call for witnesses within the the investigation in the shocking murder of Michael Massenet in Boissy-les-Colombes. Anyone who saw a white or cream-colored station wagon on Saturday, May 28, at 1:00 P.M. on the D91, in the town of La Furetière, is urged to come forward. In Sarajevo, the Serbs have begun a new round of shelling . . ."

The station changes to rock.

"Is a station wagon like our car?"

"Yes."

"And ours is white, too," Virginie continues.

"Thank you. I never would have known," Paul grumbles.

"There are tons of cars like ours," Hélène explains. "Mr. Guillaume also has a white station wagon."

It sticks in my little head. Yssart told me that the trail was absolutely insane. I've got to believe it isn't. A white or cream-colored station wagon. Either like theirs or like Jean Guillaume's. This opens up new perspectives for me. After all, Guillaume was the first one to show up on the scene when I was drowning. And who would be in a better position to be first if not the one who pushed me into the water? No, I'm blathering: poor Jean is no killer. And then, if it were him, then why would he have rescued me? To enter into my private life and watch over Virginie from up close? No, no, no, enough of this madness.

Paul is still driving just as nervously and I'm getting banged around from each direction, bumper-car–style. I hear my stomach protesting. Finally he hits the brake.

"Look at all these assholes going out to the country," Paul mutters, lighting a cigarette.

"Why are we stopping?"

"Because Daddy's gotten us stuck in some traffic jam. I think I'm going to suffocate in here. All this smoke . . ."

"Well, all you've got to do is open the window."

Nice atmosphere. Today's ride is one I'll always remember. We inch forward for quite a while before anyone says a word. Then Hélène exclaims, "Oh, look, there's Steph! There . . . in the white CX!"

"He hasn't got a CX, he's got a BMW."

"I'm telling you it's him. Anyway, I know Steph!"

"That I know. Well, excuse me, but I don't see any CX."

"Obviously he's just turned right. It must be a shortcut. That guy knows all the roads. He's not stupid enough to let himself get caught for hours in some shitty traffic jam."

Paul turns up the volume on the radio, sending decibels of rock into my ears. Finally it eases up and we're off again. I imagine hundreds of families cooped up in these cars, single file, all hollering at each other amid blaring car radios and blasts of the horn. Brrr.

Last stop! Everyone out! Yvette helps Paul pull me out of the vehicle and place me in my wheelchair.

"So, did you have a nice little ride?" Yvette inquires.

"Very nice, very nice. Well, you'll excuse us, but we've got a ton of things to do. See you tomorrow!" Paul calls out as they take off again.

"You'd think that boy swallowed a thistle," Yvette wonders aloud as she pushes me inside.

A thistle? You must mean a whole bouquet, and I have the impression that it's not over yet—Yvette seems so wound up.

RAIN, RAIN, AND MORE RAIN. TO TELL THE TRUTH, I like listening to the rain. It keeps me busy. But everyone around me is cursing. Yvette, for starters, is complaining about her rheumatism.

I smell coffee. Yvette sits down next to me and unfolds her newspaper. The rain falls harder.

"Listen to this! 'A new development in the case of the sadist of Boissy-les-Colombes. An anonymous caller telephoned the Saint Quentin Police Department yesterday, advising them to take a look in the Vilmorin Woods, in a forestry shed at the intersection of routes G7 and C9. In this shed, normally used for storing forest service tools, investigators found the bloodstained clothes of a man. The results of the analysis carried out during the night have not yet been released.' Can you imagine! But why would the murderer hide his clothes in the shed rather than burn them or throw them in the river? This doesn't hold water."

I agree, Yvette. However, there is a reason. Let's wait for the results of the analysis.

The phone rings. Yvette sluggishly gets up.

"Hello? Oh, hi, Stéphane. Yes, she's here. Okay, I'll put her on. It's Stéphane. He wants to tell you something."

Here we go, telephone.

"Hello, Lise?"

Obviously, as I don't answer, he goes on, "I wanted to tell you . . . don't believe everything they say about me. Listen, I can't explain, but I've got enemies. I have to get out of here. I . . . I love you, Lise. Farewell."

He hung up.

"He hung up?" Yvette inquires, who has admirably abstained from listening in.

Index finger.

"Is everything okay?"

Index finger. No, everything is not okay. What was he trying to say? I don't understand any of it. And to think that this nut job is in love with me is not comforting.

I slept poorly. A violent, brutal wind has risen, causing a devilish racket. I spent the night going over all the facts, in every which way, arriving at no other result than having given myself a migraine.

How do you say "I have a headache" by raising your index finger? You can't. So I get no aspirin. And so there's a dull pain above my brow, the pitter-patter of the rain, a howling wind, and a terrific setting for a scary movie. The door opens.

"Such awful weather. I'm soaked. I'm going to make us a nice hot cup of herbal tea."

Yuck.

"A nice verbena tea. That ought to pick us up."

Yuck, yuck. How about a calvados? A calvados?

"I bought the paper to see if there was anything new. They never give details on TV."

Oh, great! I'm all ears.

"There, I've put the water on. Let's see . . . where are my glasses?"

I'm sure you have them around your neck, as usual.

"Oh, look how silly I am! They're around my neck."

Bingo. She starts to read, turning the pages: "Flooding . . . the Bosnian Serbs . . . the match between France and Bulgaria . . . the Vigipirate plan . . . rebuilding the cathedral . . . oh, here it is! 'Was Michael Massenet murdered in the forestry shed? one might ask. The tests hastily carried out last night have in fact found that the blood staining the man's clothing discovered in the shed—see yesterday's report—belonged to Michael. Judging by the clothes themselves (a gray wool sweater, a pair of jeans, and black leather gloves), they would fit a man six feet tall, with size eleven shoes and large hands. "All I can tell you," claimed Captain Yssart, "is that the investigation has just taken a giant step." ' Well, with that much, they ought to be able to find him," Yvette continues. "Especially now, since they'll certainly find hair on the sweater. Nowadays, they have precision instruments in their laboratories, and with one single hair, they can find out plenty of things: the man's age, his color, tons of things. Oh, I hope they'll catch him! Six feet, how tall is that? About Mr. Stéphane's size. Yes. Much bigger than Jean, and at least a good half-head taller than Paul, too. I'll read you the rest: 'Will these new elements finally shed more light on these hateful murders perpetrated in Boissy-les-Colombes, which to this day have gone unpunished? June 11, 1991: Victor Legendre. August 13, 1992: Charles-Eric Galliano. April 15, 1993: Renaud Fansten. May 28, 1995: Michael Massenet. And last July 28, Mathieu Golbert was cruelly torn from the loving arms of his family. A monstrous series of murders, which investigators hope today to be able to rapidly put to an end.' I hope there'll be more details in tomorrow's paper. I'm calling Hélène in case the police might have contacted her."

She fidgets with the telephone. Poor Hélène! These new murders and all the agitation that goes with them must be making her relive Renaud's death to no end. It's like a recurring nightmare. Likewise for the other parents mixed up in this dreadful affair. The worst thing is that there's someone out there who has committed these murders. Behind the nickname "sadist" is someone who speaks, eats, jokes, and goes to work, as if it were nothing. A human being capable of strangling a child and tearing out his eyes or heart! Why did Yssart tell me that? I really could have done without it!

"Inspector Gassin paid them a visit. He asked them to come by tomorrow to see the clothes in case they might recognize them. All the victims' parents have been called to appear before Mrs. Blanchard, the examining judge. And he asked for the names of any friends of theirs who might match the description given in the paper. They were forced to mention Stéphane. Hélène seemed exhausted.

She told me she couldn't wait for it all to be over. I know what she means, mind you."

Five murders in five years. Victor, Charles-Eric, Renaud, Michael, and Mathieu. Out of five little boys, four were horribly mutilated. There were long intervals between murders, up until recently. From '93 to '95, nothing, then suddenly . . . What's been happening these last months? The killing machine has broken down and run off track. Why? Is it because I met Virginie? Yes, Virginie is a key, but I don't know the lock in which to place her. And what about the man's clothes left in the forestry shed? The murderer must have figured someone would find them. And who called the police? The famous anonymous call. Who could it have come from? A witness who saw the murderer enter the shed? Someone who might have discovered the clothes by chance and did not wish to be mixed up in a criminal investigation? It's exasperating to be unable to ask these questions. I can't wait for tomorrow night, to find out what the judge wanted.

THIS DAY ABSOLUTELY WILL NOT END! I'M CHAMPING at the bit. It's not even raining. Jean Guillaume has brought by two beautiful trout that he himself caught for Yvette, and now they're playing a belote. I hear them laughing. Yvette told me Jean used to look like her cousin Léon. I remember her cousin Léon, a cyclist with full biceps and a gorgeous head straight out of the Belle Epoque 1900. He was in all of Yvette's family photos until the time he was killed in a collision on the highway, near Liège. I've always suspected Yvette of having a soft spot for her cousin Léon. I know Jean Guillaume is small, Yvette told me so. If I glue Cousin Léon's head to a small weight-lifter's body, then the picture will be complete. I'm waiting for the telephone to ring, hoping Hélène will call.

Yvette: "What time is it?"

Jean Guillaume: "Four o'clock."

"I ought to go pick up Virginie from school if they're not back in time."

"I wouldn't want to be in their place. This time I deal. I wonder why the judge called everyone before him. . . . The captain didn't tell you anything, did he?"

"I didn't see him! Okay, I'm cutting the deck!"

"The guy who might really be in trouble is that Migoin. He's in good shape, sort of husky, and he's practically got sabers for hands; he was there when Elise was thrown into the water. . . . No, I really wouldn't want to be in his shoes right now."

"Stéphane? Are you kidding? Why Stéphane? And also, he didn't know those other kids."

"A guy who works on construction sites gets around. Someone told me he was the one who handled the Golberts' house, for example. Of course, you shouldn't believe everything you hear, but all sorts of gossip is going around now. There it is, the ace. Oh, you're terrible!"

"On the radio they said they were looking for a white or cream-colored station wagon, and Stéphane drives a navy blue BMW."

"Yeah, I know, but cars can be changed."

FLASHBACK: "OH, LOOK, THERE'S STEPH! THERE . . . IN the white CX!" "He hasn't got a CX, he's got a BMW." Stéphane . . . calling to tell me he has enemies, and they will certainly say "things" about him. Stéphane . . . from the start, I sensed there was something about him that was not "clean." Trust your intuitions, the shrinks say. I trust them, I trust them. I'm mistrustful.

Yvette has left to pick up Virginie. Jean sits down on the sofa, next to me. He sighs.

"Well, it's all a big mess, in any case. . . . Poor Elise, are you all right?"

Index finger.

"You know, I was thinking about you yesterday when I was passing by Romero's."

Romero's . . . They sell supplies for ambulances and the handicapped.

"They have an electric wheelchair on sale. Now that you

can use your finger, maybe you could drive it by yourself. All you'd have to do is flick a switch. Do you want me to speak to Yvette about it, so she can talk it over with your uncle?"

An electric wheelchair? I'd go bumping into everything! Unless I learned to use it inside the house . . . My God, this would be . . . this would be . . . a revolution!

Index finger.

"You're right. You can't just sit there like that, like some rag doll, waiting for a cure. I'm sure they could come up with all kinds of gadgets to make your life much easier."

That wonderful Jean Guillaume, with Cousin Léon's head! And me, suspecting you ever so briefly of being the murderer! Go ahead, pal! Tinker on! Take me out of this dark tunnel where I'm rotting away!

VIRGINIE IS WATCHING TELEVISION. I HEAR YELPS, squeals, and shouts; sounds from intergalactic battles.

"We can't let them get away."

"Captain, we can't increase our levels of neutroglyceron fusion—we'll explode!"

Biff! Bang! Pow! Jean is helping Yvette gut the trout. What the hell time is it, anyway?

Someone is ringing at the door. Finally!

"Coming! Coming! Oh, hello, Hélène, hello, Paul! Come on in. Virginie's watching *Intergalactis*. So how did it go? Would you like something to drink?"

"I'd like a beer if you have one. I'm dying of thirst," Paul answers.

"It took so, so long . . . but really the judge seemed all right. . . . Just a glass of water, please," says Hélène.

"Sit down, I'll be right back. Jean's taking care of the trout. He brought back two of them—magnificent!"

"Good evening, Elise."

"Hi, Elise."

Index finger.

They sit down. Paul sighs. Someone is cracking his knuckles.

"Here you go. I hope the beer's cold enough. So?"

I'm nothing more than one big, giant ear. Paul must be drinking a sip; I hear him gulping, and he answers, "So the judge is ordering . . . umm . . . the bodies to be . . . umm . . . exhumed. She feels that because at the time no one thought to link the murders, they should perform the autopsies again, with this in mind. No one was too thrilled about it, of course, but what else is there to do?"

"Exhumed? Oh . . . well, obviously . . ."

"They think," Hélène cuts in, "that Michael was murdered by the stream, and that the murderer went to change in the forestry shed. It's not in use at that time of the year."

"But . . . but how did someone find out about it?" Yvette promptly asks.

"Because someone saw it. Someone who's afraid, and keeping silent," says Paul, emptying his beer.

Virginie? No, the police would know the difference between a child's voice and an adult's. Could someone else know about it, then?

"It could have been a drifter looking for shelter in the shed who discovered the clothes," Jean Guillaume calls out amid sounds of frying.

"A drifter wouldn't have called the police," Hélène cuts in, her voice sounding tired.

To put it plainly, they're going around in circles. If only that bungling idiot Yssart would come by to visit. He always descends upon me whenever I least want him to.

Exhumation . . . it sends shivers up my spine. Pale little hands, caskets covered with moist earth, decomposed bodies, ragged clothing, and tufts of hair on fleshless faces revealing glinting bones. . . . Stop it, Elise, this is something you shouldn't be thinking about.

"Well, it's all so dreadful. I hope they'll arrest him soon," Yvette sighs.

"Too bad they didn't arrest him before," Paul says through gritted teeth. "Well, we'll be going now. I've got work waiting."

"Of course. Don't keep it waiting. When is it going to be? I mean . . ."

"The exhumation? The morning after tomorrow," Hélène answers. "Come on, Virginie, we're going now."

"Already? But it's not over."

"Hurry up, and don't argue."

"Good-bye, Elise. Good-bye, Yvette. Good-bye, Uncle Jean."

Go figure why she nicknamed Jean Guillaume "Uncle Jean." Everyone is saying good-bye. The sack of potatoes stays where it is, thinking. Nothing in this whole matter seems to make sense. Nothing fits together. It's as if someone were drawing a red herring across the trail, someone who had a global view of the puzzle and was sawing the pieces apart so that they couldn't be adjusted.

"Poor Paul! I wouldn't like to be in his place. To know that someone was gonna dig up my kid . . . ," Jean calls out from the kitchen.

"Be quiet, it's giving me chills. Are you getting all this, Elise?"

Index finger.

"I don't have to tell you, but some people have more than their share of grief in this world," Yvette continues.

I can only agree.

"That guy's face is ravaged," Guillaume replies. "There are times when suddenly it looks like he's aged ten years."

I can't help but wonder what feelings I would experience if I were told that Benoît was going to be dug up. Benoît, whom I never saw dead; Benoît, whom they buried without me . . . Benoît, who has been frozen forever as a man smiling beneath the cloudy sky in Ireland. And who today must be a fleshless body, on which the worms have done their work. It's too unfair; sometimes you just want to take the world in your hands and break it like a glass, until your hands are bloody.

"Does Elise eat trout?"

"I'll mash some up for her with a potato."

Well, good golly, I'm getting me some pig feed. Looks like I'm in a foul mood tonight!

* * *

SO HERE IT IS! I'VE GOT IT! THE NEW ELECTRIC WHEEL-chair. I sit atop my throne like an empress. Yvette called my uncle yesterday morning, and they delivered the thing that very afternoon. Jean got right to work on it, and this morning it's all mine! And, miracle of miracles, I can drive it without having to ask anyone, simply by pushing a button with my index finger. Jean grouped four buttons together in the shape of a cross, for going forward, backward, to the right, or the left. For the time being, I can press forward and backward, but have a hard time with right and left. When we consulted with Raybaud, he found that this mechanism could only further my manual motility, and strongly encouraged me to persevere. As if I were doing it to be nice to him! Honestly . . . So I hit the button and go forward and backward in the living room (Yvette moved the furniture against the wall). I've got to say that when for months you've been depending on the goodwill of others, it's fantastic to be able to go back and forth at will, even if it's only ten feet across the floor.

Other than that, while I'm having fun with my new toy, the cops are busy exhuming the bodies of the kids. In the presence of a family member. Paul must have gone, I suppose. A group of men in a circle, dry-eyed, throats knotted, standing in the cold wind and watching as the gravediggers shovel up the earth. Shit. It's beautiful outside, Yvette says. She left the windows open, and it smells of damp earth in autumn. It appears that the men who are opening the caskets are wearing masks, like surgeons, not so much because of the odor, but because of the fumes. Fermentation occurs in coffins. Sometimes they explode. Why do I always let myself be drawn into thoughts like these? Forward, backward, backward, forward; I don't want to imagine the cemetery, I don't want to think about those shriveled children's bodies; forward, backward.

"You're gonna wind up wearing grooves in the floor!"

Yes, my sweet Yvette, backward, forward, a groove, a trench, a ditch, a tomb, stop!

Telephone.

"Hello? Oh, hi, Catherine. Excuse me? No, no, that's all

right, you can come tomorrow, sure, I understand . . . if you have to go to the dentist. . . . What? . . . What are you saying? . . . But that's impossible! . . . How did you know? Ah . . . well, what did he say? . . . What? Really, that's crazy! . . . But why? . . . Still, that's no reason . . . Yes, I understand. Thanks. I'll see you tomorrow . . . Elise, it's horrible; Stéphane's wife . . . she, she committed suicide! Catherine was at the hospital when they brought her in."

What? What is it now?

"She swallowed a vial of barbiturates. Their cleaning woman found her sprawled on the floor. She's dead, Elise!"

Dead? Steph's wife? Committed suicide? But why the hell . . . ?

"Catherine thinks it's because he wanted to leave her. Still to kill herself over that . . . And no one knows where he is, they haven't managed to get a hold of him . . . do you realize his wife is dead, and he doesn't even know? They tried to call him because he's got a telephone in his car, but he's not answering. Oh, my goodness, it's really terrible right now. I don't know what's going on, but it just won't stop!"

You said it! Sophie's dead! And I thought people always failed with barbiturates. And where is Steph? I've got a feeling that he'll be in trouble—big trouble. What was the meaning of his call the other day—"I've got enemies"—all that, as if he had foreseen what was going to happen? Steph, who drives in unknown white station wagons . . . whose wife dies at a very opportune moment . . . and who claims to be in love with me. A guy who falls in love with a sack of potatoes has got to be a little out of whack.

Telephone. Here we go! The circus starts all over.

"Hello? Hi, Hélène. . . . Yes, I know, Catherine told me, it's horrible. . . . Excuse me? . . . But I don't understand why. . . . Oh, yes, of course. . . . And how are things for you? . . . Yes, I would imagine. . . . You know you can come to the house if you feel too lonely. . . . Come have some coffee. . . . Okay, I'll see you in a bit. It was Hélène. She had a visit from Inspector Gassin. He wanted to know if she knew where Stéphane was. They're looking for him. She said she knew nothing, he had to be at a construction site somewhere.

She seemed very depressed. She knew poor Sophie quite well, and to learn about it only this morning . . . Paul's at the exhumation, Virginie's in school, and she's all alone, so I asked her over for coffee. She said yes. She's not working today. It's all so ghastly!"

The doorbell rings.

"Definitely is. What is it now?"

The door opens.

"Oh, hello, Inspector, come in. He's not here!"

"I see that news travels fast. Excuse me . . . hello, ma'am."

No doubt he's here to see me. Index finger.

"So you know that Mrs. Migoin has died?"

"Yes, we found out about it just a minute ago from Catherine Rimiez, Elise's physical therapist."

"We're trying to track down Mr. Migoin. You wouldn't know by chance where we might find him?"

"Mr. Migoin doesn't usually confide his schedule to us. He's just an acquaintance."

"I know, but I've got to try every avenue."

"Anyway, he will be coming home eventually. Why are you going to so much trouble?"

"I'm sorry to have bothered you for nothing. Good-bye, ladies."

The door closes. Yes, why go to so much trouble? No one would nag an inspector to go hunt down a widower, they would send a policeman. I was definitely right: things are getting hotter for Stéphane.

"I wonder why the police are so troubled about this," Yvette comments. "I'm going to make some coffee."

Forward, backward . . . if only I could move this damn finger a millimeter to the side, if only . . . I feel it vibrating . . . trembling. I'm going to make it!

"You know what I think, Elise? I keep telling myself that she must have taken them that night, the pills, because otherwise the cleaning lady would've gotten there in time. She must have taken them while he was asleep. It's terrible, isn't it? To think he was sleeping next to his wife while she was dying!"

And he wasn't aware of her condition when he woke up? He thought she was sleeping in, and just slipped out on tiptoes? Why not? And why did she fall to the floor? In one final start of consciousness? One could find out by placing his hand on her. Because I'm getting the impression that good old Stéphane had his bags packed. It's funny . . . well, if I should say so, I don't think Sophie was the kind of woman who would commit suicide. With her character . . . Which only goes to show that sometimes you can be completely mistaken about people.

HÉLÈNE IS HERE. SOMEONE'S DRINKING COFFEE. NO, they're both drinking coffee. And all I get to drink is a nice herbal tea that aids digestion. I can smell the delicious scent of coffee. I'm dying to drink a good strong cup of coffee, full of sugar, but instead swallow the overheated, sluggish-tasting herb tea, cursing Yvette.

Hélène is speaking in her bad-day voice. She sounds exhausted. Sometimes I wonder if she'll wind up having a real nervous breakdown. I think she's getting sadder and sadder.

"They still haven't found Stéphane. They've gone around to all his construction sites, and no one's seen him. Do *you* think that's normal? Sophie committing suicide . . . For a long time they didn't love each other anymore. Why didn't they simply get a divorce? I knew her for five years. She helped me out a lot when . . . well, when Renaud . . . when I think about what they must be doing to Renaud . . . It's driving Paul totally crazy. . . ."

Sniffling. Yvette consoling her. Sometimes it's nice not to see anything.

"And meanwhile Virginie's having her troubles. She's chosen the wrong time for this. I know it isn't her fault, but I don't know what to do with her anymore, she's so withdrawn. . . . She seems to be obeying, but she's in her own world. Her grades in school keep dropping, but she refuses to talk about it. Sometimes you'd think she wasn't even there, that she simply doesn't hear us. She smiles and says yes, but you'd think she's empty. I took her to the school psychologist, and he says that it's normal; that she's lived through a great emotional trauma and that the murders of Michael and Mathieu have reactivated the loss of her brother . . . and that we need more time. I can't just sit and wait like that, I'm tired of waiting. All they ever tell you to do is wait, that everything will be all right, but that's not true, that's the bottom line. It won't be all right. It might even get worse!"

"Don't say that, Hélène. You're tired right now, you're going through hard times, but you'll see . . . one day this will all be far behind you. Once again you'll look ahead to the future with confidence."

I think you're laying it on a bit thick, Yvette, but in any case it was a nice thought. Anyway, what are you supposed to tell her? Yes, your daughter is nuts, it looks like your husband can't stand you anymore, your best friend has just done herself in, and her husband may be the guy who has murdered your stepson; everything's okay, Madame Marquessa?

"You may be right. . . . We'll see," Hélène answers unenthusiastically. "How about you, Elise, are you all right?"

Index finger.

"Elise has a new wheelchair."

"Oh, yes, I see! I hadn't noticed. You'll excuse me, but right now . . ."

Like she really gives a damn about my wheelchair!

"It's an electric wheelchair. You can push it, but she can also activate it herself."

"That's fantastic! Let me see!"

I've never heard anyone say "fantastic" with such despair in her voice. All right, fine, I'll play along: forward, backward . . .

"Oh, Elise! That's wonderful! You'll be able to do plenty of things!"

Right, I'll go from one wall to another.

"Jean Guillaume saw it in the window of Romero's, and got the idea to work on it for Elise."

"So, Yvette, tell me . . . you seem kind of interested in

this Mr. Guillaume," Hélène tries to joke in a funny little voice.

"Well, I've got to admit that he's quite nice, and then, a man can always be useful. Are you having some more coffee?"

"No, thanks, I'm pumped enough as it is. Paul hasn't called?"

"Paul? No . . ."

"No? Because he said he'd call home and, since I was gone, I thought he might call here in the meantime."

"He must have a lot of work to do."

"Yes, he's swamped right now. I called to tell him that Sophie . . . He was in a meeting, but the police had already been by—Gassin, that young inspector—so he said he'd call back. It's really nice out today!"

"Would you like to go out for a little walk?"

"Why not? I'll go get Virginie."

"I'll go get the lap robe for Elise."

I'm going to die from the heat with that on top of me. Hélène is right next to me. I can smell her perfume.

"Stéphane didn't kill his wife," she quickly whispers.

Well, so much the better, but to tell you the truth, I didn't think . . .

"You know the truth, don't you?"

What truth? What's she talking about?

"Ready to go?" Yvette interrupts, plunking the two-hundred-pound blanket down on my lap.

The truth . . . ? I'd really like to know the truth. It's hot outside, the air smells good, and Hélène must be thinking about Renaud, hacked up in a formaldehyde stench, and Sophie, lying in the hospital morgue. "Stéphane didn't kill his wife. . . ." Does that mean that someone killed her? Could this be a faked murder? No, what else am I going to think of! Just take advantage of the walk, young lady, and don't think about anything else!

The truth . . . why would I know the truth? And does Hélène know what it is? Does Hélène think that Virginie knows something? That Virginie may have confided something to me? Stop it, Elise, you're going to drive yourself mad. Fine, okay.

THEY STILL HAVEN'T GOTTEN A HOLD OF STÉPHANE. It's three days now. Sophie's burial is expected for tomorrow. Paul obviously wants to go, and Hélène does not. According to Inspector Gassin, Sophie may have killed herself because her husband had just left. Left *her*. Split for good. He emptied out his bank accounts, put his affairs in order, and *bang,* he was off, on his way to a new life. His departure was somewhat premeditated. I wonder if he'll react to the radio announcement the police have broadcasted asking him to get in touch with them. In my opinion, he would have no desire to know what might have happened to his wife. Besides, they have no charges against him: it's not his fault she killed herself. But I've got a feeling they have a ton of questions to ask him, and that his wife's death is only a pretext. Another hypothesis: What would you do if you were to discover that your husband was a murderer? If you recognized him in the descriptions of certain clothes? Would someone commit suicide over that?

The doorbell rings. Yvette runs to get it.

"Oh, hello . . ."

A disappointed tone.

"Hello, Mrs. Holzinski. I suppose Miss Andrioli is here?"

"Where do you expect her to be? She's in the living room. You know the way."

"Yes. Thank you."

Yssart! His soft footsteps on the wooden floor. I wonder how he's dressed. An impeccable three-piece suit? He smells of eau de cologne.

"Hello, Miss Andrioli."

Index finger.

"I was passing by, and thought I might visit you. Don't worry, I have no questions to ask of you. No, you see, I've come to give you some information. For I'm convinced that you've taken quite an interest in this whole sad matter. The laboratory exam has revealed hair on the collar of the sweater found in the forestry shed. Light hair. Belonging to Stéphane Migoin. We've compared it to a sample taken from a hairbrush in his house. This is what I wanted to tell you."

So it really was true?

"What's more, it would seem that Mrs. Migoin's death was not necessarily accidental. The way I see it, someone may very well have used force to make her take these pills. She has a bruise on her jaw, which would give credence to this theory, or else she might have done it to herself falling out of bed, obviously. I'm told that Mr. Migoin was interested in you."

There's a pause. I'm waiting. He must be observing me. He continues, "I'm also told that he may have been seen at the wheel of a white CX station wagon."

Paul and Hélène! They gave him that!

"I'm told so many things that I have to put out a warrant for his arrest. So, in case you might have some idea of his whereabouts, I would be quite obliged if you would inform me. It would save time for everyone."

Again! This guy really believes I know the whole town's secrets! If I knew where Stéphane was, I'd be the first to say. Well, to try to make them understand.

"Do you know anything about this?"

No index finger.

"Do you think little Virginie might be so attached to Mr. Migoin to the point of not revealing what she may know about him?"

Virginie? Attached to Stéphane? Seeing him murder her brother and saying nothing? No, impossible, unless . . . unless . . . my God, yes! Unless Stéphane were Hélène's lover! If this were true, then Virginie would not have dared to speak! But Hélène loves Paul. Why the devil would she go sleep with Stéphane? And Stéphane loves me. Oh, my, I'm getting mixed up . . .

"Do you understand that Stéphane Migoin will be accused of the murder of Michael Massenet?"

Index finger.

"Do you think he may be behind this crime?"

What does he think? That I'm the Delphic Oracle? Since when do the cops worry about what paralytics think?

And, besides, what *do* I think? I can't bring myself to raise my index finger. I realize that I cannot believe that Stéphane killed these children. I can *think* it, but can't *believe* it.

"Thank you. I needed to know what your feelings are on this matter. You see, Miss Andrioli, contrary to what you might think, I trust your judgment enormously."

He really takes my breath away! I've never said a word to him, and yet he trusts my judgment! I must be dreaming! This cop is another nut job! I'm surrounded by nut jobs! Perhaps I'm in an asylum and no one has told me.

"I'll be taking my leave. Be well."

Like a charm. Thank you, and a good day to you. Send in the next one! The asylum's open every day! I can hear his soft footsteps grow distant. I'm sure he's wearing hand-sewn leather shoes.

"Has he gone?" Yvette inquires in an arrogant tone.

Index finger.

"Pretentious!" she calls out before returning to her kitchen.

Forward, backward, thinking. I've never done so much thinking in my entire life. Before, everything was so simple. I complained like everyone else, but when I think about how easy it was compared to now . . . forward, backward. . . . What if I crash into a wall? "A quadriplegic woman went charging into her living-room wall at 150 miles per hour and smashed her skull!" Forward, backward. "Attention, ladies and gentlemen, welcome to Boissy-les-Colombes's grand rodeo starring the incomparable Elise Andrioli. The crowd's going wild!" Fortunately, no one knows what I'm thinking. I'd be quite ashamed. My poor father always wondered how I could laugh about everything, even in the worst of situations. One must think of it as a gift. The other hypothesis is that I'm a complete asshole. Let's be serious: Where could Stéphane be? Why has he fled? Why did he decide to leave, and empty his bank accounts, and everything else? And, above all, is he stupid enough to have left his sweater full of Michael's blood in the shed? Maybe he's no Einstein, but still . . .

EIGHT

YET ANOTHER BURIAL. BUT THIS TIME I'M TAKING part in it. Since it's nice out. Yvette decided to attend and is rolling me there. We're going there by foot, taking our time. Paul and Hélène were driving and offered to give us a lift, but Yvette preferred to walk. She says it will soon be winter, and that we should take advantage of the weather. So we're taking advantage.

When the road is straight and empty, Yvette lets me press the button and roll by myself. Vroom vroom. . . . The worst thing is that I'm delighted. The crisp sound of the wheels upon the asphalt, the rustle of the leaves, the sun's warmth on my arms, and the wheelchair gently moving forward this way are all so nice that I might forget the reason for our walk.

As we approach the cemetery, Yvette resumes her commands, calling out a brief "We're here." Our bucolic interlude is over.

"The cemetery's filled with people," Yvette offers.

The whole town is here, and the gossip is flying all around. Since Sophie has no family, the mayor is taking care of everything. This good man Ferber—for whom I

never voted—is running from right to left, shaking hands
and checking out the sprays of flowers. . . . Well, I must say
he's got quite a task ahead of him if he wants to bring
money into this town.

It seems that Inspector Gassin is present, with two po-
licemen. No doubt they're expecting the widower to appear
at the funeral. Paul has confided to us that Stéphane's parents, old farmers living in the Eure region, have had their
residence under constant surveillance.

"Hi. How's it going?" Hélène whispers. "Paul's over
there, with Ferber. Neither Michael's parents nor Mathieu's have shown up. They knew Sophie well, but what
with everything they're saying about Stéphane today . . ."

The ceremony begins. The wind has picked up. A brisk
little autumn breeze. I feel it caressing my neck and
cheeks. For once, I'm grateful to Yvette for wrapping me
up like a newborn. It's hard to make out the voice of the
priest, who is reciting vague old sayings with no convic-
tion. Fortunately there's some wind to keep the gathering
awake.

I hear the dull sound of earth as it falls on the casket.
Heels scraping, movements, nervous coughs, a brief pa-
rade in silence, people fidgeting, and finally it's over: Sophie Migoin will be resting underground forever.

"Ah, our Elise!" comes Ferber's fat, jovial voice. "How
are we doing? You seem to be in fine form!"

No, actually I'm not. Excuse me, Ferber, but if you
think it will make me vote for you . . .

"Miss Andrioli is making great progress."

Look! It's Raybaud! All proud of his student.

They all start to talk together, no longer worrying about
me. So much the better. I'm listening to the noises going
around, the busy buzz of the living. Stéphane's name keeps
coming up, accompanied by a thousand hypotheses. At
random, they bring up bankruptcy, murders, drugs—at this
rate, he'll soon be a mafia don and a terrorist. Someone's
tapping on my shoulder.

"Miss Andrioli, it's Florent Gassin. Still no news from
our friend?"

No index finger. This is definitely turning into an obsession for them.

"Too bad. Excuse me."

People start to head off. The cold, cutting wind is not conducive to long discussions. Yvette grasps the wheelchair.

"Poor Sophie . . . and to think just last Monday I ran into her at the butcher aisle . . . she was buying scallops. And now . . . The mayor invited Paul and Hélène to lunch; I told them we were going home. This wind's a cold one. . . . Let's go!"

We're off again. Stéphane hasn't shown up, appearing out of the blue, disheveled, in a deep sweat, yelling "Sophie!" to give us the final word on this enigma.

Paul and Hélène are having lunch at the mayor's house, and life goes on. Life always goes on. Well, for the living, of course.

On the road going home, Yvette keeps quiet. So much the better, as it allows me to ruminate calmly on the latest news. Let's review: A murderer attacks some children. It's assumed that he drives a white station wagon. In a shed they discover a sweater covered with the blood of one of the young victims. The sweater's collar has Stéphane Migoin's hair on it. They said Stéphane Migoin was seen at the wheel of a white station wagon. And disappeared the very night his wife committed suicide, but not before emptying his bank accounts and liquidating his assets. I call for a life sentence!

To the attorney for the defense:

Your Honor, would you still please consider that:

a) It was an anonymous call that informed the police of the location of the shed that contained the bloody clothes. What if someone had planted them there? And what if someone had planted hair belonging to Stéphane Migoin on the collar of the sweater?

b) Virginie Fansten claims to have been present at one or more of the murders. However, she has never accused Stéphane Migoin, for whom she seems to have no particular affection.

c) Could Stéphane Migoin be so dumb that he would
   run away and leave everything pointing to him?

I call for his acquittal, based on lack of evidence.

Gentlemen of the jury, what is your opinion? Guilty or
not guilty? Your verdict, please?

We arrived back at the house without my realizing it, as
I was so caught up in my imaginary trial. I understand that
the only chance for the defense would be for them to make
Virginie talk. There's no more time to procrastinate. I've
got to inform Yssart.

But still there's one question: If Stéphane were the murderer and Virginie knew, would he have left her alive?
That's a good question; I'm proud of myself. But how am I
to explain all that to the captain? In bees' language, making
figure-eights on the wooden floor with this goddamn
wheelchair? If only Benoît were still here . . . if only. . . . A
great depression overtakes me; I feel a lump in my throat,
and my lips are starting to tremble. I'm crying. This hasn't
happened to me since the accident. This must mean I'm
getting better, that my muscles are unlocking. I'm crying.
Shit! I can feel tears roll down my cheeks, wetting my
mouth. I'm having trouble breathing. It's gripping me,
choking me. I'm crying like a baby about this whole mess,
yet at the same time I'm happy to be able to cry. There are
times when really small things can be satisfying.

"Elise? Oh, my God, what's wrong?"

Wiping my tears with a clean handkerchief.

"Is it because of all these funerals? Breathe deeply, it
will be all right. You'll see, you'll make it through, don't
cry."

Yvette is babbling into my ear, and I'm not listening,
because I'm off, very far away, with Benoît, to those years
that will never return, and I can feel my tears flow like a
river to the sea, a sea still warm with memories.

I'M ALONE. I'M GOING FORWARD AND BACKWARD. I
feel calm. All those tears the other day emptied me out.

Our little town is in turmoil. The succession of tragic events have won us celebrity, and they talk about us on television and all the scandal sheets. The only ones in this scandal are the murder squad, as if the local police and investigators hadn't done a damn thing.

The one person making a big noise is the young Inspector Gassin. He could never put up with Yssart's arrival on the scene. He told Hélène he just couldn't see what these guys who were thrust upon us could understand about the subtle ramifications in any of these matters. As for Yssart . . . no comment.

I listened to the latest news with a sort of detachment. Stéphane's picture was broadcast on the TV news, on every channel. An all-points bulletin has been put out on him. But for the moment Steph has slipped through their net.

The exhumation of the bodies of the little victims has demonstrated once and for all that they were in fact killed by the same murderer. They've found nothing that might incriminate Stéphane or find him innocent.

Mathieu Golbert's father punched the face of some journalist who would stop at nothing for an interview, and stomped on his camera.

But above all, Sophie Migoin's autopsy has led some to think that her ingestion of sleeping pills was not voluntary. Someone held her mouth and forced her to swallow. I found that out from Hélène, who found it out from the ever-charming Inspector Gassin.

It's cold. It's raining. Yvette and Jean Guillaume have driven to the superstore. The rain has started up again, with the dull sound of hundreds of tennis balls. The telephone rings. As always, when Yvette steps out, she turns on the answering machine. I come to a stop so that I can hear better.

· "Hello, We cannot answer your call right now, but please leave a message after the beep . . ."

"Elise? Listen, I haven't got much time."

Stéphane!

"You're in danger, Elise, great danger. You've got to get out of town. I don't have time to explain, but believe me, it's a horrible frame-up. If you knew . . . I've gotta go, I've gotta hang up. I love you. Good-bye . . . I . . . no, no, let go of me, no!"

There's a violent crash, the sound of something smashing into the wall of the phone booth, and then nothing else. Only gasps for air, and the obsessive *beep beep beep* of a call cut short.

What in God's name is this? Am I dreaming? The strangled cry, the silence. . . . Does that mean Stéphane has just been . . . there? As he was talking to me? A crackling outside startles me; my nerves are as tightly wound as strings on a violin. "In danger . . . leave town . . ." And then he was cut off. Nervously, I pace the room in my wheelchair, repeating to myself Stéphane's words. The rain beats the roof like a tambourine. What does that call mean? What a pain in the ass it is to be unable to speak about anything to anyone! Good God! The answering machine recorded the conversation, and that's evidence. Yes, evidence in Stéphane's favor! Unless this is all just a clever put-on. What the hell is Yvette up to? She's got to come back, listen to that piece-of-shit answering machine, and call the cops! I'm waiting impatiently, keeping watch. Minutes flow by like drops falling from a faucet—slow and exasperating.

Ah! There's a sound of footsteps on the gravel! I get ready to roll over to the front door, but it's not opening. I hear the doorknob turning, but then nothing. If Yvette has lost her keys, well, then, here we are. I hear footsteps along the dining-room wall. Then they come to a stop. Why isn't she calling out to me? She's got to call me, to explain. I'm still alive, after all! *Unless this isn't Yvette . . . Unless this is someone who knows that Stéphane called me . . .*

The walking resumes. In the rain. Going around the house. Someone is looking at me through the windows. Yes, there is definitely a face pressed up against the glass. I feel naked. I ridiculously back my wheelchair all the way to the sideboard, as if I could somehow get beyond the sight of this gaze that has settled on me, unbeknownst to me, and which I imagine as cold and having no other expression than the interest a predator has for its prey.

Stéphane! Call back! Tell me it was just a stupid game, an idiotic nightmare. Call back!

More crackling on the gravel. I can't stand the thought of these eyes I can't see, and yet are looking at me. I'm afraid. This fear runs through my bones and veins, cold and chilling.

Is that goddamn front door locked?

Someone is shaking the doorknob. I can recognize the sound. My saliva is having a hard time clearing a path down my throat. Someone's scratching at the window. I imagine fingers sliding along the panes—long, curvy, impatient fingers.

Then no more sound. Has "he" left?

Ah! The blow has been struck without warning. Broken glass crashes onto the wooden floor, right in front of me. "He" is going to slip his hand through the hole and turn the catch. I'm petrified. My throat hurts so much from wanting to scream. "Who broke the glass? Go away! Go away, whoever you are, leave me alone! For Pete's sake!"

There's someone in the living room. The glass is crunching under his furtive steps. I activate my wheelchair to back up and hear a little laugh. Virginie? Someone passes before me. If I could hold out my hand, if I could see . . . I shrivel up in my seat, waiting for the blow to fall, the pinprick, or maybe worse . . .

A metallic noise.

A voice abruptly rises through the room and it takes me two seconds to understand that it's the answering machine.

Footsteps again, approaching me. No, I don't want to. . . . This silence is more unbearable than anything. . . . And what if he plunges a knife into my body, my eyes, my mouth . . . he can do whatever he likes, I . . .

A car horn. Just nearby. Three familiar blasts of the horn. It's Jean Guillaume! A sudden rush of steps toward the window, onto the gravel. Behind the house, a car door slams shut. I feel so relieved I think I might faint.

"What is this? Have you seen this, Jean? The living-room window's broken."

"Well . . . let's see. That's no surprise, have a look at

this! It was with this stone. Lucky thing poor Elise wasn't hit right in the face with it!"

"Just another stunt by those dirty little hoodlums who hang around by the train station."

"I'll replace the window for you this afternoon. Otherwise, with the rain, the floor will get soaked."

"Are you okay, Elise? You must have been scared."

As far as being scared goes, I was scared to death. I feel about as spruce as a shriveled soufflé. Yvette's putting things back in order, cursing the hoodlums. I try to breathe normally, without choking. Jean Guillaume is fiddling with the window. And suddenly I understand what my mysterious visitor came to do: to erase Stéphane's message. If he had the time to . . . to hurt Stéphane and run over here, then it must mean that Stéphane called from somewhere close. Or that two people are operating together. What did Stéphane say? "A frame-up." It seems that way to me. But why get me mixed up in it?

In any case, I'm the only witness again.

FOR TWO DAYS I'VE BEEN LISTENING ATTENTIVELY TO the news, each moment expecting them to announce that Stéphane Migoin's body has been discovered, but there's nothing. The rain won't stop, and everyone is edgy, nervous, and agitated. Too much has happened in too little time, and everyone is anxiously, impatiently waiting for it to unfold. Virginie hardly comes by anymore. Her parents have enrolled her in after-school classes so that she will catch up with what she has missed. Sometimes when I hear Hélène discuss things with Yvette, it seems that her voice is husky. I wonder if she's drinking. It appears Paul has a crazy schedule; he comes home late, leaves early, and constantly seems in a bad mood. Even Jean Guillaume and Yvette had an argument over the recipe for coq au vin, and he left without coffee, muttering into his mustache. It seems ridiculous, but it translates quite well the general state of mind: exasperation and waiting for who knows what. Why haven't they found Stéphane? Did he want to play a trick on me? Well, after all, a trick . . . it's a way of saying something. A guy who's capable of this type of trick deserves to be put in a straitjacket.

This is how the time has been going by—tensely.

The Great Catherine finds that I'm holding myself much better. She feels a certain tension in my muscles, a shudder, which has led Raybaud to order new tests.

Hospital. Odors of formaldehyde, ether, and medications. They roll me through cold corridors, where metallic sounds resound. They stretch me out on a table, plant needles in my body, and place electrodes on my chest and temples. They sound my chest, sit me up, and tap on my joints with a rubber hammer, making dubious "hmms." It takes all day. It all ends with a body scanner. Everything will land on the desk of Professor Combré, who is currently attending a symposium in the United States. They put my clothes back on, settle me back into my precious wheelchair, and we go back home.

"So?" asks Jean Guillaume, who has come to pick us up.

"According to the consultant, there's incontestably an improvement. Now, we've got to wait for the professor's opinion to find out if we can attempt an operation."

Jean Guillaume lowers his voice so that I won't hear, but I hear him say, "And if the operation succeeds, how would she be?"

Yvette then lowers her voice and says, "They don't know. They think she could recover her sight and perhaps movement in her upper limbs."

I feel a mix of frightful despair and fierce hope: despair in knowing I'll be condemned to a wheelchair, and hope that I'll be able to see again, and move at least a little bit.

Wait . . .

NINE

NOW, THERE'S A STROKE OF BAD LUCK! YVETTE HAS
slipped on the damp sidewalk and sprained her ankle, the
same one she twisted this summer.

I was having visions of myself shipped off to some air-
conditioned vegetable patch when Hélène and Paul kindly
offered to put me up during the time it would take for
Yvette to get well. "Should be about fifteen days," said the
doctor.

Yvette has gone off to be with her cousin. And I've been
moved into a room in the Fanstens' home. Yvette left
Hélène with all the instructions concerning me. I ought to
survive.

Being in this house again brings to mind that famous
night when there was a barbecue, and a stranger came and
felt me up while I was on the sofa. Let's hope it wasn't
Paul. Otherwise, I would really be in the wolf's lair.

It's night. I'm lying down. The bed is narrow. The quilt
is heavy on my feet. I'm convinced this is Renaud's room.
It smells of dust and darkness. I'm imagining toys perched
on a shelf, observing me with their empty, unmoving eyes.
I've got to get to sleep. The first night in a strange house is

always difficult. Elise, old girl, relax. Fifteen days will go by in no time. Time enough for one or two children to be murdered, and a few suicides and a rape to take place. Why not?

Is the moon full? Am I resting on a child's bed, suffused with soft light? Like in a horror movie?

I've got to relax. I've got to think about the operation. I've got to galvanize my strength to step out from this nothingness. Concentrate upon it. And sleep. As the Persians say, "The night is pregnant; who knows what dawn will bring into the world?" Amen.

LIFE IS GETTING ORGANIZED. LIVING AMONG THIS family is having a funny effect on me. Hélène wakes up at seven-fifteen in the morning, wakes Paul, makes breakfast, and then wakes up Virginie. Paul doesn't stop wailing that he's going to be late and runs all over the place. Virginie dawdles and gets scolded. At eight-ten, Paul and Virginie are out the door. And at eight-fifteen Hélène comes to attend to me. I'm given my basin, washed, and then dressed. Then she usually rolls me into the living room and turns on the television while she attends to her housework. I listen on and off to the morning programs. At eleven we take our coffee break. It's wonderful! I'm entitled to some coffee! When I rediscovered the delicious taste of coffee on my lips, I might have kissed poor Hélène!

She talks to me during our coffee break—she keeps me up-to-date about the latest gossip and the progress of the investigation; she expresses her worries about Virginie, and complains about Paul. She feels she can confide in me, as there is no risk of my contradicting her. I hear some gorgeous stories. It feels as if I were discovering a world other than that which is visible, going on a deep-sea dive into the brain of an ordinary housewife. She's a real Mount Vesuvius. When I was with Benoît, did I have as much pent-up anger, overflowing resentment, or as many hidden fears? I don't remember.

At one-thirty we leave for the library. She rolls me in

and sets me up in a corner of the room. I hear people turn-ing pages, shoes squeaking on the floor, and children gig-gling. At five forty-five, we go back to the house, but make a stop to pick up Virginie from after-school. The Great Catherine, tsarina of the powerless, has arrived: I'm mas-saged, stretched out, and oiled. It's the anti-bedsore pre-vention hour. Paul comes home somewhere between seven and seven-thirty, it depends. We have dinner around eight. Virginie goes to bed at nine. Everything is well organized, there's nothing to say.

Once again, I'm back in my little bed in the dead boy's room. Virginie was kind enough to confirm for me that it was in fact her brother's room. And to describe it for me. On the wall by the bed is a Teenage Mutant Ninja Turtles poster, and on the opposite wall, above the desk, is a poster of Magic Johnson. On the desk are books from the Pink Collection, notebooks, bags of marbles, and boxes of un-finished models.

Under the bed is a big drawer full of toys. Virginie never touches them. "Boy toys," she says, with a touch of scorn. The only thing she has picked out is the Nintendo console. She plays with it for hours in her room, confronting imagi-nary warriors, striking them down, one after the other.

Virginie has also told me that there are marks on the wall, where they used to measure her brother. Pencil marks that reach a maximum height of four feet three inches and go no higher.

I really don't like sleeping in this room. I'm not afraid of ghosts, but knowing that you're sleeping in the bed of a little boy who is dead, surrounded by all his familiar ob-jects, can have a funny effect on you. Fortunately I'm feel-ing a deep, heavy slumber coming on now. I wouldn't want to wake up in the middle of the night here.

It's incredible how people so quickly forget that I am present. They talk in front of me as if I did not exist. Like-wise, they say that people quickly forget they're being filmed, that a camera has been planted in their house for purposes of news reporting. Insofar as I'm concerned, you would talk not so much about a camera as a tape recorder. I hear and keep silent. This morning, there's a storm going, in Dolby stereo.

Hélène: "I'm fed up, you hear? I'm fed up with all your criticism."

Paul: "Well, what about me? Do you think I'm not fed up? You think I'm having a good time? He was my son. Don't you understand that?"

"And what about Virginie? She's here, isn't she? You don't give a damn about Virginie. She's alive, and she needs you!"

"That's not the problem. The problem is, you're losing it. Get a grip, goddamn it!" Paul screams.

"It's easy for you. You're never here. You don't give a shit about anything. If we all disappeared, you wouldn't even notice!"

A dish breaks.

Paul: "Goddamn it! Get me the broom."

"Get it yourself."

"Daddy, we're gonna be late."

"Virginie, go into the living room and get your book bag ready."

"It is ready, Daddy."

"Okay, then, let's go."

"Paul! We've got to talk!"

"Not now."

"When? Tell me when!"

"I'm late, Hélène, you'll excuse me. Virj! Get your sweater!"

"Don't you see I'm at the end of my rope? Paul! *Paul!*"

The door slams shut.

In my bed, I make myself small. Outraged crashes come from the kitchen. Something has just tumbled down. Glass? Doors are slammed violently, and brooms are swept against the furniture. And then silence. I imagine she's crying. I hear incoherent words. "My little boy . . . why did they take him from me? . . . They don't understand a thing." Then a long silence. Footsteps in the corridor, heading toward me.

"Good morning, Elise, did you sleep well?"

Her voice is crisp and incisive. Without waiting for an answer, she picks me up to pass me the basin. Then she places me in my wheelchair, and without saying a word, rolls me into the bathroom. She cleans my face, neck, and torso, then puts a T-shirt over me.

"There. Let's have breakfast."

We're in the kitchen. I roll over something that crunches. There's a smell of coffee and something burning. She brings a cup up to my lips, but so abruptly that the coffee—boiling—spreads over my chin.

"Oh, I'm sorry, I'm a little nervous this morning."

I know, I know, but still the boiling coffee is hurting me. She vigorously wipes it off, which is even worse than the burn. I hope she won't stick the teaspoon into my eye.

No. I'm conscientiously chewing their notorious oatmeal, made from vitamin-enriched cereal. Another sip of coffee, this time without knocking anything over.

"I had a bit of an argument with Paul."

To say the least. . . . More oatmeal. When I think about all the poor kids who are forced to eat this every morning . . .

"Paul thinks Stéphane killed his wife. I'm sure he didn't. Stéphane would be incapable of such a thing. He didn't love Sophie, but he didn't kill her. I know who it is."

Look, here's a new revelation. Go on.

"It was her lover. Sophie was cheating on Stéphane for months. Once, as I was arriving at her place, I heard her on the phone. She was in the middle of saying, 'He won't be back until after tomorrow, I'll see you at our usual place.' She saw me, got flustered, and changed her voice: 'Okay, I'll call you back,' and hung up. I didn't say anything to anyone about it. It's none of my business, is it? But as we wait, I'm sure it was that guy, the one on the phone, who killed her. Not Stéphane. They must have argued, or maybe he was married and she threatened to tell his wife everything, something like that. She was bad news, that Sophie, a real instigator."

She interrupts herself to scratch at something in the sink.

Let's meditate on this latest information. Sophie cheating on Stéphane. Why not? Sophie's lover killing her. Again, why not? After all, I'm starting to believe that anything's possible in this town. If someone told me that the butcher was selling the flesh of children and that the police were running a white slave-trade network, I could almost believe it. So, Sophie's lover had a score to settle with her . . . that's pretty routine. Hélène's putting away the dishes. I can hear the silverware clink.

"I've often wondered who the hell that guy was on the phone, but I never managed to find out. She never gave herself away. I observed her when we'd all get together; I watched the way she would speak with men who were there, but, no, nothing. Maybe it was someone who doesn't live here."

I've got a better idea: What if Sophie's lover were the one killing the children? And what if Sophie had found out? Wouldn't that be reason enough to rub her out, in an attempt to pin it on poor Stéphane? Yes, but then why kill Stéphane, if he is in fact dead, as I am beginning to sense? Oh, I know, but this is burning me up! I'm sure they'll find Stéphane, having "committed suicide," with a confession note! That way the whole matter will be closed, and the murderer will rest easy. The only obstacles left in his way will be Virginie and . . . me. Why the devil has he not turned on Virginie yet? How can he be sure she won't give him away? I'm going back to the theory I had from the start: Virginie knows him and loves him. And he loves her, too! Yes, he loves her; that's why he hasn't done anything to her! And if I pursue this line of reasoning, then . . . then I arrive at the conclusion that the person Virginie loves most in the world after her mother is . . .

Paul?

Paul? Sophie's lover? Paul, a murderer of children? Paul, friend of Stéphane, aware of his every move . . . Paul, who is subject to mood swings . . . Paul, who has a white station wagon. . . .

Could this be?

"Now I'm wondering whether or not I should tell the police, talk to them over the phone," Hélène continues. "You think I should?"

Index finger. Yes, I think you should. And right away.

"Once I told Paul I thought Sophie had a lover. He got furious, and accused me of spying on everyone and that I'm turning into a cantankerous old shrew. A shrew. I think it's true. It seems that I'm constantly mad. Unsatisfied. Filled with hate. I don't know what to do anymore. Raybaud prescribed some tranquilizers for me. They worked at first, but now I have to increase my dosage, or else I can't sleep. And when I do sleep I wake up feeling completely addled. And Virginie . . . Virginie is such a burden. . . . There are times when I'd love to be able to change my life, just like that, with a wave of a magic wand, and find myself far, far away, all alone."

That happened to me. I found myself far, far away, all alone, so alone that you couldn't imagine, Hélène, and I swear to you, there's nothing enviable about that. I would still prefer to have your life, to have lost a child, to have my husband cheating on me than to find myself where I am, deprived of my body and senses.

"Well, I'm going to do some cleaning, and I've got a ton of ironing waiting."

She sighs heavily before rolling me into the living room. The vacuum cleaner gets going. On TV there's a scientific program about the sea, and I conscientiously listen to the specialist speak to me about the migration of starfish, thinking about Paul, Steph, and the children who were murdered, the mutilations they suffered. What meaning could these horrible wounds have? To cut off the hands and hair, and tear out the heart and eyes—why? So that their eyes would see no more, their hands could not touch, and their beating hearts and soft hair would no longer attract him?

Hélène stops the vacuum cleaner and the speaker's voice gets back its intensity: *"We have a special report. The police have just discovered the body of Stéphane Migoin, one of the witnesses sought in connection with the murder investigations in Boissy-les-Colombes. From the earliest findings, it would seem that Stéphane Migoin took his life by shooting himself in the head, after parking his car at the rest area in Hêtraie, on Highway A12. A letter found next to him, on the driver's seat, might shed some light on the reasons for his act, as well as some other charges apparently hanging over his head. . . ."*

"What's that he's saying? Stéphane?"

Hélène runs over and turns up the sound, but it's too late. Time for the commercials.

"Did I hear right? Stéphane's dead?"

Index finger.

"He killed himself?"

Index finger. Just as I had predicted. With a letter next to him. Poor Stéphane. He was talking about a frame-up. He was right.

"That must mean . . . he was the one who was the killer! . . . Oh . . . I've got to call Paul."

That's it! In my opinion, he already knows. Because it seems my little theory has turned out to be right on target. And if it's right on target, then your husband is none other than the man who killed Stéphane and Renaud! But how could a man kill his own child? Well, they just arrested a couple in England suspected of killing their own daughter, but still . . . Paul. . . . Someone had to have done it, however. No one seems guilty, and yet someone is.

"Hello, I'd like to speak with Mr. Fansten please. . . . Yes, it's his wife. . . . Hello, Paul, have you heard the news? They've found Stéphane, he's dead, committed suicide. . . . What? On TV, just now . . . he left a note . . . shot himself in the head, yes, I'm sure, on TV, I'm telling you, okay, yes, I'm calming down, okay, I understand, yes, bye-bye . . . Paul?"

I guess he hung up.

"Paul's going to try to find out some more. He was in a meeting. He'll call me back."

Practical. The old meeting alibi. It allows him to cut short those unpleasant conversations. I suddenly realize that I'm coldly constructing the hypothesis that my best friend's husband may be a monster. Yet I can't help it. Perhaps it's because I'm so locked up in solitude. Endlessly going over what I think of a world I can no longer see, but which is perhaps making me insensitive. Hélène's right behind me, and she won't stop fidgeting, muttering words that make no sense. After the death of that Massenet boy, then Golbert, and Sophie's suicide, it's now Stéphane's turn. Four violent deaths in less than six months . . . I'm convinced that Stéphane got himself killed when he was calling me the other day. The murderer came into the phone booth and assaulted him. Then he dragged the body all the way to the car, fired a bullet into his head, and made the murder look like a suicide. What about the letter? The experts will see for themselves if it really was written by Stéphane. Only then could I accept it.

The telephone rings.

"Hello! Yes! Yes? . . . Who is it? . . . Excuse me, I'm having a hard time hearing, there's some static on the line. . . . It's terrible. . . . I know, but still . . . to imagine that Stéphane. . . . Oh, Paul, do you realize that . . . okay, I'll see you soon."

She hangs up slowly.

"It was Paul. He got to talk to Chief Guiomard, from the station house. He knows him well, he has an account at the bank. They found Stéphane this morning, at around eight o'clock, in rest area four. He shot himself in the head with his rifle. He left a note asking forgiveness for what he did to the children . . . it's crazy!"

Her voice is getting dangerously out of hand. I hear her dashing out of the room, no doubt to cry. Stéphane, putting a bullet into his head . . . With his rifle. Did he take it with him? On the other hand, who would have access to his apartment if not, in fact, Sophie's lover? All the trails are converging. Either Stéphane really is guilty, and has carried out justice upon himself, or perhaps it's a plot set up by the murderer to scatter all suspicion. This brings us back to Paul, his best friend . . . The future will tell what part he has in this.

The one o'clock news elaborates in great length on the

matter. Briefly, they summarize Stéphane's life, recall his wife's suicide, the murders, the sweater found in the shed, go to the opinion poll taken over the past fifteen days, and play an interview with Chief Guiomard. Hélène suddenly cries out.

"I'm sorry! It's just seeing the body lying on the stretcher, knowing it's Stéphane under that sheet . . . and the car filled with blood. . . . They shouldn't show that."

She quiets down when she recognizes Inspector Florent Gassin's voice:

". . . can't tell you anything."

"What about the letter found next to Stéphane Migoin? Does it contain a confession?"

"I'm sorry, but I can't answer that."

"Is the investigation over?"

"I'm sorry, but I can't answer that."

"Shall we say that serious charges were hanging over Migoin, and that today it seems they were confirmed, but still we have to wait for the examiner's final report before we can be sure . . . ?"

"Excuse me, I have to go . . ."

There it is, just as I thought! The trick has been played! Bravo, Death from the Woods. But now how will you satisfy your instinct for murder? For if Stéphane Migoin is supposed to be the one who has killed the children, then he cannot go on, since he is dead. That is true, I had not even thought about it. Does this mean that the murderer wishes to put an end to his career? That he has peacefully gone into retirement after pinning it on someone else? Unfortunately, maniacs like these rarely can stop.

"Oh, it's late, I didn't see the time. We'll have to get going."

Hélène puts away the dishes, turns off the TV, and we're off, I with my twirling thoughts, she with her anguish and pain.

* * *

AT THE LIBRARY, EVERY CONVERSATION IS CENTERED around Stéphane. Most people are convinced that he really was the murderer, and their comments are making their way around.

"He seemed so nice . . ."

"I never would have believed it. . . . And to think he was in charge of the soccer club."

"He could always make us laugh. . . ."

"When you think he killed five kids!"

"He was a sexual pervert . . . his wife used to complain how he'd demand strange things . . ."

"I always thought there was something weird about him. . . ."

"He was a Leo, with Pisces rising. He had a dual personality, bound to be torn apart. . . ."

They try to whisper because Hélène is there, but they can't keep their voices from breaking loose, for the emotion is so great—it's just too thrilling—knowing that a murderer was there, in their midst, in their town, and not just anyone, but a businessman known by all. Hélène's coworker asks her if she'd like to go home, offering to handle everything for the afternoon, but Hélène refuses. She simply says she would like to take care of the archives waiting to be dealt with, and leaves Marianne, her coworker, to greet the readers.

I stay there listening. I'm thinking about poor Yvette, who must be quite shaken. And Virginie, when she finds out.

HÉLÈNE HAS MADE MEATBALLS AND MASHED POTAtoes in no time. Virginie, who apparently hasn't heard a thing, is playing in her room. Paul is watching the regional news. When he came in, Hélène ran straight to him. I guess he held her tight in his arms, for they were silent awhile. Then he said, "I'm going to have a drink. I'm beat." I heard whiskey poured, ice splashing into the glass, and his body plopping onto the sofa.

"So, Lise, have you seen? As far as surprises go . . . this one's really incredible."

There are times when I'm almost happy to be unable to react, to remain impassive. On TV, they're replaying the same reports from this afternoon. Hélèna's busy in the kitchen.

"Virginie! We're eating!"

"Did you tell her?" Paul asks in a low voice.

"No, I didn't have the courage."

"You've got to tell her."

"But, Paul, if she knew what they were accusing Stéphane of . . ."

"You shouldn't hide the truth from children."

"What are you talking about? Well, Daddy?"

Virginie has just come running over.

"Listen, precious, it's about Stéphane."

"Has he come back?"

"No, not really. He . . . he had an accident," Paul answers in a gentle voice, the voice he uses when he speaks to his daughter, and the one that charmed me from the beginning.

"Is he in the hospital?"

"He's dead, precious, he's gone up to heaven."

"Has he gone to join Renaud? He's lucky!"

Dismayed silence. When will they accept the fact that this child needs psychological help?

"What kind of accident was it?"

"A car accident."

"At school they say he's the one who killed everyone else."

"What?" Hélène exclaims.

"Yes, but I know it's not true, so I don't care. What are we eating?"

"Mashed potatoes and meatballs," Hélène answers mechanically.

"Great!"

And so we're back to chewing our meatballs, with no appetite, except for Virginie, who's scoffing them down.

After our meal, she slips over to my side to say good night, and whispers, "I'm going to call Renaud tonight to find out if he's seen Stéphane. Maybe he needs help getting up there. . . . Good night!"

One day, if I can move again, I'm going to catch the little brat and torture her until she gives up the whole truth.

WHAT TIME IS IT? I'VE JUST AWAKENED WITH A start. I don't think it's morning. Everything is too calm. What was it that woke me? I'm listening attentively.

"Elise!"

My heart skips a beat, and then I recognize Virginie's voice.

"Elise, if you're up, raise your finger."

Index finger.

"Renaud says Death from the Woods killed Stéphane. For sticking his nose where it doesn't belong. Do you hear me?"

Index finger.

"Renaud's here with me. He thinks you're very pretty. He says that if you were dead, you'd be a real pretty corpse."

I immediately imagine Virginie leaning over me, with her brother's glacial specter behind her, all pale in her white nightshirt, and holding a long knife, which she's preparing to thrust into my heart as she repeats, "A real pretty corpse . . ." This kid is driving me mad. I'm getting goose bumps.

"Renaud's hungry. He wants some of Mommy's chocolate cake. I'm going to take him to the refrigerator."

Yes, take him, please do. Go away!

"They're going to say it was Stéphane who made them all die, but it's not true. Renaud knows it, too, and then there's you. So the three of us know. You know, it's because Renaud is dead, I'm alive, and you're somewhere in between. Well, I'm going. I just wanted to tell you . . . you shouldn't be afraid of being dead. Renaud says it's not that bad."

Thanks, terrific. Her muffled little steps grow distant. I force myself to breathe slowly. The poor kid is delirious. Fine. Let's forget all about this nocturnal interlude. I had better get back to sleep or else I'll start ruminating.

"Virginie, is that you?"

Hélène's voice.

"I went to pee."

"Go to bed right now!"

"Good night."

"Good night, honey. It was Virginie," she goes on, in a low voice.

"I don't like her wandering around at night," Paul answers.

They're both whispering, but in the night's perfect silence I can hear them distinctly.

"Hélène?"

"Yes?"

"Hélène, we've got to talk."

"It's late."

"Hélène, do you realize that Stéphane is dead?"

"What's got into you?"

"Are you doing this on purpose or what?"

"Don't talk so loud, you'll wake Elise."

"I don't give a damn. I'm sick and tired of always having her under our feet. I'm sure she's spying on us."

"You didn't seem sick and tired of her this summer . . ."

"You're being stupid!"

"Why? Maybe you like her? It's true, isn't it? You think I didn't see that little stunt of yours, caressing her neck and all that?"

It was him! I'm sure of it now, on the couch, that dirty lecher!

"Hélène, for heaven's sake, can we talk seriously?"

"We're talking, aren't we?"

"Oh, well, too bad. Never mind, forget it."

They must have closed the door, because I'm not hearing anything anymore. What did that lecher Paul want to talk about? Anyway, there's no longer a place in his heart for me. No more squeezes on the shoulder, no more kind words. I feel like an old aunt who's come to visit, whom they can't wait to get rid of.

Nothing left to do but count sheep.

TEN

"GOOD MORNING, ELISE. DID YOU SLEEP WELL?"

I wake with a start. I must have fallen back to sleep after the 3,255th sheep, and I'm completely out of it.

"It's magnificent outside. A real autumn day," continues Hélène, opening the shutters.

I don't know why she is wasting her time opening and closing them. It doesn't change anything for me.

Someone's at the door.

"Oh, someone's at the door. I'll be back."

Quickly, I hope, because I really feel like peeing. I'm pricking up my ears—it's a man's voice. Florent Gassin. Well, well.

"I'm sorry to disturb you so early in the morning, but I'll need to ask you and your husband some questions."

"He's already left. He's dropping Virginie off at school before going to the bank."

"Ah, that's too bad. Listen, this is off the record, but I'd like to know if you've gotten wind of any rumors of Sophie Migoin having an affair . . ."

"Would you like some coffee?"

"Uhh . . . no, thanks."

"Sit down, please. Excuse me just a minute, I'll be back."

"Uhh . . . yes . . ."

She bursts into my room.

"Here's the basin. Inspector Gassin is here. I don't know what to do. He wants to know if Sophie . . . Do you think I should tell him?"

Index finger. She pulls away the basin.

"I'll be right back."

She returns to the living room.

"Okay, I'm all yours."

"Well, about Sophie Migoin . . ." Gassin continues, audibly embarrassed.

"I did hear about it, in fact."

"And was it true?"

"Yes, I think so. In fact, I once heard her calling a man and talking about a rendezvous."

"Do you know who it was?"

"No, and even if I did, I wouldn't tell you. Sophie's dead, and so is Stéphane, and it wouldn't do any good to drag their names through the mud."

"We have to establish clearly whether Stéphane is innocent or guilty. Don't you think so?"

"I don't see what that has to do with Sophie."

"The examining judge isn't really convinced by Migoin's suicide. She'd like to be sure that this isn't some setup to have him shoulder the responsibility for this series of murders."

Her Honor is no dummy. Good thing she's there!

"Well, what about the letter Stéphane left behind?"

"Yes, the letter, there's no getting around it, in my opinion. That's also what the experts in the judicial police believe. It was typed on the same typewriter he used for his professional correspondence, therefore typed before he left, with the margins he normally used, and he was the one who signed it."

Typed! That changes everything! As if a guy like Stéphane would type out his confession! Intellectuals do that. I could see Stéphane uncapping his gold pen and writing it out carefully, making a double copy on graph paper.

"Why are you telling me all this?"

"It seems to me it would concern you. After all, it was your stepson . . . well, what I mean is, you'll forgive me, but . . ."

"Renaud is dead, Inspector, and nothing's going to bring him back. I've heard enough of these stories. All I'm asking for is a little peace."

"But peace can only come through knowing, ma'am. Knowing the truth might bring you peace—"

"What do you know about it? Sometimes knowing is much more painful than not knowing, especially when the truth is unbearable. And what you're telling me is unbearable."

"You may prefer the judge's theory, but I don't think it stacks up."

"Are you done? I've got a lot of work to do."

Gassin's voice sounds confused. He's young and apologetic, and stammers, "All right, I'll be leaving then. I didn't mean to disturb you . . ."

"Good-bye, Inspector."

"Good-bye, ma'am, I—"

The door slams shut, setting off a racket.

"Dirty little asshole! They're all just dirty assholes! Will you all just give me a break already, goddamn it! Shit, shit, shit! Why don't they all just go fuck themselves!"

She screams and pounds the furniture. Of course, I'm no help, lying in this bed like a beached sea lion. I hear her rattling around some more, and then nothing. She must be exhausted. Anger can be exhausting, just as grief can be exhausting. When I grasped what my situation was, it was hard being unable to shout, scream, cry, scratch my cheeks, pull out my hair, or pound the furniture; it was hard being unable to make myself exhausted, or get drunk on sadness; and it was hard being alone, locked up inside my brain, inexorably aligned with never-ending thoughts, images, and words.

Calm has returned. Through the silence I can hear a constant moan—a faint, painful moan—and I imagine Hélène, with her head buried between her arms, letting a

long moan of suffering fly out, sounding at once like a
wounded animal and a helpless child. It's very upsetting to
witness someone's personal pain so intimately. I swallow
my saliva. The moans have not stopped, but have ampli-
fied, clawing their way through the high notes, abruptly
breaking into raucous sobs, the dry sort of sobs that tear
the throat, and then there is nothing more.

Footsteps. A door. Running water. She must be splashing water on her face. The water stops. The footsteps head
my way.

"He's gone. They're convinced Stéphane was guilty.
Only the judge doubts it. The whole thing's such a mess. I
can see us again, seven years ago, when we decided to live
here. Calm, quiet countryside, quality of life and all. . . . A
lot of bullshit that was."

She seems to be collecting her thoughts for a moment,
and then continues, "You know, I always wondered what
my son would do when he grew up. I don't know why, but
I used to imagine him at the helm of a sailboat, with the
wind in his hair . . ."

"My son . . ." She was really attached to him, as if he
were her own child.

". . . and yet at the same time, deep down, there was this
foreboding that something would go wrong. Maybe it was
because he was a boy. Boys die more often than girls,
they're more fragile. In fact, I was always afraid for him, as
if something bad were watching him, as if something evil
were hidden in the shadows. And it was true. Someone
stole him away from me."

She gets back her breath. Her breathing relaxes.

"Some days you find yourself wading through the debris
of your life. But then what can you do about it? No one can
be master over his destiny, right? Look at you. Would you
have imagined what happened to you? This town brings
sorrow, that's the truth. We've got to get out of here. Paul
says we can't. He's afraid he won't find another job that's
as interesting as the one he's got. He'd prefer to sell his
soul than make less money. He doesn't realize it. I think I
hate him deep down. Yes, I think I've been hating him for

quite some time. It's often that way, isn't it? What time is it? It's crazy the way time goes by when it's devoid of hope. Well, all right, I'm going to get you dressed."

Now she's humming something, a tune I don't recognize, all perky and nervous as she ineptly puts my clothes on. I must be quite heavy, inert as I am. I try to make myself light. All this buzzing about imitating joviality is pitiful; poor Hélène is cracking up. Okay, I'm all dressed and heading toward the dining room.

IT'S A PRETTY MOROSE BREAKFAST—MASHED POTATO leftovers and frozen fish sticks. I'm not that hungry. Hélène's not talking; she's still humming that annoying tune and cramming the spoon into my mouth. I can sense her tense, nervous movements, and keep getting the impression that she's going to hurt me. I chew rapidly to be done with this chore as soon as possible. There's no cheese or dessert, but there is coffee. Strong, black, and tasty, but too hot. It's burning me, and I'm unable to protest. Boom, we're on our way.

I can't wait for Yvette to be cured so that I'll be able to go home. Especially after hearing Paul call me a spy. The wheelchair comes to a brutal stop. What's going on now?

"Hélène! I just wanted to call you!"

Oh, look, it's Miss Perfect, a.k.a. Claude Mondini, who lowers her voice and adds, "An inspector came by this morning, asking questions about Sophie's private life. Of course I told him I didn't know anything was going on. Everyone's got their own life to live, right? And when I think about the things they're accusing Stéphane of! I couldn't sleep at night. Jean-Mi made me take a pill. It's terrible—*terrible!*"

Louder now, "So you're the one taking care of Lise?"

"Yvette twisted her ankle."

"Oh, yes, that's right, I forgot, what with all these events, and then on Sunday there's the treasure hunt with the worshippers at Saint John's; you should come, it'll be great. So listen, if you want, I could take Elise for a walk and drop you off at the library in just a little while?"

"Why not? Lise, would you like to go for a little walk?"

With this chatterbox? No, thank you. No index finger.

"Maybe she's dozed off. Listen, I'll leave her in your hands. See you soon, and thanks. I've got to run, I'm going to be late," Hélène concludes.

Help!

"Elise? Elise, yoo hoo, it's me, Claude, do you hear me?"

Index finger, resignedly.

"We're gonna take ourselves a nice little spin! For once it's not raining. I need to walk, I feel so tense. Hélène seems ravaged, she's aged ten years! Jean-Mi met Paul last night. He's very worried about her, he's afraid she may be going into a depression. When you think that Stéphane was their best friend and that he . . . poor little Renaud . . . and all the others . . . And to say how I'd seen him at the wheel of that white station wagon and didn't think for a second . . . according to the police, it was the vehicle his foreman used to go to the construction sites. Everyone thought it was normal that he would use it, too. Those construction sites are messy; he didn't want to have his BMW cleaned every day. The inspector told me they were going through the station wagon with a fine-toothed comb. Especially the trunk. Jean-Mi refuses to talk about it; he says I'm too impressionable, but it does no good to turn your face from it. Poor Sophie . . . it's because of her that I lied."

She whispers dramatically, "Yes, I guess I can tell you, I knew she had someone."

I was right! Once again I was right! Turn the investigation over to me, goddamn it!

"I saw her one day, in her car. In the woods, behind the Cluster. I had come to look over the grounds for the VTT races on Palm Sunday. It had to be three or four o'clock in the afternoon. At first I noticed the car parked behind a copse of trees, and I thought right away it might be lovers. So of course I made myself discreet. And then I recognized it was Sophie's 205. I didn't think anything bad, but it struck me as odd, like a shudder, you know? The sun was beating down on the windows, so I couldn't see inside. Normally I would've gone over to say hello . . . but something held me back—instinct, no doubt, it's crazy the way I'm so intuitive—and at that moment the passenger-side door opened up, and he got out, fixed his hair with his hand, and then went to relieve himself against a tree—I thought he was so vulgar! Anyway, what was he doing there, inside Sophie's car? Not that I want to speak ill of my fellow man, but there are times when you can't help but draw conclusions, am I right? So, of course, I didn't move. He got back in the car, she took off, and they passed right by me, without seeing me, I was crouching down in the nettles, I won't tell you about all the stings, but to make a long story short, I saw them from up close. Sophie was smiling, she seemed all blissed out, and he had a satisfied, almost beastly look on his face. I would never have thought that about him."

Who, goddamn it?

"I didn't say anything to Jean-Mi; I didn't want to hurt him, but I spaced out our meetings, which was insensitive. I'm not supposed to be party to their acts. When I think about it, Sophie and Manu, it just makes no sense."

Manu? Did she say Manu? Well, what the hell was he doing in there? It shouldn't be Manu, it ought to be Paul! You're goofing up!

"And that poor Betty, thinking she can fulfill that spiritual void of hers with wheat germ, she'd be better off if she just watched over her husband. I always thought he had piercing eyes, like Rasputin, and with that white beard of his . . . brrr . . . But I'm just babbling away, I must be boring you."

Not at all. For once you're fascinating. Go ahead! Go on!

But no, now she's talking about trees and falling leaves, the coming of winter, onions peeling, which heralds in the colder weather, the war in Yugoslavia, the famine in Africa, and the difficulties in gathering clothing and medication, how people are so cold, insensitive, while I keep repeating "Manu and Sophie, Sophie and Manu" like a mantra that's supposed to bring me the Revelation.

After a day like today, I am aspiring toward a state of calm, and can't wait to go home, even more so now that I know Paul has called me a spy. Those days of nighttime fondlings are over. Does dear Paul have other, more urgent concerns? Fortunately, Yvette called last night, and she feels perfectly back to normal, and will be driving by to pick me up the day after tomorrow, with the inevitable Jean Guillaume. It's getting worse here. Paul and Hélène don't stop screaming at each other. She pops pills to calm down, and he yells at her when she does. He keeps repeating that she needs medical help. I'm parked in the dining room. Virginie is watching television and seems to notice nothing.

"Virj! Will you please turn down the TV!" Paul screams.

She turns up the sound. I have a feeling there's going to be a blowup.

"Do you hear me? Turn that damn TV down!"

No reaction. The Penguin continues to shout insults at Batman.

"For heaven's sake! Damn it, you think I'm funny?"

"Ow! Leave me alone! Mommy! Mommy!"

Biff, bang, pow! A firm hand there and back, and Virginie goes off like a siren. Hélène, outraged, intervenes.

"Let go of her, you son of a bitch! I forbid you to touch her. You have no right over her!"

"Watch what you're saying, Hélène!"

Things are really heating up now. He must have let go of Virginie, because I hear her sniffling in her corner.

"I'll say whatever I like. You don't scare me!"

"Please stop it!"

I "see" them standing face-to-face, with their hackles up, nostrils pinched, lips pursed and pale, like all couples caught in the anger dance. Paul withdraws from the battle: "Oh, well, fuck it, I'm out of here."

"Paul! Where are you going?"

"What the hell do you care? Just take care of your daughter."

The door slams shut.

"Mommy!"

"Yes, honey, Mommy's here."

"When are we eating?"

"Go look in the kitchen. There's pizza."

"Can I watch *Batman* while I eat?"

"If you want, but don't get anything dirty."

The warrior episode is over. Virginie settles in with her pizza and sniffles for the last time. I sense someone's presence behind me. It's Hélène, gripping my wheelchair and rolling me into the kitchen.

"Do you want some beer?"

Index finger. Yes, ma'am! A nice cold beer . . .

The bottle opener clicks, the beer glug-glugs into the glass, and I'm drooling. You'd think we were in a pub. Finally. It flows down my throat, nice and frosty. I've been waiting a year for this sip of ice-cold beer. She gives me a bit more, and then I hear her drink some herself.

"Paul's right. I take too many pills. But it's because I can't sleep. I can't take it anymore, turning over and over in my bed, thinking about all this. I'm getting the feeling that my marriage is on the rocks, like they say. You must think we're nuts."

No index finger.

"You know, I'm going to tell you something I've never told anyone"—she lowers her voice—"Paul isn't Virginie's father."

I almost choke on my beer.

"Virginie had just been born when I met him. He married me, legally recognized her, and promised me he would take care of her as if she were his own daughter. He's kept his word. I'm the one who's screwing up, I know, like just now. Virginie doesn't know he's not her father, and I haven't told her anything. Anyway, she'll never see her other father. Do you want some more beer?"

Index finger. We drink.

"It's all so far away now . . . it's all in the past. I was

young. I was an idiot. I didn't have an easy childhood, you know. Oh, it's not what you think. I lived in a good household, but my father wasn't a very affectionate man, if you know what I mean. And my mother . . . my mother didn't say anything, she was afraid. She would drink to forget. She let him beat her for thirty years. When my father died, it was really liberating for her, but she didn't outlive him by much. She died of cancer six months later. A real soap opera, isn't it! Understand, though, she wasn't the only one to take her share of beatings." Her voice is tinged with sarcastic bitterness. "When I think of my father, I see him looking so dignified—he was a doctor—while my mother and I were so pale, covered with black-and-blue marks under our torn clothes. . . . Why am I talking to you about all this? Oh, yes, to tell you that when I met Tony . . . if only I could have known what to expect . . . I'm getting one of those headaches, as usual—whenever I talk about my parents or Tony, I get a headache. But it's awfully late. I've got to put Virginie in bed. Some more beer?"

Index finger. I swallow the foamy liquid without even thinking. So, Paul isn't Virginie's father. What does that change? Nothing. And what about this Tony? What the hell could he have done to her to speak of him in such terms? Did he beat her, perhaps? Where is he now? In jail? No, that's enough. I'm constructing a novel out of all this.

Are they sure Virginie doesn't know what's going on? Kids often know much more than one might think. In any case, my stay here hasn't been useless. I've picked up enough to chew on for eight days. I'm imagining, with disgust, this bourgeois family, with a sadistic father. . . . After ten minutes Hélène returns.

"Okay, all done. There's a report on Colombia. Are you interested?"

Index finger. Why not? It will take my mind off all this. All aboard for that green hell, with drug cartels and the peaks of the Andes, although I would much prefer a full report on Virginie's true father!

* * *

"HELLO! OH, YOU LOOK TERRIFIC! HELLO, HÉLÈNE! Did everything go okay? It wasn't too much work?"

Yvette! My Yvette! Come here, let me kiss you!

"No, no problem. What about you? How is your ankle?" Hélène asks.

"Everything is in order. So dumb of me, anyway . . ."

"And how is Mr. Guillaume?"

"He's in the car. You know how men are, always in a hurry."

"Uhh . . . well, let's not keep him waiting. All of Elise's things are ready."

"You seem tired, Hélène. You're sure this didn't make a lot more work for you?"

"No, no, it's just that I'm not sleeping well these days. I'll come with you."

They roll me out, and though I'm happy to be leaving, I'm still a bit sorry I won't be at the heart of this household anymore, especially with Hélène about to make some startling revelations. They hoist me into the station wagon, and place the wheelchair in the rear.

"Hi, Elise!"

It's Jean Guillaume's jovial voice. He takes my right hand and presses it between his.

"Still as pretty as ever!"

Laughter, politeness, bye-bye, so long, thanks so much, let's keep in touch. And we're off. Right away, Yvette takes it upon herself to give me a fully detailed account about her stay with her cousin: "Nothing to report."

IT'S TOO COLD, SOMEONE OUGHT TO TURN UP THE heat. Yvette drains the radiators, checks the boiler, and hurls invectives at the sky for being so prematurely harsh. She changes my cotton sweatshirt for a sweater. I'm vaguely listening to the weather report when the anchor suddenly announces, *"Tomorrow, October 13, the sun will rise at . . ."* October 13! A year! It will be a year! Tomorrow will be one year since I pushed open those glass doors in Belfast; one year since Benoît . . . one year since I've been transformed to the living dead. . . . How could this be? Can time have passed so quickly? It feels as if I've just come out of the coma. But, no, there were all those dead children, and all those new people I met. Summer went by so quickly . . . my brain hasn't stopped humming like a turbine. Now, it's time to move! I've got to move, I want to move, and if I could move this lousy finger, then I should be able to do better. A year! Enough already! Starting tomorrow, I'm going to stop thinking and start acting!

IT'S GOT TO BE WORKING. THE GREAT CATHERINE can't get over it.

"You know what, Miss Yvette? It looks to me like every now and then her muscles are getting stiff . . . no, I swear, it's like she's stretching them. Come have a look for yourself."

If only you knew how I'm stretching them, if only you knew how much energy I'm mobilizing to stretch these fucking muscles—it's enough to burst a blood vessel!

"Touch her, there and there. I've got to talk to Raybaud about this. I think she's getting a whole lot better!"

I'm knocked out from the effort. I'm dripping with sweat. The Great Catherine doesn't think to sponge me down. She trumpets, "They found blood in the trunk of Stéphane's car."

"No?"

"Yes! They announced it this morning on the radio. It was type AB, like what that Massenet boy had."

"So then he would have killed Michael in the shed and carried him over to the stream?" Yvette inquires, eagerly.

"I dunno, that's all they said. They're still looking. And then there were also stains of type O blood, like Mathieu Golbert's, but it looks like Stéphane himself was type O, so it all seems complicated to me."

Let's meditate upon this. If, and I'm saying if, Stéphane is innocent, then it means the murderer used his car. It means that he knew him well enough to borrow it from him, but under what pretext? I'm always falling back onto this problem with Sophie's lover. Was it Paul or Manu? Or every guy in town? Why not?

"Okay, try to make an effort, Elise. Stretch, stretch . . ."

So once again I'm immersed in my thoughts and have neglected to muster my strength. "Stretch, stretch." She's got some of her own. I feel like a curtain rod. Finally the torture is over. I slowly get my breath back. Silence. Yvette has turned on the boiler, and I listen as the water gurgles through the pipes. If, according to my theory, Sophie's lover is the murderer, then why not Manu? But if it were Manu, why would Virginie keep silent about it? With Paul, I would understand, for she believes he is her father, but with Manu? Here I am, making assumptions about a perverse relationship between Manu and Virginie. This is pathetic. One can imagine everything and anything. Still, it should be noted that there's someone in this town capable of killing and mutilating children, all while keeping up the appearance of a normal citizen. Now, that's crazier than anything I could imagine. As Benoît used to say, "It's all out there, and anything can happen. All you've got to do is read about it in the papers."

I've read a lot of whodunits in my time, and like to think I'm a good amateur detective. One of the last books I got to read before entering the Miss Vegetable pageant related the story of an FBI investigation on a serial killer. It explained that there are two types of pathological murderers: if all of them are moved by irresistible urges, then there are some who are fully aware of what they are doing and take great pleasure in outsmarting the police and their fellow citizens, while others forget their crimes as soon as they are committed, and can swear in all good faith that they are innocent. It's a separate part of them, an unknown part of their consciousness that has committed the murders. However, if I am to presume that Stéphane was killed by the true murderer within the framework of a precise plan, then I would have to imagine that this murderer knows perfectly well that he is one. So it's not just some sicko we're dealing with, it's a pervert who must enjoy watching us as we all cast about—a pervert who must get off on my anguish. And why not a pervert who could be controlling Virginie?

I'm ashamed to be thinking these thoughts.

But . . .

Someone's ringing the doorbell.

"Hello, Captain. This way. We were just getting back."

I can hear the disapproval in Yvette's voice. Poor Yssart really isn't that nice to her. As for me, I'm delighted by his visit.

"Hello, Miss Andrioli."

Index finger.

"I'll be in the kitchen," Yvette calls as she walks out.

"I'm sorry to be dropping by unannounced again, but in light of the circumstances . . ."

Make it short.

"No doubt you've been following the latest developments in the case."

Index finger.

"You know that we've found blood in Stéphane Migoin's car."

Index finger.

"After analysis, it would seem that the oldest stains come from Michael Massenet, and the most recent from Mathieu Golbert. What's more, the employee at the shopping-center parking lot confirmed that a large white station wagon did leave at approximately the time of the murder of Mathieu Golbert. No one has any doubt that Migoin is the murderer. The only other alternative is that someone used his car, or more precisely, the car from the construction site, unbeknownst to him. However, only someone who knows him well would have had access to this vehicle. The foreman at the construction site has airtight alibis, and so do the workers. So I'm going to ask you one question: Did Sophie Migoin have a lover?"

Index finger.

"Do you know his identity?"

I half raise my index finger.

"Very well. I'm going to go down a list of names. Raise your index finger when you recognize what seems to be the

right one. Jérôme Leclerc. Jean-Michel Mondini. Luc
Bourdaud. Christian Marane. Manuel Quinson."

Index finger.

"Well, well, well. You're definitely always well informed.
I'm never wasting my time when I come to visit you. You're
the Miss Marple of these woods. The problem is that
Manuel Quinson was out of town when the Golbert boy was
murdered. He was in Paris for a training seminar. He spent
the day at his company's headquarters, with twenty-five
other members of upper-level management. I've spent a lot
of time checking on the alibis of the people gravitating
around the Fanstens, Virginie, and yourself, because I'm
convinced that the guilty person is moving in this small circle. The only ones who really might have committed these
murders are Jean-Michel Mondini, Paul Fansten, and Jean
Guillaume. Win, place, and show, if you ask me. Not to forget the late Stéphane Migoin. You seem confused. I understand. It's always unpleasant to imagine that someone close
to you could be dangerously ill. In fact, we're going to close
the investigation. We are going to have to conclude that
Migoin was guilty. Everyone's accusing him. But that
doesn't satisfy me. I wanted to tell you that. And I sincerely
believe that we're going to let some monstrous murderer
frolic about in nature. I would recommend that you make
your winter quarters somewhere else," he continues with
poise. "With your uncle, for example. But of course you are
free to do as you wish. Well, I've enjoyed our little conversation. I'll be leaving you."

He's got a funny conception about what conversations
are, but fine, let's not quibble.

"Good-bye. See you soon. Good-bye, madam," he calls
toward the kitchen, getting no response.

The door closes again. As I sit here, I'm turning these
three names over in my mind: Jean-Mi, Paul, Jean Guillaume. It's got to be one of them. Going free. Paul! Everything points to Paul!

If only I weren't stuck in this wheelchair, if only I were
myself again, I'd go poking into their past, because I'm
sure I'd find the solution there. You don't become an insane

murderer just by chance. Jean-Michel Mondini . . . no, that's ridiculous. . . . But after all, his wife told me that Sophie was having an affair with Manuel. What if she had lied? What if Jean-Mi were sleeping with Sophie?

"Are you thinking about your exercises?" Yvette calls to me, pulling me away from these reflections of mine.

The Great Catherine left me with a series of exercises to do, for half an hour, three times a day. Bit by bit, I have to concentrate on my body and try to feel it, visualizing my toes, calves, thighs, et cetera, and at each stage I must try to feel my blood, muscles, and skin, and send an impulse: "Move." Let's get to it.

ELEVEN

JEAN GUILLAUME AND YVETTE ARE HAVING COFFEE
and watching a variety show on TF1. Every now and then I
hear Guillaume laugh at some comedian's jokes. He has a
nice laugh. It's not the laugh of one who is mentally ill. Are
he and Yvette holding hands? Are they sitting with their
arms around each other? Are they lovers? They can do
whatever they want right under my nose, since I can't see
them. Could Yvette and Jean Guillaume be wildly rolling
around on the table, amid the dirty dishes, and throwing
sideways glances at the vegetable sitting in her wheelchair? . . . No, not my Yvette. I'm sure she would put me
back in my room first. I'm vaguely listening to the jokes,
and now, replacing the comedian, is some girl screeching
in English with a voice that's about as pleasant as chalk
across a blackboard.

"Do you want another glass?" Guillaume asks.

"No, not for me, thanks," protests Yvette, who must be
drinking very little.

"What about you, Elise? A bit of wine?"

Index finger. You're crazy if you think I'll refuse.

I feel the glass making contact with my lips. The wine

flows into my mouth, over my gums and palate, thick and red and absolutely delicious—after all these months of abstinence, it's about as heady as a hit of LSD. The doorbell rings imperiously, and Guillaume starts, sending a stream of wine rushing down my throat. I'm swallowing, suffocating—shit, it went down the wrong way! I'm choking! Shit! I'm struggling to get my breath back. Oofah! It goes its way, only to be followed by a fit of hacking. I take in a lungful of air.

The doorbell rings again. But there's deadly silence all around. What's the matter with them? Why won't they open up? I cough again and spit up some wine. Well? The doorbell rings. Move it, will you? All this ear-splitting noise is exasperating me.

"Elise . . ."

It's Yvette's voice. It sounds soft and gentle, as if she were about to announce that someone just died.

"Your hand . . ."

What about my hand?

My hand. *My hand is by my face.* I raised my hand. I raised it. I raised my goddamn left hand! Just like that, in one fell swoop. The doorbell.

"Coming!" cries Yvette.

She runs to the door.

I moved my hand.

"Try it again," says Guillaume, with his nice encouraging voice.

I hesitate. What if it were just a reflex? A muscular spasm? Go ahead, Elise, raise it!

I feel a shudder run through my wrist, and think hard about a plane on a runway. There it goes, gently rising—a wonderful left hand in perfect working order, climbing at least four inches before getting stuck.

"Try to move your fingers," Guillaume murmurs.

My fingers? I swallow my saliva. I'm vaguely conscious of a bustle of activity by the doorway. I concentrate on my hand—on the tendons, the nerves, and the pretty little phalanges. I abruptly order it to bend, but nothing happens.

"Try again!"

I calm down. Breathe. Gather momentum. Nothing. Just a slight pain in the middle finger. Well, that's too bad, but I'm not complaining. My hand moved, and that's fantastic. And as for the fingers, we'll see about them later.

"I'm sure you'll get there soon," Guillaume whispers.

Suddenly I become aware that Yvette is discussing something with someone who's talking very loud.

"I've got to find her, you understand?"

I recognize Paul's voice, filled with anguish and anger.

"But I don't know where she is," Yvette protests.

"What's going on?" Guillaume asks, getting up.

"Paul and Hélène got into an argument, and Hélène took off, slamming the door behind her," Yvette explains.

"She'll be back, don't you worry. It happens to everyone," Guillaume offers reassuringly.

"She was very worked up. I've got to find her. She hasn't been very well lately, I'm afraid that . . ." Suddenly he goes silent.

"How bad is it?" Guillaume asks, surprised.

"She's very depressed, and I'm worried," Paul confirms.

A horrible suspicion runs through my mind: would he want to bump her off as well? "My wife was depressive . . . she jumped off the bridge. . . ." I raise my hand.

"What is it, Elise? Do you want to tell us something?" Guillaume asks.

"Elise was just able to move her hand," Yvette beams.

"Great," Paul says, though obviously he doesn't give a shit. Then, suddenly, he gets an idea: "Lise, do you know where Hélène is?"

He could almost shake me. The great thing about being able to move your hand is that you can a make a no—a weak no, just a minuscule wave of the wrist from left to right, but still enough to mean no.

"Shit. Listen, if she calls, tell her I'm sorry and that I'm waiting for her at home. And if she comes over, keep her here and call me. I'm going home. Virginie's all alone."

He's gone as quickly as he came.

"Oh, well!" Yvette and Jean Guillaume exclaim together.

"Elise, this is marvelous!" Yvette goes on.

"Poor Hélène," Guillaume comments.

"I hope she doesn't do anything crazy. I've seen how she's been losing it for quite some time. She looks terrible. She's got giant rings under her eyes."

"I've got to say, he doesn't make her life easy. I know men have got to stick together, but . . ."

"Well, anyway, everything's going well for us. Oh, Elise, honey, I'm so happy! I'm sure that Professor Combré will want to operate now!"

From your lips to God's ear, Yvette. I'd cross my fingers if I could. But the thought of Hélène, all alone on the empty streets, darkens my clouds of joy. I'd feel much calmer if someone were to go looking for her. As if hearing me, Guillaume suggests, "I'm gonna take a drive out and see if I can spot Hélène. . . . You never know. That way we'll feel more assured. I'll be back."

"You're right, that's a good idea. I'll wait up."

He goes out. Yvette turns up the TV, the way she does whenever she's worried and doesn't want to speak. We listen in silence as some announcer makes stupid jokes. I know the program ends at ten-thirty. So it's earlier. I enjoy raising my hand and putting it back down, just like that, for my own pleasure. You can get used to miracles very quickly. So quickly that I almost forgot how this damn hand refused to obey no more than fifteen minutes ago. Up, down. Up, down. It travels throughout my arm, but even this pain from moving is fine. The terrible specter of bedsores grows distant. And constantly I command my fingers: *Bend! Bend, you assholes!* Perhaps they don't like being insulted. I try to sweet-talk them: *Come on, babies, make Mommy happy.* Oh, go on! They're just laughing it off, those ingrates. They're not thinking about all the times I soaped them up, applied red nail polish, plunged them into the warm sea, hot sand . . . detergent, dish water, ice-cold water, snow, mud, dirt. Cut it out! I realize they've gone on strike! I feel foolishly cheerful, even though I should be worried for Hélène's sake, but I feel like laughing all by myself.

The door slams shut.

"Nothing. I didn't see her. It's coming down in sheets. There's not even a cat out there."

"I can see that. You're soaked. I'll go make you an herbal tea."

The commercials come thundering out. Someone turns down the sound. The telephone rings, and Yvette picks up: "Hello? Oh, yes, that's good, okay. Good night." She hangs up. "That was Paul. Hélène's just come home," she announces. "That's a load off my mind."

Mine, too.

"Well, now, everything's all right," Guillaume concludes. "This herbal tea's excellent."

THIS MORNING, AS I WOKE UP, THE FIRST THING I thought about was my hand. What if it refused to move? Immediately I tried, my heart pounding. And the miracle was reproduced. I wished I could dance for joy. The pain in my middle finger is becoming clearer; I'm getting the impression it's starting to bend. As I basked in the prowess of my new hand, Yvette walked in.

"Raybaud will be here soon. I caught him on his way out, just before he left for the hospital."

She coughs nervously.

"There was an accident last night."

I felt a knot in my stomach.

"The Cabrol boy. Joris."

Joris Cabrol. I remembered him right away. He was a boy of maybe twelve, and very small for his age. He was a fan of cop movies. He came often, either alone or with his father. Several years ago his mother took off with a traveling salesman.

"He fell onto the railroad tracks. A train ran over him," Yvette continued.

How awful! I thought. How did it happen? I thought a second later, just as Yvette was explaining it: "He went to the movies last night. You know how his father is a male nurse, he works at the hospital three nights a week. The boy was all alone, and he went to see the Stallone movie, and on his way home—no one knows why—he got the idea to go the railyard and continue along the tracks. Maybe he lost his balance. In any case, the ten o'clock express train was coming along at full speed and Joris jumped out in front of the locomotive. The conductor didn't even have time to brake. The poor kid was killed instantly. They just announced it on the radio. Obviously, the troubles in this town will never cease! I'm going to empty that; I'll be back."

She goes out, and I continue to lie in bed, petrified.

The monster's back at it, I'm sure of it. It's too much of a coincidence. Yet another child and, as if by chance, so mutilated by the train that no one will ever know what he might have gone through. The child was small for his age, so the murderer must have believed he was younger, the way he likes them. And, as if by chance, Paul was out last night. Guillaume, too. Both of them acting so eager to go after Hélène! How can I find out what time Paul got home? Let's see. He must have rung here around nine-thirty. And Guillaume got back around ten-thirty, because the variety show had just finished. They both had the time to be at the yard by ten o'clock—at night it takes only five minutes to get there. But no one could know that Joris would be going that way. Unless . . . unless the murderer went past the movie theater slowly, glimpsed his prey from among the moviegoers on their way out, and followed him until just the right moment.

Guillaume came home soaked. Why is that, if he didn't get out of the car? And what about Paul? Was he wet? I think I'm getting hot. I've got to be on the right track!

When Yvette comes back and gets me ready, I still haven't stopped ruminating on all this.

Someone's at the door. It's Raybaud. I demonstrate my flying hand. He congratulates me. He presses my fingers, palpates my palm, and practically dislocates my thumb.

"Good, very good. I'm very happy to . . ."

Thanks, chief!

"I'm going to speak to Combré about this. It's a good

sign, in my opinion. I don't want to say this for sure, but if she spontaneously regained some movement . . . I've got to make these fingers work. I'm convinced they're just asking to bend! I've got a mind to prescribe a series of electric stimulations for her . . . Let's see . . ."

He's concentrating on my prescription. Yvette squeezes my shoulder. I raise my hand over and over like a cheerful, obedient dog bringing a ball back to its master. What about Raybaud? Could he kill children? Plunge his scalpel into their flesh? Atrocious visions of tortured bodies pass before my eyes. I force myself to pull a big black curtain over these unbearable images and concentrate on my fingers. There, all gone.

". . . good you're keeping me abreast. See you soon," Raybaud was just saying.

He leaves.

"I'm so happy!" says Yvette, kissing me on the cheek.

And I think, Quick! The local news.

Time passes too slowly. At each moment I expect to see Yssart, Hélène, or someone else pop out, but there's nothing. Finally the news:

"A terrible accident . . . the body could only be identified thanks to a bracelet with his name engraved on it . . . father is destroyed. . . . But what could Joris have been doing in this seedy, deserted neighborhood so late at night, in the pouring rain? . . . It came as a great shock to the conductor. . . . Rail traffic was interrupted for two hours. . . . And now for the weather: finally, we'll be having sunshine!"

We eat, feeling depressed—veal liver and green beans, all mashed up for me. It's a real treat. I'm really getting to understand those brats who grumble about their baby food.

Joris Cabrol. The sixth little victim of a crazy murderer. No one suspects a thing? Or am I going delirious?

"A litte sunshine couldn't hurt," Yvette mutters as she clears the table.

Did Paul get home at around ten o'clock? Only Virginie could say, but no one's going to ask her. I can't. Why didn't

I make my career with the cops? Captain Elise Andrioli. Ace of aces. What would Benoît have thought? All I do is think "Benoît" and I'm crying again like a fountain. The tears come spilling down my cheeks, as if on a darkened path.

"What's the matter? Oh, poor Elise! It's hard, I know," Yvette assures me, dabbing at my eyes with a Kleenex.

I feel ridiculous, but it should do me some good to get my tear ducts open. So I cry my eyes out, for myself, for Benoît, and this whole disaster, still raising my hand. I feel like I'm four, playing a game of Simon Says.

Finally I stop crying, and sniffle profusely. Yvette wipes my tears, and wipes them again, until I must have gone through three tissues. All the while the killer is still on the loose.

Someone's ringing. Yvette dashes over. I try to look dignified. Hélène enters, with Virginie.

"Hi, Lise! I got nine out of ten in dictation."

My hand flies up.

"Oh, that's great! Did you see that, Mommy, she can move her hand! Do it again!"

I go through it with pleasure. Hélène comes near: "That's wonderful! I'm so happy for you, Lise. Well, at least someone's having a good day today."

Yada, yada, yada.

"What do you want to drink? Juice? Beer?" Yvette asks to change the subject.

"Beer!" Virginie calls out, all excited.

"Certainly not!" Hélène cuts in. "Juice for Virginie, and a beer for me."

Yvette leaves, followed by Virginie, babbling away. Hélène turns to me: "Have you heard? The accident little Joris had?"

My hand flies up.

"This town is cursed. I'm not kidding, Lise, something weird is going on. This chain of catastrophes . . . it sends shivers up my spine. I've already experienced it, you know, and I thought . . . I thought I'd never have to relive it. But it looks like this curse is following me. Unless"—she comes close, and I can feel her shuddering, her mouth to my ear, her skin moist—"unless Tony . . ."

Again with this mysterious Tony! Evidently Yvette has returned, and Hélène immediately steps away.

"One cold beer coming up! And a nice glass of grapefruit juice for Virginie, and for you, Elise."

I sigh for Hélène's beer, but have to swallow the grapefruit juice. Fortunately I like it. Unlike grape juice—"It'll revitalize you, Elise"—which I've had to knock back every morning and night until I can spit it out.

Virginie climbs up on my knees.

"What are you doing? Stop it, will you?" Hélène protests.

I raise my hand twice to let it be understood that it doesn't bother me.

"It doesn't bother you?"

I raise my hand.

"Soon you'll be able to move your arm, your leg, and then everything!" Virginie calls out. "And then you and me will go for walks. Renaud, too," she whispers. "And Joris. Everybody thinks the train ran him over, but I know what happened. Death pushed him under the wheels. Pfff."

What does she know? She was at home. But if Paul is the murderer and she saw him leave, then she could guess. . . . Yes, this is getting more and more plausible.

"I'm so dumb! I forgot the *TV Guide* at the bakery," Yvette suddenly exclaims. "Hélène, can you stay here another five minutes?"

"No problem."

"I'll go with you! Wait for me!" Virginie cries, jumping to the ground.

They're barely gone when Hélène approaches. Her breath smells of beer, and suddenly I suspect that this wasn't her first of the day.

"Nobody knows about Tony, Virginie's father—her real father . . . we weren't married and he didn't legally recognize his daughter. Tony's locked away. He was dangerous. Once he broke my arm. Can you believe that? Because I dared to stand up to him. That's why I can't stand it when

Paul raises his voice or acts brutal. I've known it too well. I've seen my mother beaten black and blue, kicked in the stomach by my father, and it was the same for me . . . for stupid things, stupid little things. He would tie me to his desk, and at the slightest noise. . . . Sometimes I had trouble walking because I was hurting so much, but no one ever guessed a thing, not in school, not during my piano lessons. . . . My father was sick. He should have been locked away. Tony was also disturbed. Later on, the psychiatrist told me it was normal, that women who had a troubled childhood often married men who resembled their violent, alcoholic father. After that, when I thought I was finally over it, there was Renaud, and it all started again, everything. This curse is following me, Lise, and I can't take it anymore. Now Paul is changing. He's getting mean, he's drinking, I'm afraid of him."

Well, maybe you have a reason to be afraid. And what about this Tony? Why is he locked away? Breaking an arm, brrr . . . this guy's not very tender, is he? Poor Hélène's life is a real soap opera. I might almost forget about my own.

"If he touches Virginie, I'm calling the police. I told him so the other night. There's no question it might start again. I would never stand for that."

Tell me about Tony, I feel like yelling.

"Sometimes I get these ideas. I can't confide in anyone, but I'm wondering . . . I say to myself that maybe Tony . . . but that's impossible, he's in Marseilles, he'll never get out. They put him in with the criminally insane, you understand? But what if he ever . . . if he ever got out? What if he ever came to take back his daughter? He told me he would kill me if he ever found me again, he would kill anyone who got in his way."

This is getting better and better. First we had a child killer, and now we've got ourselves the mentally ill ex-boyfriend.

"That's why they locked him up. For murder. And now . . ."

"We're back! We didn't take too long, did we?"

You were too short, Yvette. Hélène is already on her

feet: "No, not at all. We were just having a nice little chat.
We'll be leaving you now, we just came by to say hello.
Coming, Virginie? Thanks for the drinks, Yvette. See you
tomorrow."

"See you tomorrow! Good night."

"I hope so!" Hélène calls out sarcastically before walking out the door.

"Is everything all right?" Yvette asks.

I raise my hand. I'm running full throttle, Yvette. Picture
a new character, someone named Tony, who has entered
upon the scene and who seems like one hell of a problem.
Because who would Virginie protect more than Paul, huh?
Her real daddy! So here we have a child killer, served up on
a platter! But while I'm entertaining all this brilliant reasoning, they're getting ready for Joris's burial. Life isn't as
funny as novels are.

I would even say, coming from my own personal experience, that sometimes life is shit.

Would I prefer to be dead? Well, no, I've got to confess.
Even if life is nasty, sad, cruel, and injust, I would prefer to
live it.

Okay, our fifteen minutes of philosophy are over. Let's
get back to the subject. Hélène said something about a
murder! Virginie's real father would be in an asylum for a
murder he committed! If he had escaped and Virginie
recognized him . . . that would explain everything, why
she's protecting him, why she's. . . . Why hasn't Yssart examined this possibility? Does he even know that Tony exists? Hold on a minute, old girl: How could Virginie
recognize a father she hasn't seen since her infancy? And
how could he find her? I'm guessing that Hélène didn't
leave him a forwarding address.

Let's assume that he somehow managed to get it . . .
No, even better, let's pretend he escaped and just came
here by chance. He settles down in the area, feels over-
whelmed by his irresistible urges, and starts to kill children. One day, Virginie sees him and . . . No, that doesn't
work—she can't recognize him. Unless he recognized
her. . . . Yes, perhaps he had heard news about his daughter

using the hospital, a photo, or in short something. So he recognizes her, tells her who he is, and Virginie can no longer denounce him, and there we have it! I'll write "The End" on it and go looking for a publisher.

Nevertheless, it's easy for me to elaborate on these theories, because to me all these people are no more than voices and faces I can only imagine, and really I know nothing about their smiles, their gaze, the texture of their skin, or their attitudes.

If I'm ever able to use my hand again, I'll be able to ask questions, to write. To think it was such a burden to write postcards! Now I could sign thousands of them without complaining, even if I would also have to lick the stamps.

Yvette has finished cleaning up the kitchen, and I hear her rummaging through the buffet.

"So when is this sunshine coming? My back hurts, and my rheumatism's acting up, what with all this rain we've been having. . . . Catherine's late."

Shit, I forgot about her! Right on cue, she rings.

"Sorry I'm late."

"Yes, I was just saying to Elise . . ."

"I ran into Hélène Fansten, and we got to talking, you know what it's like," she continues as she lays me upon her massage table. "So, it looks like we're getting better? We can move our hand now? That's really great!"

And when the day comes that I can really move it, I swear I'm going to clock you one right in the face, dearie, I say to myself with my typical elegance.

"Mrs. Fansten didn't look good," Catherine goes on, in a stentorian voice that makes me think Yvette is in another room. "I was even wondering if she'd had a bit too much to drink."

"Hélène?" Yvette says, indignant.

"Yeah, she really stank from beer!"

"She drank one here half an hour ago," Yvette explains, relieved.

"Anyway, she seemed kind of weird. Or maybe she's on drugs. You know anything's possible these days. In any case, she was telling me some things that were pretty strange. About her husband. That he was very tense, that he scared her sometimes, and he'd have to go see a doctor. I was thinking to myself that maybe she needed to be cared for. . . . Paul Fansten's a great guy, always smiling . . . and besides, it's not like fate's been kind to them. By the way, did you hear about little Joris? That was so awful!"

She flips me over like a crêpe and gets to work on my back. I have to acknowledge that this does me good. Sometimes I get the impression that my body is just one single cramp. I feel her hard fingers dig into my limp flesh, and she won't stop talking for a second in her high-pitched voice: "Can you imagine what a person might look like after falling under a train? And then the father was obliged to go identify the body! Nothing's going right these days! They're laying people off at Carbonnel, we're living with some crazy killer in our midst, the weather's completely off track, everything's gone wrong. . . . Like poor Stéphane. He was too nice. He should have been watching over his wife. I don't like to put other people down, but when I think about it . . . That woman did the right thing when she killed herself!"

"Catherine! People shouldn't say such things," Yvette says, indignantly.

"I know what I know, that's all. In any case, it's not possible he would do those things, no, not Stéphane Migoin, it's all a big setup."

Look, we've got a meeting of the minds! If the Great Catherine is starting to see things as I do, then maybe I should rethink my opinions right away!

"It was one of Sophie's lovers who did it, I'm sure of it!"

"You shouldn't listen to all that gossip," Yvette protests.

"But it's not gossip! I saw her with my own eyes in Saint-Quentin, in a crêpe shop with Manuel Quinson."

Manu again! Get Manu out of the picture, he's just mixing everything up! It would be so much simpler if her lover were Paul!

Finally, Catherine gets to my fingers—pulls and stretches. I ought to give her a demonstration of my new ability.

"Fuckin' A!" she exclaims, like a little kid. "I never would've believed you'd manage to do this one day. Okay, let's get those joints of yours working. Let's go . . ."

It feels as if someone has placed a red-hot wire inside my muscles. It's spreading all the way to my wrist.

"Okay, now bend! One, two, one, two!"

The wire is running just beneath my skin, and my hand is nothing but pain—pain that's delicious, pain that's alive. Alive.

Well, that's it. All done. The Great Catherine puts her things away, tosses me into my chair, and wipes off my face.

"She was sweating. That proves something's going on!" she calls to Yvette. "Well, I've gotta run. See you tomorrow!"

I'm left all alone. I enjoy rolling around in my chair. I'm getting much better at it. I raise my hand and bring it down with all my strength on the electric controls. It's terrific! The wheelchair jumps forward and backward.

I hear Yvette behind me, sighing, though she dares not say a thing. I feel like a four-year-old. Things have gone haywire all around me; for entire families, things are falling apart; but I'm moving forward, rising back to the surface. By necessity, I'm out of step with the general atmosphere, but what else can I do? Must I be forbidden from hope and rejoicing?

TWELVE

THEY'VE BURIED LITTLE JORIS. YET ANOTHER.
Another small coffin. The mere thought of it nauseates me.
And no one here suspects a thing!

There's a terrible wind blowing. It seems as though a giant were out there, shaking the trees for the fun of it. The
sound of humid leaves is sinister. Yvette has gone out to do
her shopping and has put on an audio book for me—Zola's
La Bête Humaine. I adore Zola, though, under the circumstances, the title is not in such good taste. The cassette was
a gift from Guillaume. He brought it by the other night. I
was very happy for it. Except I couldn't help wondering
whether he, in fact, was the killer, and if his reasons for
giving it to me were less than innocent. What's happening
now? Well, it's stopped, of all things, and right in the middle of a sentence! This is so annoying! There's nothing I
can do about it but wait for Yvette to return. Ah, someone's
here! Nope, wrong. What's the tape recorder doing now?
The lousy piece of junk is making all sorts of clicks and
snaps. Ah, there, it's working again.

"It was neither a pleasure nor a joy, but rather a neces-
sity, a terrible necessity. I had to kill them. I had to hold

them tight until they moved no more and were at
peace. . . ."

Funny, but I don't remember that.

". . . looking all around, in order to choose the right vic-
tims, imagining their tender young flesh, so tender, pressed
close to the heart, listening to their shouts, seeing exactly
the moment at which life left their bodies and they would be
no more than a pile of rags, unmoving. How is it possible?
How can one die? How can one be warm and supple, and
then cold and stiff? Does anyone really die?"

What the hell is this?

". . . how could I know? How would I find out if not by
moving here, to this tranquil suburb, being among others,
talking about rain and lovely weather, paying membership
dues to local sports clubs, mowing the lawn, and smiling
into the mirror, a bloodstained smile, and running my
hands over my treasure, my precious treasure, who was
taken from my little angels . . . my little squealers . . ."

My God! It's another cassette! The voice isn't the same.
This one is raucous, dull, assumed, yes, an electronic
voice . . . and what it's saying. . . . It's not possible, and
yet . . .

". . . some might say it's hatred, sadism, but I loved
them. I wanted to love them, hold them, just hold them tight,
hug them, but they don't want me to. They fight back, they
try to get away. They don't understand that I just want to
help them rest . . ."

No! I don't want to hear this! Who put this thing into the
tape player?

". . . but no one understands. I have to hide. I have to
push poor Elise Andrioli's wheelchair, thinking how nice it
might be to cut open her abdomen with a scalpel, and reach
into the wound, knowing she could not fight back or cry
out, and tear her heart out, nice and gently, to watch her
mouth fill with blood, and see her die, so ironically, with
her blind eyes gazing upon her murderer's face. . . . I hate
you, Elise. I didn't hate the others. No, I loved them, I loved
them very dearly. But you I hate. . . ."

Stop this thing!

Who put this cassette in? Who stopped Zola to put this on? A terrifying idea occurs to me: He's here—*here*—*next to me.* He's listening to himself speak and laughing, I'm sure of it, with his scalpel in hand, listening to the cassette and looking at me.

"*. . . yes, that's what I've got to do. Kill her, get rid of this useless creature, inflict horrible suffering upon her, punish her . . .*"

For what? What have I done? It's gone silent. I hear nothing else, except the sound of his breathing. Is it on the tape or in the room? I don't know. I don't know anymore. I'm scared to death, I . . . it's starting again . . . that electronic voice again, and—

" *'Hi.'* "

"Hello."

Oh, no, not that, not that. I don't want to hear this.

" *'What are you doing?'*

" *'I'm gathering some ripe ones for my mom.'*

" *'I'll help you if you want. . . . You're very cute, you know.'*

" *'I've gotta go home.'*

" *'Wait a minute . . . stay here with me.'*

" *'No, I've gotta go home, I'm late.'*

" *'Come here! I've got a surprise for you.'*

" *'No!'*

" *'Come here, will you! Come over here!'*

" *'No! Aahhh! Aaaahhh!'* "

The screaming rings out. I can't stand it, I can't stand it! Stop it! Stop! It stops. This bastard recorded himself! He recorded the murders and must play them back at night, at home, to get off! He should be killed. He's a monster and . . . *he's here!*

There's a hand on my arm. *Warm. Real.* I'm not dreaming. On the inside I'm screaming so loud it seems I'll burst my larynx. A hand is tightening around my throat, and now there's something else, something cold. The scalpel. My God, the scalpel! He sticks it into my flesh. It hurts. Please, help me. He sticks it in again. It's burning. Please, help me, someone, I beg you, I'm begging you! No, you bastard, you bastard! He's going to cut me up alive! I'll kill you, you bastard! Take that! Take that, in the face, you bastard.

"Miss Andrioli? Are you there?"

Yssart! Quick! Quick!

"I let myself in. It was open and no one was answering . . ."

Close it and get over here, quick!

"Ah, you're here . . . I wanted to have a word with you about . . . what's happened to you?"

Yssart! He's here! The madman is here! He must be hiding in a corner. He's armed. Be careful! Careful! My God, why the fuck can't I speak!

"I'll call an ambulance. Everything will be all right."

No, it won't be all right. He'll kill you, then me, and he'll cut me into pieces, and I won't be able to cry out. That's what he'll do, just as he did with those children. I feel tears of rage and terror rolling down my cheeks.

"Don't cry, everything will be all right now. The ambulance is coming. Do you know who did this?"

No index finger. How can I tell him that the killer is definitely here . . . unless he hid behind the door and fled while Yssart was attending to me. If only . . .

I feel something warm trickling down my arm.

"Don't move. Just raise your finger. Were you alone?"

Index finger.

The cassette. He's got to hear the cassette. In spite of the pain I raise my hand and try to point it toward the tape player.

"Slowly . . . what do you want to tell me? That piece of furniture?"

I lower my hand.

"No, not the furniture. The wall? The vase? The painting? The stereo?"

Index finger.

"Something that was in the stereo?"

Index finger.

He goes to it, and I hear him rifling through the tape recorder.

"There's nothing inside, just a cassette of *La Bête Humaine,* next to the tape player."

The bastard took it out before Yssart came in! The ambulance siren approaches, and I feel soft and cold. Yssart puts his arm around my shoulders. He smells of cologne.

"The ambulance is here. They're going to help you. Don't worry."

Why would I worry? I wonder.

Footsteps and voices . . . they place me on a stretcher and pick me up. My head rolls a bit; it's so cold. Have I lost much blood? Doors slam shut; they're talking to me. Someone injects me with something. Yssart's calm voice is saying, "Don't worry."

I WAKE UP IN A BED. I'M LYING DOWN. THERE'S NO noise, except for a buzzing to my left. It smells like flowers. For a second, the frightful thought comes to mind that I'm exposed in an open coffin, and then think back. I must be in the hospital. My right arm seems heavy. It rests upon the blanket, beside my body. My left arm is folded over my chest. I try to raise it, and it works, but it hurts like hell, tugging on me from all over. The door opens.

"Gently! They've just stitched you up!"

It's a woman's voice; she seems to be in her forties, a nurse, of course.

"Your arm was cut wide open about four inches, and there were nicks on your left forearm when you hit him."

Hit him? I hit somebody?

"Don't worry about your thighs. It wasn't very deep. You won't have any scars."

How could I have hit him? Someone else is coming in.

"You had us so scared!"

Inspector Gassin. He must be very close. I can smell his leather.

"So, what happened?"

What? Does he think I'm going to sing for him? "Yvette fainted when we told her the news," he continues. "She was coming home from her shopping and saw the ambulance heading off. She's feeling better now; she's waiting to see you. Your friends the Fanstens are here, too. As far as the investigation goes, it's running its course. The guys in the lab went through the living room with a fine-toothed comb, and we'll have results tomorrow. Did the guy talk to you?"

Not really. How should I explain this to him?

I raise my hand.

Did he tell you what he wanted?

I raise my hand.

"Did he want to . . . well . . . what I mean is . . . did he try to abuse you?"

No hand. Suddenly I understand that for him this is a simple assault that has nothing to do with the case of the murdered children. Perhaps Yssart himself did not make the connection. They'll chalk this up to a man who attacks women who are alone, and the trick will be complete. Anyway, I won't be able to have them listen to the cassette where he recorded . . . Just thinking back to it makes my stomach contract. What? What is he saying?

". . . let you rest. I'll be back tomorrow."

And what about Yssart? Where is Yssart? He's the one I want, the only one who understands anything!

Yet obviously Gassin leaves without hearing my silent plea.

"Elise! My child!"

Yvette! I know she's crying.

"Oh, my God, I was so afraid! I thought you were dead!"

So did I, Yvette.

"It's my fault. Still, I was sure I locked the door. I'm getting old," she mutters, sniffling.

He would have come back anyway. Poor Yvette! I feel like taking her in my arms and consoling her.

"Fortunately you were able to move your arm. If he had come eight days earlier, he would have killed you. They found some knife on the floor. You must have hit him right in the face and he dropped it."

Hit him . . . that's what the nurse was talking about. Yes,

I remember, being immersed in anger and the sensation of hitting, hitting . . .

"The police are hoping he bled, too. They took blood samples, dusted for prints—you'd think you were in *The Last Five Minutes.* Paul and Hélène are here, but the nurse doesn't want them to come in. She says you need your rest; because of the shock, your blood pressure dropped way down, you were all white. Oh, I'm so happy there was nothing serious."

Impulsively, she leans over and kisses me on both cheeks—two big, fat smacking kisses. Am I crying? It's possible; I feel moisture on my cheeks.

"I'll be back tomorrow morning. Get some rest!" Yvette calls out again before leaving.

I sniffle deeply. The flowers must be from her. Or are they from the Fanstens? Or from Guillaume? Guillaume . . . He's the one who gave me the Zola cassette. Perhaps some-one had tampered with it. No, wrong, because Yssart saw it. That proves nothing; he didn't listen to it. Shit, there I go again. The squirrel is back in my head. My arm is calling. They found the knife on the floor. So much the better. I hope I broke the bastard's nose. I hope I hurt him, the way he hurt me. Oh, if I could, I'd . . . Well, in any case, terror is very effective as a cure. If I could get back the use of a limb with every murder attempt, then I'd ask to be taken on a drive at night through the bad parts of town.

He prepared this recording with me in mind. He insisted that I listen. He wanted me to be frightened. He likes to frighten. This cruelty, the very idea that he recorded the murders—how could a human being do such a thing? You're going to tell me that the Nazis filmed their execu-tions in the death camps. Perhaps once you get past a cer-tain barrier you're capable of anything. He must have changed his voice with one of those devices they sell through the mail. Once I saw an ad where some guy on the phone was laughing while talking into a small device: "Fool your friends with the vocal modifier. Your own mother won't recognize you." I'd even told myself that this sort of invention would please "raven"-style maniacs.

I'm sleepy. They must have given me a tranquilizer. I feel about ready to go to sleep. I'm safe here. Under no risk. It's the hospital.

"ELISE! WAKE UP! WAKE UP!"

Hmmm, what's going on?

"Listen carefully!"

Suddenly I feel totally awake. It's Yssart. He's leaning over me, holding me by the shoulders.

"I don't have much time. The lab tests haven't yielded a thing: they haven't come up with any fingerprints other than Yvette's, or Guillaume's, or the Fanstens. And there were no prints on the knife—it was a very sharp Laguiole, they say. And no other blood besides your own. Your attacker must have been wearing gloves."

Just like you. I can feel the leather of your gloves through my fine hospital gown.

"We're at a dead end. No one wants to admit that the attack you've been through is linked to the series of murders. They want to stick with the theory that has Stéphane Migoin as the man behind these crimes. So the true murderer is free to go on doing as he pleases. I can't continue pursuing him within a legal framework. I'm held prisoner by contingencies. So listen carefully: I'm going to have to carry it off through other means, but don't worry, I'll be watching over you, I promise."

What's he talking about? Is he going to take to the bush or something?

"You and I know that he's very close to you. And to Virginie. He is very close. I know it, I can feel it, I'm hot on his trail, right on his heels. That's why he has become so enraged. He's afraid. I can recognize the smell of fear."

Yet another who's losing his marbles. Not you, Yssart, logic made flesh!

"Do you know why we always find the solution to every enigma? Because there's no lock that doesn't have a key, and no key that doesn't have a lock. To even conceive of an enigma, one must know its solution, for it is part of the very essence of the enigma. Knowing this is enough to no longer be afraid."

I have no idea what he's talking about.

"Do you know the legend of Isis and Osiris?"

Isis and Osiris? From ancient Egypt? While I'm waking up?

He gets up again. "See you soon, Elise."

A draft of air, then nothing else. He's vanished into thin air. Perhaps he has turned into a bat and is floating through the pale sky. What time is it? Everything is so calm.

A door opens, followed by the sound of footsteps. I hold my breath. Someone's leaning over me. A hand lifts the bedsheets and I raise my hand.

"Oh, you're awake? Look, you've got to sleep. It's three in the morning. Don't be afraid. I'll come back every hour on the hour."

The nurse leaves without a sound.

Three o'clock in the morning. Yssart was in my room at three o'clock in the morning. Am I hallucinating? And he called me "Elise" and was saying such strange things. Could he be on drugs? Or perhaps it's my fatal charm that makes every man I meet fall apart. Isis and Osiris . . . As far as I can recall, Osiris was killed and dismembered, and Isis sought to reconstitute him, to find all his scattered pieces to give him life again. I fail to see their connection with the murders we have here in Boissy-les-Colombes, in the twentieth century . . . For Zeus' sake! Pieces! Eyes, hair, hands, a hand . . . but to reconstitute what? Renaud? Could it be Paul, gone mad after Renaud's murder, looking to reconstitute him? But the murders started before then! No, I mustn't get lost down the Egyptian track.

I should go to sleep. Well, this good lady knows some good ones. But she hasn't received visits from completely wired detectives in the middle of the night after almost being bumped off that very same afternoon. She should have given me some sort of shot, a nice little shot that could make me dream . . . without anxiety, without anything. When I was little and couldn't sleep, I would imagine a rubber ball bouncing in the hall, on the stairs. I followed it with my eyes. I glided with it, glided . . . glided . . .

MY HEAD HURTS. I'M IN BED, AND THE NURSE HAS just washed me, passed the bed pan under me, and changed my bandages. She told me it was overcast and not very cold. The wounds seem to be healing. This bastard cut open my whole right arm and hip. Some gorgeous gashes—a good half inch deep. My left forearm, the one I swung in his face, was hit in the act, suffering superficial lacerations. Actually, I'm not feeling any pain; they must have given me painkillers.

Why the devil did Yssart burst into my room in the middle of the night? It reminds me of Stéphane calling me when he should have been fleeing. The nurse asks if I would like to listen to the TV, and I lift my hand; it's just as well to have a distraction. She goes from one channel to another until I settle on a science magazine on FR3 for kids. At least I'll learn something. I listen attentively for a half hour and then the door opens.

"Elise! How are you?"

Yvette. I lift my hand.

There's a voice behind her: "Hi, Elise." Hélène.

"Are you okay now?" Virginie.

"Not so loud, Virginie. Lise is very tired." Paul. All three of them are here, those shit fuckers. Why am I thinking that? I don't know, it just came to me.

"You really had us so scared!" says Hélène.

"Does it hurt much?" asks Virginie.

"The room's pretty calm," comments Paul, who I imagine is shifting from one foot to the other, as men often do when they're in a hospital.

I casually lift my hand, to show them I'm all right.

"I told Inspector Gassin that I was sure I locked the door, and then I remember being distracted by a fallen branch. You know how all this wind upsets me," Yvette explains, feeling guilty.

"The captain's dead," Virginie announces.

My heart skips a beat.

"Virginie!" yells Paul, visibly annoyed.

Yssart? Dead?

"He died of a heart attack last night, at home, in Paris, at around nine o'clock," Hélène explains through the uneasy silence. "Mind you, we didn't see him that often, anyway, maybe two, three times."

A cold sensation, from head to toe, invades me. If Captain Yssart had died at home last night at around nine o'clock, then *who* came at three in the morning to speak with me? Did I dream up this whole conversation?

"I've got to say, he didn't look well," Paul adds. "It was clear to see, he drank too much."

Yssart? He never smelled of alcohol. Who are these people talking to me? Are they real? Am I real? I feel my hand spasmodically clutching the sheet. The sheet seems real. My hand. Clutching. I can feel it wrapped around the sheet. That's fantastic!

"Look! Elise can close her hand!" Virginie announces triumphantly.

"We've got to notify Raybaud! Nurse!"

Yvette runs out, all excited.

"I'm sorry to hear about the captain, of course, but in any case, from what Gassin was saying, it looked like the old guy was losing it for a while. He was supposed to retire in a couple of months. To tell you the truth, I got the impression that Gassin was being a bit critical of him; he thought he was going a bit soft in the head, if you know what I mean."

Yssart? A man in his sixties? With a voice like that?

"I told the nurse to notify Dr. Raybaud. After all that's happened, I don't even know if I'm up or down anymore," Yvette says, sadly. "And now the captain. You'd really think we've been cursed."

"Come on, things will get better, they've got to. A time always comes for things to get better," Paul interrupts, patronizing. "And with the captain it's not the same thing. For someone his age, he must have been really overworked."

"That's true. And of course there was that mustache of his, yellow and all. He must have smoked like a chimney," Yvette acquiesces.

He never smelled of tobacco. This isn't possible. They can't be talking about Yssart.

I lift my hand.

"Yes, Elise? Did you want to tell us something?" Paul inquires.

I clench and unclench my fist and swing my arm out to the side. I want a pencil! I want paper and a pencil. Stiff as justice, my arm leaves me and goes bumping into clattering objects.

"Lise, watch out!"

A glass shatters. I can hear their whispering: ". . . nervous . . . shouldn't have talked about the captain . . . notify the nurse . . ."

That's right, notify her! Damn it, I need to know what's going on!

The nurse arrives, cleans up, and gives me a shot.

"You need to be careful. You mustn't get so excited."

Clearly I understand her implied threat: "Or else I'll have to give you a nice, big dose of tranquilizers."

"Come. I think she needs to be left alone. She needs her rest."

They all leave in funereal silence. My arm hurts. Once or twice again, I clench my left hand, imagining that it's tightening around the neck of that bastard who slashed me. That ought to do me some good. If this goddamn hand could grip a pencil, then finally I'll be able to communicate with others. I feel so soft. From the shot, no doubt . . . Soft . . . soft . . .

I wake up and go back to sleep. I have nightmares that leave me bathed in sweat. They can let up on the tranquilizers already, I've earned the right; it must be at least two days that I've been struggling through this gauze of muffled sounds. Vaguely I hear a voice telling me, "We've got a package for you."

A package? Can't open it, much too tired. What time is it? Is it night or day? I'm cold. I'm warm. I want to wake up and move my legs, scratch my feet. I want to run! I feel completely wiped out. Need to sleep. Dreamless sleep. To sleep.

I FEEL MORE CLEAR-HEADED TODAY. I MAKE SURE TO appear calm. I move my hand only when questioned, and this seems to have borne some fruit. They have me drink a lot of water. They sit me up in bed, supporting me with pillows and a back strap. I'm used to these preventive anti-bedsore exercises, so I just let them manipulate me. I open and close my hand, and lift my arm on demand. They compliment me and leave me alone. And then I'm off, plunged back into these dark thoughts of mine.

Yssart. Dead. It's impossible. He can't be dead and yet speak to me. Or perhaps it's true what Virginie says: the dead are just roaming among us, spying on us. All these dead children are around me, with their hollow eyes. And Benoît, with his throat slit . . . having a laugh with them, about me . . . And Yssart, a tall corpse with a soft voice and long pianist's hands. Impossible. A pencil. If I had a pencil . . .

"Do you want me to open it up?"

That idiot nurse just scared the hell out of me! I was so lost in thought. What's she talking about?

"The package. Do you want me to open it up?"

So I wasn't dreaming? A package? For me? Delicacies from my uncle? I lift my hand to tell her she may go on.

"Hold on a second. . . . How come they always put on so much tape. . . ."

The paper goes *scratch, scratch* as it unfolds.

"Here we are. What is this? Ahh, it's a thick pair of men's glasses, with tortoiseshell frames, and then we've got black leather gloves, and this . . . it's a yellow mustache, a fake one, and—what's this?—oh, yes, a white wig that's turning yellow. It's kind of strange, but you must know what this is about, I suppose."

No, dearie, I have no idea. I'm not in the habit of receiving packages containing assorted tricks. Did a clown send it to the wrong address? A clown. A yellow mustache. Black gloves. Yssart! Good God, *Yssart was phony!* For months a phony detective was roaming through town with complete impunity! That's why he came to talk to me that night! To tell me he couldn't go on! Because the real Yssart was dead! He could no longer come to my house. Well, then . . . who is the phony Yssart? And how did he gather so much information about everything? And why did he come speak to me?

"I'll be leaving now. See you later."

Fine. Bye-bye. A perfectly disagreeable thought has just come to mind. Yssart showed up just when that guy was slashing me with his knife. What if . . . *what if he were the one who found it amusing to play with me like a cat with a mouse for all these weeks?*

How am I to warn the others? How can I make them understand?

But if Yssart is the murderer, then why did he come to speak to me that night? And why didn't he take advantage of the occasion to kill me?

Enough! Enough of these questions! I would like some answers!

I'm feeling tears of powerlessness and frustration well up in my eyes. In my rage, I'm crumpling the sheet between clenched fingers.

"So, Elise, I hear we're making progress every day!"

Raybaud.

"That's great! I never would have believed . . ."

He stops in midsentence and coughs nervously.

"I've scheduled a meeting for next week with the neurosurgeon. We shouldn't get our hopes up too much, of course, the progress might end there, but still it would be nice, wouldn't it?"

Fabulous. I'm sure you'll love that.

"Well, get some rest while we're waiting. I'll be back tomorrow."

Pfff. He's gone.

"Hello."

Gassin!

"I haven't got much time. I believe you've already heard about the captain."

I lift my hand. Honey, if only you knew about the captain!

"Do you remember the knife we picked up? The Laguiole? It has a yellow tortoiseshell handle, with a blade about four inches long. It's one of the finer models. That doesn't ring a bell with you?"

I'm thinking about it. No. It says something to me, vaguely, but what? My uncle has a Laguiole with a dark wooden handle, but this . . . no, not offhand.

"That's too bad. It might have helped us find out who the owner is. The guy must have been hiding in the garden. He saw Mrs. Holzinski leave the premises, and took his chances. He must have been surprised when you moved your arm, because he took off without waiting. There's one thing I don't understand. Who called the paramedics? The ambulance technicians claim that when they got there, there was a man next to you. Here is his description: about six feet one, very thin, with black hair and black eyes."

Yssart! The real one! Without his disguise!

"The man told them he stayed there to wait for the police. No one heard from him again. Do you know who this might be?"

Yes, I do. But what am I to do? I lift my hand and pivot my arm to the side.

"Uhh . . . Wait . . . do you want to show me something?"

I lift my hand.

"Okay, but what? Is it in the room?"

I lift my hand. I pivot my arm again.

"Uhh . . . the cardboard box over there?"

I lift my hand, exultantly. I hear him crossing the room and rummaging through the cardboard box.

"Shit! What the hell is this? Could it be . . . Damn it, this can't be!"

Oh, yes, it can, my sweet. I hear him rooting about with something, and then an electronic beep. He must have a cellular phone: "Hello, this is Gassin. Yes, get me Mendoza. It's urgent. . . . What do you mean, he's in the can? Okay, I'll wait.

"Mendoza? . . . Listen, frankly, I don't give a damn, because I've got something here that's really weird. I'm at the hospital, with Andrioli. . . . Yes, her. Well, you know someone told us that some guy called for an ambulance, a guy no one knew. Well, there's a package here in her room, delivered by . . . wait, let's see . . . Parcels Express, 25 Place Thiers, Saint-Ambroise, and inside the package there's a wig, a mustache, and tortoiseshell glasses. You know what? These are the same glasses the chief used to wear! And the same mustache . . . No, I'm not bullshitting you. Send someone over to Parcels Express right away, understand? . . . No, she's blind, she couldn't possibly be aware. . . . No, nobody knew Yssart. Police captains aren't exactly movie stars. All he had to do was vaguely resemble him, that's all. . . . Okay, later!"

He pauses momentarily before speaking to me. "Excuse me, I've just notified my office. Did a nurse bring you this?"

My hand goes up.

"Still, this is incredible! Something this ridiculous would have to happen to me! I'm gonna be the laughingstock of the whole force. But you've got to realize, this doesn't quite stand up!"

He calms down and clears his throat, still furious.

"Okay, well, I've gotta go. I'll be taking the package. I'll have a cop sent to guard your room. You never know."

Ah, he's starting to understand that this here isn't a simple case of assault.

"I'll keep you posted."

He walks out, and I hear him speaking in a dry tone of voice with a nurse in the corridor.

Could the man who passed himself off as Yssart be the one who killed these children? I liked his voice, his inflections. Wouldn't I have sensed it? No, I won't get started again with these endless calculations. Now the investigation will progress, I'm sure of it.

He's tall, with brown hair. A bit how I imagined him. I'm daydreaming. Imagining myself in the Caribbean, lying on a beach of fine sand, feeling the sun's warmth on my tanned skin, and listening as the waves lazily crash upon the shore. A white sailboat out at sea, rocking upon the waters; the smell of grilled lobster . . . I'd knock back a bottle of cooler. An ice-cold cooler in my left hand, and a juicy mystery novel in my right . . . yes, that should do me fine. A siesta in the sweltering heat, far, far away from these gray suburbs teeming with insane human ants, running in all directions, full of atrocious questions and sinister answers . . . I want to stay in the Caribbean!

The problem is, this isn't working. This isn't the sun warming me. I don't hear the sound of the waves, but rather the monitor on the night table, and that ice-cold cooler has dwindled to three pills with warm water every two hours.

IT'S IMPOSSIBLE TO STAY IN THE CARIBBEAN. I CAN'T stop ruminating: Did Jean Guillaume bring me an altered cassette? If so, then he would be the murderer. But why would he have it in for me? That's what I don't quite understand. Captain Yssart was a phony detective. How is it that the real one never came to see me? Because I had nothing significant to offer to his investigation. Only the phony Yssart established a relation between Virginie, the murders, and me. Which leads me to another question: Why did he pass himself off as Captain Yssart? Who the hell is this guy? Either it's the murderer himself or perhaps . . . who? A journalist looking for a great scoop? A private detective hired by the family of one of the victims? In any case, the murderer can't be Jean Guillaume and Yssart at the same time. If only someone would go through the trouble of listening to that awful cassette . . . But how could Inspector Gassin ever guess that it's got something abnormal on it? In fact, all the murderer's maneuvers rest upon the base postulate that I am incapable of communicating with anyone else. What if I were to get my speech back? Or if I managed to write? He would have to kill me, because all the little tidbits I'd recount would certainly lead to his downfall. So that means extreme concentration and nonstop hand exercises.

THIRTEEN

THE NURSE HAS MANAGED TO UNTANGLE MY HAIR.
It involved some pulling. She makes sure I look proper,
and that my vest is buttoned. She's very nice. Her name is
Yasmina, she told me so while changing my bandages. I
know her father is Kabyle, and her mother is from Pas-de-
Calais. She flunked her B levels due to family problems—
translation: her mother was an alcoholic. She decided to
become a nurse so she could look after others and try to
help them, but finds it doesn't pay so well here, and thinks
the union should be more active. She has long, curly brown
hair and has a boyfriend named Ludovic, who also works
here as a male nurse. I don't know why, but as soon as people are alone with me, they start telling me their secrets. It
must be like talking to their dolls.

"There. You're as pretty as a heart!" she beams as she
sets me down in my wheelchair. "It's ten o'clock. They'll
be here soon. I hope we won't have to see you here for
quite a while."

Me too. Even though my brief stay here wasn't unpleasant . . . I got to rest, in spite of all those gnawing questions,
and of course, knowing there's a cop standing guard outside

my door has a tranquilizing effect on me. Speaking of tranquilizing, they haven't stopped making me swallow them.
What a dirty little habit. Three-quarters of the time, they
put me right out.

There are footsteps in the hall, and then the door opens.

"You really look good!" Yvette exclaims, giving me a
kiss. "Paul's waiting downstairs. Bye-bye, miss, and thank
you!"

"You're welcome! Bye-bye, Elise!"

I amiably lift my hand and bend my fingers three times
in a row, which could resemble a perfectly acceptable
"ciao."

Yvette grasps the wheelchair and rolls me toward the elevator, giving me a running commentary of the latest news.
I feel like a race-car driver, back on track after a brief pit
stop.

"Oh, my poor thing, quite a few things have been going
on! First, Inspector Gassin discovered that Captain Yssart
wasn't a real detective. Can you imagine? We had ourselves
an impostor! Jean changed all the locks in the house, and
I've had a bolt placed on the bathroom window. You're not
safe anywhere nowadays—a fake detective! For all we
know, he might even be the one who attacked you or killed
those poor kids! Inspector Gassin told me he might have
some clues, because he may have left prints on a cassette . . .
you know? The audio book Jean gave you."

The elevator stops with a mild jolt, Yvette pushes me
out, and we're surrounded by people, hospital smells, and
ringing telephones. A fingerprint. The phony Yssart may
have left a fingerprint when he touched the cassette.
Wouldn't he find that somewhat disturbing? Or is it a false
fingerprint left there deliberately? Anything is possible. In
any case, the cassette does not contain anything unusual; if
it did, Gassin would have noticed.

"Hello, Lise! You seem to be in good form!"

Paul. I raise my hand. I'm hoisted into the station
wagon, and the door slams shut. We're off.

Back to the house.

I enter with a certain bit of apprehension. It seems

soiled, it's no longer safe. It exudes evil and danger. Yvette rolls me into the living room and starts scurrying about. Paul sits down on the sofa, near me.

"Well, here we are. I hope things will be all right now." He lowers his voice and leans over: "We don't know what to do. Should we talk to the police about Virginie's real father? Hélène told you I wasn't her real father, didn't she?"

I lift my hand. Suddenly I wish he would leave; I don't know why he's making me feel sick, his voice seems so gentle.

"The guy was a real son of a bitch, and in fact, what you don't know, and what Hélène confessed to me, is that—"

"Would you like something to drink, Paul?"

"No, thanks, Yvette, that's very nice of you. I've got to go. I have a meeting. See you later, Elise. Bye-bye."

It's insane how people are so casual with me. They toss me bits of information I didn't ask for, then cut the transmission short just as abruptly, as if they were talking to themselves, all alone, like those people you see delivering monologues to their pets. What the hell could Hélène have confessed to him about Virginie's father? Can't be too pretty, considering the character . . .

I'm back in my living room for barely an hour, trying to talk myself into a little snooze, when someone rings the doorbell. Here we go again! Ladies and gentlemen, welcome to the Andrioli merry-go-round! Open every day, even at night, for kids of all ages!

"She's in the living room."

"Thank you. I have to see her alone."

I hear the sound of sure-footed steps.

"Hello. I have to speak to you. It's important."

Gassin. In just two days, he's taken on an air of authority. I hear him close the door separating the living room from the entrance hall.

"Do you remember the package that came for you in the hospital?"

My dear inspector, I'd have to be lobotomized not to remember it. I lift my hand.

"Good. My partner, Inspector Mendoza, went to Parcels

Express to ask a few questions. The person who sent the package was fairly tall, skinny, and had dark hair. The same, we believe, who called the ambulance and came looking for you. Of course, he left a false name and a false address: Stéphane Migoin."

Oh, my, now I'm really floundering. What has poor Stéphane got to do with all this?

"So it's obvious that this is someone in the know about what's going on here, and that we're not looking at a simple case of assault. Fortunately, he slipped up, just once: he left a thumbprint on an audiocassette that was right next to your stereo, *La Bête Humaine*. We've looked in the central registry, and bingo! Do you know who the man is who's been passing himself off as Captain Yssart? The man who sent the package? The man who most certainly assaulted you before calling the ambulance himself?"

He gives me a second or two to wait patiently before going on.

"Antoine Mercier, also known as Tony; thirty-eight years old, arrested in 1988 for murder, declared incompetent to stand trial, and held in the Saint-Charles psychiatric facility near Marseilles, in the Bouches-du-Rhône province."

Tony! Yssart was Tony! Wow! . . . The arm-breaker, disguised as a cop! Tony, the same guy who was incarcerated for murder!

"Hold on, you haven't heard everything," Gassin continues, unable to contain his excitement. "Just guess who Tony Mercier is. . . . Tony Mercier is Virginie's real father. Hélène Fansten has just told us. He was seeing Mrs. Fansten from 1986 until the time he was arrested. And do you know why he was arrested?"

He leans over toward me, and I can smell the menthol on his breath: "*For the murder of an eight-year-old child committed in his neighborhood*. He was denounced by an anonymous letter. My colleagues down in Marseilles carried out a search at his place and found a rope similar to the one used to bind the kid, as well as wool fibers matching his sweater."

I feel myself going soft. Gassin continues, full speed ahead: "Tony Mercier was known to be unstable, with a record as long as my arm: car theft, burglaries, you name it. He was often mixed up in brawls, and had a deplorable family history: he was taken away from his alcoholic parents and placed with social services, he ran away over and over, and so on and so forth. He was unemployed and had even gone into detox several times, but with no results. Everyone knew he beat Hélène and that he'd recently broken her arm. To make a long story short, even if he were innocent, his fate was sealed. Mercier's lawyer pleaded not guilty, on the pretext that anyone could have placed the compromising evidence at his place so that he would be accused. The experts declared him incompetent to stand trial. He was placed in custody. And that's not all: since 1991, Mercier has been granted leave, and two years ago he slipped away from the psychiatric hospital!"

Gassin was so excited, he practically shouted the last words. I can understand him, poor thing: imagine, some nut job suspected of murder is passing himself off as your boss, gleefully running loose through town, leading his own inquiry, especially when the nut job in question happens to be the father of some kid who seems to know quite a bit about the murders perpetrated on the outskirts of this same town . . .

Obviously, a guy who's capable of breaking his own woman's arm could very well drill holes in my head with needles or cut me up with his Laguiole. Some would say that this mystery is well on its way to being solved. It seems to me that Tony/Yssart is our designated culprit. That would explain why Virginie said nothing. He must have revealed to her that he was her father. Then he killed Migoin to lay the blame on his shoulders! How did Hélène not recognize him? Because he never went to her house— only the real Yssart did! And I listened to all that sweet talk from the impostor, who must have been laughing, wondering when he'd knock me off. I just narrowly escaped.

Gassin grabs both my hands: "My theory is that Tony Mercier is our child killer. He came back here to prowl, looking for his daughter and the woman he continues to consider his wife. All reports show he's extremely possessive, and that he's often made threats against her. Once back in the area, he couldn't keep himself from killing again. He took on Captain Yssart's identity so that he could be at the heart of the events. He tricked you and all of us perversely. He's dangerously ill, and I fear the worst for your safety and for Hélène Fansten's. I don't want you to stay here. I want you to go stay with your uncle. I've warned Hélène's husband: he'll take all the necessary precautions. Understand that for the time being I can't prove a thing, I don't even have letters rogatory, but I know this much: you're in danger."

He gets up. Go to my uncle? Well, honestly, why not? It's far away from it all. I won't be present when they'll arrest poor Tony, and won't hear Virginie cry or Hélène's shouts of rage or all the acerbic comments.

"Do you agree?"

I lift my hand.

"Good. I'll go speak to Mrs. Holzinski about it. Goodbye."

He goes to the kitchen and consults with Yvette. Gassin hasn't cooled off. This episode of the phony Yssart must be humiliating for him. I've got to say that. . . . Yvette bolts the door behind him. Behind me, I can hear her racing, and I'm sure she's running to make sure that the bathroom window is shut tight. What is she doing? Ah, she's on the telephone. I'll give ten-to-one odds she's talking to my uncle. I win. And so on and so forth. We'll be arriving tomorrow night. She picks up the phone again. To the Fanstens, no doubt.

"Hello. Good evening. It's Yvette. I'm sorry to disturb you. . . . Yes, just now. . . . It's terrible. Who could have known? . . . What an ordeal it must be for you, poor thing! What about Virginie? She doesn't know a thing, I hope. . . . Oh, yes, it's better that way. . . . With your mother-in-law? . . . You're right. I still can't believe it. . . . No, I didn't know. . . . Yes, I understand, it's not the type of thing you'd feel like talking about. . . . And how is

Paul? . . . Yes, he's solid, you're lucky. . . . Oh, that's good. . . . Excuse me? Okay, I'll let you go. I'll call again tomorrow."

Click.

"I got Hélène. It's all so terrible . . . Virginie's father, can you imagine? A madman! Escaped from an asylum! It's incredible! I wonder what this world is coming to. They're going to send Virginie to stay with her grandmother. Hélène doesn't want to leave. She wants to stay with Paul. You know how she gets nervous. I understand better now, mind you, how when the father of your child is a murderer, it can't really help your nerves."

That's for sure. Good thing they're sending Virginie far away. I'm dismayed. Instead of feeling happy to see the light at the end of the tunnel, for surely Tony Mercier's arrest is imminent, I feel depressed. It's all just too ugly.

WHAT TIME IS IT? I CAN'T GET TO SLEEP. IF I COULD move, I'd roll over and over, every which way. I'm content to open and close my hand nervously. Yvette put me in bed at around ten, and I've got the feeling it's at least two in the morning. It's impossible to close my eyes.

If Tony Mercier has come to live here, then he must have settled under some identity or other. He didn't just show up disguised as Captain Yssart. First, he must have moved in, then started to kill, and then decided to take on Yssart's identity.

Why would he kill Migoin? Why not Paul? It seems to me that if I were mentally ill and insanely jealous, I would see to it that my ex's husband would be accused of murder, and not someone as brave as Stéphane . . .

Unless (1) Stéphane had suspicions about me, or (2) Stéphane were my ex's lover . . . or had been Hélène's lover.

This opens up some new perspectives.

We may even imagine that there may have been a combination of hypotheses 1 and 2.

When I think that I went as far as to suspect my best

friend's husband and my nurse's devoted fiancé! Paul
Fansten and Jean Guillaume.

What about Sophie? What has become of Sophie's cadaver in all this? Was it really a suicide? For the banal reason of adultery? Was it a dispute with Manu? Or did Tony
kill Sophie as well to increase the charges weighing against
Stéphane? Could an escaped madman be so Machiavellian? Yes. If he couldn't, then he wouldn't be capable of taking on the captain's identity. On the other hand, as Gassin
was saying, even if he were innocent, he had no chance, with
all his baggage from the past.

What if he hadn't committed that murder in Marseilles?
Why would he settle down here? Why would he disguise
himself as the captain? No, it's got to be him: there's no
other rational explanation. But I'm obstinate about finding
some bubbles in this stagnant water.

Still, why wasn't he suspected from the very beginning?
After all, knowing that the stepmother of one of the victims
had lived with the murderer . . . no, I'm being stupid. They
didn't know: Hélène didn't speak to anyone about Tony, and
in any case, she could not guess that he'd run away from the
hospital. She thought he was locked up. There was no reason
to stir up all this mud.

"WHAT LOVELY WEATHER!" YVETTE CALLS OUT AS SHE
opens the shutters.

I don't remember falling asleep. It feels as if I were
dreaming all night long.

We have our washing and breakfast ritual. Yvette's not
so talkative, which is just as well, as I'm feeling a bit glum.
She moves me into the living room, near the window, so
that I may benefit from the sunshine coming through the
windows. I feel the warmth against my skin. Yvette must
be packing my things to go to my uncle's. Will they catch
Yssart soon? He's slipped through their fingers for six
months. Perhaps he won't let himself be trapped so easily.
Especially now that little Gassin has to convince the judge
and his superiors of his extravagant theories.

The telephone rings.

"Hélène and Virginie will be coming by at noon to say good-bye," Yvette informs me after she hangs up.

If Yvette hadn't moved me to the shade in the super-market parking lot that day in May, I would never have met Virginie, and I would know no more about these goings-on than what they say on TV. Instead, I've been caught up in a maelstrom of events, feelings, and fears. If . . . if . . . if . . . you can't look back.

Yvette's grumbling about something. She's afraid she's forgotten something or other, and checks the suitcase a hundred times.

The doorbell rings. Greetings. Two small arms close around my neck.

"I'm going to Gramma's!"

"Virginie, we say hello first!"

"Hello, I'm going to Gramma's!"

I lift my hand and tighten it into a fist. Virginie inserts her finger.

"That's great. Look, Mommy, she can hold me!"

If I can hold a finger, then why not a pencil? Virginie smells of apple-scented shampoo, and I imagine her silky, well-combed blond hair.

"If you'd like, we could drop you off at the airport on our way to taking Virginie to her grandmother's. It's not too far out of the way," Hélène offers.

"Oh, I wouldn't want to disturb you," Yvette protests.

"It was Paul's idea. We could come pick you up at around five."

"Really, I don't know . . ."

"But still you're not really taking a taxi, are you? That would be dumb!"

"That's very nice of you. Virginie, would you like a bit of apple pie?"

"Yeah!"

"Yes, thank you," Hélène corrects her, sounding tired.

Yvette slips off, followed by Hélène, speaking to her in a low voice. Are they sharing secrets?

"Now that the captain is dead, they'll never catch Death

from the Woods," Virginie whispers. "And Death won't be there when I go to my gramma's house. I'm really glad to go. Renaud, too. He always liked Gramma. Did you know there were two captains? A real one and a fake one? The young policeman told Mommy. He's nice. He gave me strawberry gum. He wanted to know if I knew the phony captain. It was a stupid question. Of course I knew him, because he was the captain. He asked me about tons of things, about everybody: my parents, you, Jean Guillaume, Yvette, Stéphane, Sophie, all the kids. I was sick and tired of it. I didn't know a thing about any of that. Like I was going to tell him! Renaud was behind him the whole time. He was making funny faces over his shoulder. It was making me laugh."

I imagine a half-decomposed Renaud making funny faces. Hilarious.

"Finally, I told him I was tired. He was mad. He told me that if I were hiding things from him, then I could go to jail, but I don't hide things, and I haven't stolen from anyone. And I'm sure Death from the Woods is going to hold still now."

"Here you go. A nice big piece of pie!"

Virginie dashes over to Yvette, who has her sit at the table. Why is Death from the Woods (what a retarded name) going to hold still now? Because Tony Mercier has been unmasked and cannot continue with his little game. Yes, everything is holding still.

"No, thanks, no pie for me," Hélène says firmly.

She seems nervous. Suddenly she places her hand on my arm and whispers, "When I think that bastard was here, so close! And as if that weren't enough, in Marseilles . . . When I think how he must have been spying on all three of us, spying on Virginie . . . he must have really gotten a thrill out of that! I hope they get him real soon!"

There's so much hate in her voice, it makes me shudder. They chat with Yvette a few more minutes, and then they're off, with kisses, "see you tonights," and "bye-byes."

"Poor Hélène. She looks like death warmed over." Yvette hesitates, then continues, "Of course I may be

wrong, but sometimes I get the impression that she's over-
doing it a little with the beer. And those big black sunglasses of hers . . . it's not summer anymore. Those are the
kind of sunglasses you put on to hide a drawn face. I had a
cousin who didn't hold her alcohol very well. She was always falling down the stairs or in the shower, and she wore
big sunglasses like those to hide her black eyes."

Is it the alcohol or Paul's quick hand? I've already heard
him slap her. And isn't it true that battered children often
reproduce this type of relationship with their spouse, and
that Tony, her first man, in addition to being a murderer,
was also a violent alcoholic? This is a real Zola novel!

No, don't bring up Zola, *La Bête Humaine,* or anything
of the kind.

It's a long wait. It's boring and yet at the same time ex-
citing. Irritating. Backward, forward, right, left. I'm drawing arabesques with my wheelchair, stopping only to lift
my arm and make a fist. I must seem like Pasionaria in a
wheelchair. "Boissy-les-Colombes: a friendly handicapped
woman turns out to be a dangerous terrorist." Forward,
backward, for the *Mazurka for Quadriplegics.*

I'm sick of waiting. I wish time would just speed up
and Gassin would ring the doorbell and say, "All right,
we've got him!"

Someone is ringing at the door.

"All right, we've got him!"

Shit! It's Gassin!

"I've got a warrant out on Tony Mercier. We've got
roadblocks set up all over, and we've notified all the air-
ports and train stations. We've got him!"

Well, that's better than nothing.

"You know, I often said to Yssart—the real one, I
mean—to keep an eye on the little girl, Virginie Fansten,
but he didn't listen to me. To him, it was all just so much
malarkey. Well, today I'm sure he was wrong, there was a
connection, I could feel it, and the proof is that Mercier is
Virginie's father. My God, when I think that they didn't
follow this lead when Renaud died! If only Hélène Fansten
had talked about Mercier back then! She said she wanted to

make a complete break with her past, that she knew he was interned, and that deep inside she thought she was the victim of some sort of curse. But no! You realize this?"

I realize that things are never as simple as one thinks.

"Get lots of rest at your uncle's. Everything will be taken care of by the time you get back," he sighs.

That boy's an optimist. I lift my hand. Exit Gassin and his arrest warrant. I wonder why he came to tell me that. What if this Gassin were phony? After all, a game like this could go on forever. What if I were a false Elise? Then right now the real one would be prancing through meadows, gathering daisies.

Outside, a car horn honks twice. That must be Hélène and Paul!

"Coming!" Yvette shouts out the window. "Where are my glasses? Where's your wool shawl? I'm sure I left it over there . . ."

She whirls around me, rushes out, comes back, dashes toward the kitchen, grips my wheelchair, and rolls me outside.

"Sorry I'm late," Hélène calls, spilling me onto the seat. "We'll put the wheelchair in the trunk."

"Paul's not here?"

"He's waiting at the bank."

"What about Virginie?"

"She's at school. We'll pick her up on our way," Hélène answers.

Yvette gets into the backseat. I hear her sigh as she sits down heavily. Hélène then sits down, and leans over to strap on my seat belt.

She takes off. The tires crunch over the gravel. We ride in silence. Hélène turns on the radio, and rap comes booming out. I hate rap; I can never understand the words, and it makes me feel like shaking my head like a dromedary.

We stop. Hélène gets out. Oh, yes, the bank. Yvette's rather silent! Has she fallen asleep? The back door opens: "Hi, Elise," Paul calls out over the rap.

The back door, then the front door slam shut.

"Okay, let's go," says Hélène as we head off once again.

It's a long way to go. Where is that fucking school anyway? It must be the new one, on Route D56. No one is saying anything. If only this rap music would end . . .

"Oh, my God," Hélène suddenly shrieks.

What's going on?

"Noooo!"

My heart starts racing. She slams on the brakes, the car swerves, and I'm thrown forward. My head bangs violently against something, and everything goes black.

MY HEAD'S KILLING ME. IT SEEMS TO HAVE GROWN TO twice its size. I've got a raging thirst and a coated tongue. Where am I? Sitting, I guess. In my wheelchair, because I can feel the electric button under my finger. I hear a leaky faucet. There was an accident. It couldn't have been too serious. I'm sure I'm not in the hospital. I'd be in bed, and it would smell like antiseptic. Where's everybody else? I'm listening. Nothing. With each passing second my headache gets worse. I must have an enormous lump at the back of my head, where it's pulsing. If only someone would give me something to drink. Or would speak to me, explain what's happened . . .

It smells like wood. I guess I'm in a wooden house. Is it a chalet? What the hell would I be doing in a chalet? My uncle lives in a modern villa, which he had decorated using everything from his construction sites. And besides, there would be some sound in his house.

Let's see. We were on the road, going to pick up Virginie. There was an accident. Perhaps some people took us in. Some very quiet people—mutes, for example. Or maybe I'm the sole survivor. Shit. This can't be.

I press the button, and the wheelchair slowly moves forward. I roll over the floor and recognize the sound. Boom! That was the wall. I back up, roll for three seconds, and boom! The other wall. It's a small room, about three seconds wide. Without furniture, I guess. Is this the entrance hall?

"Don't worry. Everything will be all right!"

Ahh! My hair stands on end until I recognize Yvette's voice.

"Hélène is coming."

What about Paul? Why hasn't she said anything about Paul? Why hasn't she explained anything to me?

I feel something against my lips. A glass. Of water. Thank you, dear Yvette. I take a long drink. The water tastes gross, but all the same, it does me good. I feel so tired. I'd like Yvette to give me an explanation . . . and this headache . . . swelling . . . swelling . . .

WHY CAN'T I SEE ANYTHING? I WISH I COULD OPEN my eyes. I bat my eyelids. My eyes are open, but I can't see anything. I'm thirsty, still thirsty. My lips feel enormous. Yvette gave me something to drink. Yvette. The accident. I can't see because I'm blind. For just a moment I forgot, I returned to a year before, to a time when none of this had happened. I lift my arm. No one turns up. I'm still sitting. The back of my neck hurts; it's all stiff. I must have fallen asleep. I'd really like to lie down. I've had something to drink and have fallen asleep. What about the others? I lift my arm again. They haven't all disappeared, have they?

"Everything's all right."

It's Yvette again, showing up without warning. Is she trying to kill me or something? Usually she makes so much noise when she moves!

"I'll go make you a nice pie."

But I don't give a shit about your pie! Where are Paul and Hélène? What's happened? That's what I'd like to know!

"I've notified your uncle."

Well, that's fine, but notified him of what? And then there's this fucking headache that just won't quit. The more excited I get, the worse it becomes. It's as if I had a boiler inside my head, and some crazy mechanic kept filling it. *La Bête Humaine,* and *pop!,* into the machine goes a nice lump of coal, and *pop!,* my skull starts smoking and overheating. If I could move my arms, I'd lock them around Yvette and shake her until she told me where we are.

"Paul called."

Paul? He's not with us? Or perhaps she means to say that he called somebody? Called for help? Yvette! I lift my arm and make a fist again and again. Can't you see my signal?!

"Paul called."

I know, I'm not deaf. For goodness' sake, Yvette, make an effort. My God, maybe she's hurt; maybe she's lying on the ground, at my feet, half-dead . . . but no, her voice hasn't changed, she's not gasping for air. She's speaking in her everyday voice.

Everyday. Not even excited. And what if . . . no, it's impossible, but still what if . . . *what if Yvette were not in her right mind?* This odd way of pronouncing short little sentences, completely calm . . . perhaps she's suffered a serious blow. Here's the catastrophe scenario: Paul and Hélène are dead or dying, and Yvette has lost her marbles and dragged me into a shed by the side of the road. She believes we're at home and attends to her duties. We're going to die here, me in my wheelchair, and Yvette pretending to cook.

But she's not attending to her duties. She's not moving. If she were moving, I would hear her, especially on the wooden floor.

So the question is, where is Yvette?

I move forward and hit the wall again. I back up and bump against the wall. To the right—the wall. To the left—the wall. I make crosses—walls.

Yvette? At no time did I touch her. Nor did I hear her move. I hear only the pounding of my heart. Move, Yvette, please, move.

"Paul called."

A great chilling sensation invades me. She must be off her rocker. But where is she? Her voice is coming from somewhere on my right. I advance toward the voice. Nothing.

"Paul *creeaak*."

Then there's no more. What was that gurgle? I've known Yvette for thirty years, and she never said *"creeaak."* For God's sake. . . . Silence, short sentences . . . it's starting to dawn on me . . .

It's not Yvette. It's a tape recorder.

That must mean I'm at his place. In the monster's lair. He's kidnapped me.

He caused an accident and then kidnapped me. And that must mean that Paul, Hélène, and Yvette are dead, for if they weren't, they would have called the police.

I must be going nuts. No, I'm not . . . because if I were going nuts, then where are they all, and why does Yvette keep repeating the same thing, like a broken record?

My uncle will worry when he sees we haven't arrived. He'll call all over. They'll conduct a search. They'll be here. It's just a matter of time. Like in *Blue Beard.*

But why this tape recorder? Why does he want me to believe that Yvette was here? So that I'll stay calm? And what about that glass of water? I fell asleep after having the glass of water. I was drugged, no doubt, but why? Why not kill me right away? The more I think about it, the less I feel like knowing the answer.

"Elise?"

Hélène! I'm so wound up that I swing my arm against the wall, and it hurts like hell. Hélène!

Is it the real one?

"Elise! You're here! Oh, my God, if only you knew!"

That's the real one, all right. She throws herself around me and holds me tight.

"Paul . . . he . . ."

She cries so hard it seems she's laughing. I don't think I need it spelled out for me. I swallow.

"He's dead . . ."

I try to lift my hand.

"His neck was broken . . . ," she manages to say in one breath.

What about Yvette? What about my Yvette? My heart's beating a mile a minute.

"Yvette's in a coma. When I came to, there was blood

all over, and Tony was dragging you away, down the road. He took your wheelchair and was leading you away. I didn't know what to do."

She interrupts what she was saying to get back her breath, while I'm hanging on her every word. Yvette, in a coma . . .

"I knew right away that Paul was dead. . . . I flagged down a car and I asked them to call for help. I ran back for you, and came here, to the forestry shed."

The forestry shed? But that's not on the way to the school. Well, fine, it doesn't matter. Is this the forestry shed where Michael was killed?

"He just left here, about ten minutes ago. He got into a white Renault 18 and left. So I took a chance and made my move and came inside. We've got to get out of here right away."

Tony Mercier was here? He took me out? An uneasy feeling washes over me, but still I won't faint! I would like to tell Hélène she ran an enormous risk in coming this far, and to thank her, but I can't; I can only clench my fist. I can't quite understand how she could go so far from Paul's body only to think of me. Paul dead . . . and Yvette . . .

There's a sound of a motor outside.

Hélène. Where's Hélène? She must have gone out to have a look.

Someone cuts the motor.

Footsteps.

Someone walks into the room.

Furtively moves around me.

My mouth goes so dry, you couldn't even stick an olive inside.

A hand rests on my arm. "Don't be afraid. I'm here."

My hair stands on end, because I know this voice. It's the voice of Yssart—the false Yssart—the voice of Tony Mercier, the voice of the killer.

"Don't move!"

It's Hélène's voice, strong yet trembling.

"Leave her, Tony. Back off!"

"Hélène . . ."

"I said, back off!"

He obeys. I hear the floor creak. Hélène must be armed.

"Why'd you do it, Tony? Why did you come back?"

"You know perfectly well. I had to see Virginie."

"You're completely insane! Let me tell you a little story, Elise. Once upon a time there was a young man who had a little boy. At the age of eight, the little boy was murdered by two teenagers who were completely stoned. The father couldn't bear it, and just fell apart. He left his wife. He could no longer look at little boys who resembled his son without having an irresistible urge to destroy them. His new girlfriend realized what was going on and wanted to leave. He broke her arm. Then he turned his thoughts into action. He was sentenced. She fled to Paris and started a new life, but he managed to escape from the psychiatric hospital and came to pursue his mission—to kill, again and again."

"That's a very nice story. It may lack some solid grounding, but what the hell . . . What about Elise? What are you going to do with her?" asks Tony/Yssart's tired voice.

"Elise? What you don't know, Elise, is that you look a lot like me: you've got the same size, build, and hair color—you're exactly his type of woman. He kept hounding you because you represented me, and because you were tied to Virginie, who knew exactly what he was doing!"

"You're lying. She doesn't know a thing!"

"But she does. She definitely knows everything. What do you think?" Hélène laughs bitterly. "She's my daughter, after all."

"Put down that weapon, Hélène."

"Never! I'm going to make you disappear, Tony. Get rid of you, like the wicked animal you are. I'm going to kill you."

No! Hélène, no, don't do it! We haven't got the right! I lift my arm and frenetically open and close my hand.

"It's too late, Elise. There's no other solution."

But there is. We've got to notify the police. Even though Mercier may be crazy, he still has the right to a fair trial.

Hélène is ready to shoot. I can hear it in her voice. What can I do?

I can tell by the click of the hammer that she has cocked the gun. I want to yell "No!"

"If you pull that trigger, you'll never see Virginie again," Tony calls out.

"What are you talking about?"

"Did you think I'd come here with no defense? Virginie is being held somewhere she can't escape from. If you kill me, she'll die from hunger, cold, or thirst. Because no one besides me knows where it is. She can't cry out because she's been gagged."

"You're lying!" Hélène screams.

"I picked her up as she was coming out of school. I told her I work with Paul. She believed me. She followed me. If you kill me, then she'll die, too."

That bastard! Who would dare bind and gag his own child?

"So go ahead and shoot me!" Mercier cracks, trying to provoke her.

"Where is she?" Hélène cries.

"In a place where she's cold, afraid, and alone. Is that all right with you?"

"Son of a bitch!"

"Put down that weapon."

"Never!"

Don't give in, Hélène, or he'll kill us both. What if I were to charge at him with my wheelchair? Maybe he'd fall. I've got to be attentive so that I can locate him exactly.

"I'm going to kill you anyway. I think you're bluffing," Hélène suddenly decides.

"Call the school, then. You'll see."

"There's no phone here."

"Here."

He must have thrown her something, a portable phone, because I hear her pressing the keys.

"Hello, this is Mrs. Fansten. I'll be a bit late in picking up Virginie. . . . What? You've let her go? Are you completely out of your mind?"

I hear a dull thud; must be the telephone landing on the floor.

"Okay, you son of a bitch, where is she?"

"Drop your weapon."

"Absolutely not. You know what I'm gonna do? I'm gonna shoot you in the legs. I'm gonna smash one leg after the other, and then the arms—"

"And then what? You're gonna tear out my eyes?"

"Listen to me good: If you don't tell me where Virginie is, I'll shoot Elise, you hear me?"

What? No, but . . .

I hear Tony sigh, and then, in a tired-sounding voice, he answers, "She's at Benoît Delmare's place."

A lead weight has just been dropped in my stomach. *Benoît? My Benoît?* I must be going mad. *What does Benoît have to do with any of this?*

Someone grips my wheelchair.

"Thank you, Tony, and good-bye—forever."

A deafening explosion. The smell of cordite and gunpowder. And the dull thud of someone collapsing to the floor, groaning in pain. She shot him! She shot him anyway!

I'm briskly rolled toward the exit, slapped with cold rain and jolted along the path as we dash away. She fired. Did he die? And what about Benoît? My head's going to explode! How is it that Tony/Yssart had the keys to Benoît's apartment?

The car door clicks open. *Ouch!* She just lets me fall onto the floor—*click-clack*—with the wheelchair right on top, half crushing me. She takes off like a madwoman. She must have taken Tony's car, and Yvette . . . my God, did anyone call an ambulance for her? Mercier's blood is emptying out on the floor of the shed, Yvette's lying in the road, and Paul is at the steering wheel, covered with blood. It's all too much. It feels as if someone's given me a shot of adrenaline. My head's spinning.

What about Benoît?

She slams on the brakes. The door opens, the wheelchair clangs onto the pavement, and with a sudden rush of strength she grabs me around the waist and tosses me in. I'm crooked and sliding about, but she seems unaware, violently pushing me and constantly murmuring, "That bastard. They're all bastards. Bastards. Rapists." I hold on with my good hand as we take a corridor. We're in the elevator. Her impatient palm hammers against the wall of the compartment, and I make myself small. It would be terrible if anything were to happen to Virginie. Could it be any more terrible than what has already happened?

The elevator hisses to a stop. We're out in the hallway. I can recognize the smell of Benoît's hallway. I never would have thought so. That I could recognize the smell of a hallway. How many times have I gone down this hall, laughing? A lump forms in my throat. I have a hard time breathing. Stop. Someone's shaking keys. She's got the keys to Benoît's apartment. For God's sake, by what miracle did she get them? With a sinister squeal the door opens. It's cold and stuffy in here.

"Virginie? Are you here, honey?"

No answer. She plants me in the middle of the living room and runs through each room. It's not a big place. There's one bedroom, a living room, a kitchen, and a bathroom. A bedroom, with a large bed. I'm so sick to my stomach I could vomit. It's stuffy, but something else smells. It stinks. Like something rotting. Rotting meat.

"She's not here. He lied to me!"

What could be stinking so badly? A terrifying vision of Benoît's corpse rotting on the bed crosses my mind. No, Benoît was buried, Yvette told me herself. And . . . no, this thought is too horrible to be allowed to come over me, but still . . . the children . . . those organs that were removed from the children . . . what if the murderer hid them here, in this unoccupied apartment?

"He lied!" Hélène screams, throwing something against the wall.

A crash of shattered glass. Is it the photo of Benoît taken by the pool, when he was laughing as he came out of the water?

"I've got to get back there."

No, you've got to call the cops! Bang! Am I dreaming or has the door just slammed shut? Has she left me here? I hear the sound of heels in the hallway. I roll straight ahead and bump against something hard. I raise my arm and tap against a flat surface. Is it the buffet? Hélène! Don't leave me here! Shit!

There's no more noise. She's gone. I'm alone in Benoît's apartment. Alone with his phantom. With the phantom of our love. Alone with the smell of putrefied meat. She's going to return to the shed and finish off that fucking nut job, and I've got to wait here, in the dark, in the dust, with these rotting, stinking things! You have no right, Hélène. You have no right to do this.

I know this apartment by heart. Why couldn't I open the door? If I could get to the side and manage to turn the doorknob . . . First I've got to get my bearings. I advance and run into the coffee table, back up, and hit the sideboard. Good, I've got to pivot to the right. Yes, I can feel the wood from the door at the tip of my hand. Awkwardly I extend my arm and make blind sweeping motions against the smooth surface. Ah, the knob, I've got it. I clutch it with my fingers—hard, harder—and turn. Nothing. I try again. Nothing. That asshole turned the key in the lock! The bolt is too high for me! I don't want to stay here. It's as if someone has thrown me into Benoît's cold grave.

I've got to get out. I'll turn the wheelchair so that it faces the door, and hit the controls. And go bang, bang, bang against this lousy door until I bring out the whole building. Boom. Come out of your apartments! Boom. I'm going to knock this door down!

It opens.

My stomach is pounding.

It shuts again, without a sound.

Hélène? There's a dull thud, as if someone were sitting down. Is someone to my left moving? I'm breathing so heavily, I can't hear.

Someone's trying to drive me crazy. I'm pivoting, going in circles through the room. Who's hiding in the dark? I crash into the table. I back up. And feel them. Legs. Legs wearing pants. Someone's sitting on the sofa. I scream in silence. I back up again. Another leg. Without pants. It's a leg in a stocking. My fingers brush against nylon. A second leg sheathed in nylon. I don't believe it. This just can't be. I back up yet again along the sofa and feel more legs. Skinnier. Shorter.

There are three people sitting on this sofa. And I know in an instant who they are, oh, yes: Paul, Yvette, and Virginie. I imagine them sitting, their empty eyes turned toward me; their dead, sightless eyes, staring wide open into nothingness. But how is it that Hélène did not see them?

Someone's breathing. One of them is breathing. I approach these people sitting here. I make a superhuman effort to lift my arm and touch. Touch them. Touch these unmoving things. The first one isn't moving. He's cold. His shirt is sticky. My fingers brush against the crocodile sewn on the left side. Paul. It's Paul, and he's dead. The second one doesn't move, either, but she's warm. I can feel her woolen vest. Yvette. Passed out. The third one is hot. I extend my arm toward her chest. She breaks out laughing and calls, "Bravo, Elise!"

Darkness.

FOURTEEN

"ELISE! YOU'VE GOT TO UNTIE ME! QUICK!"

Who's that talking to me? Where am I? I don't want to wake up, I don't want to hear this shrill little voice in front of me. I don't want to be here!

"Elise! Untie me or both of us will die. Renaud says it's urgent."

So what? I thought being dead was wonderful. I see you've changed your mind. But what's come over me? This is no time to settle scores with a kid. What's worse, the poor kid is sitting next to Paul's cadaver, and she's been tied up, probably by her own father. But why at Benoît's apartment? The question keeps throbbing back, like a raging toothache. There's no time to think about it. My number-one priority is to get out of here. If I could free Virginie, then she'd be able to open the door and free me, but I've got to do it fast.

"I'm so sleepy . . ."

Well, not me.

"How are you going to get me out?"

If only I knew . . . I approach her legs, fumble over them, and feel the nylon wire coiled tightly around her ankles.

I haven't got the dexterity necessary to undo the knot. It must be small and tight, and my fingers don't obey me enough to untie it. I back up, avoiding the overstuffed leather chair where Benoît liked to sit when he read. If my memory serves correctly, the kitchen is on my left, with the door about twenty inches from the sofa. I move ahead.

"Elise! Where are you going? I'm here!"

I raise my arm to reassure her. There. I must be facing the door. I advance slowly. That's good. Just a little more. Now I'm bumping against what must be the kitchen stove. I pivot my wheelchair and move beside the dishwasher. Stop. I'm by the countertop. I raise my arm and sweep it over the surface. Will my hand be able to touch the wall? Yes. There should be a rack where Benoît hung his knives. There it is. I can feel a round handle. I grip it. Lift it. I've got it! The butcher knife. Benoît's big butcher knife. I lower my arm and return to the living room, bathed in sweat.

"I think I'll go to sleep."

That's out of the question. In spite of my urge to charge ahead, I advance slowly. This is no time to drive a twelve-inch blade into Virginie's legs. The coffee table, Paul's pants, here we are. I tug on her skirt.

"What are you gonna do? Are you gonna slice me up?"

The worst thing, in my opinion, is that she really is asking herself that same question. I'm getting a good grip on the handle and flattening my arm along the wheelchair, with the blade lifted, in the hope that Virginie will understand. I know the right side of the blade is facing upward because the knife's handle is notched. It's an ergonomic handle; it said so on the plastic wrapping. Virginie yawns heartily. "Do you want to saw through the string?"

I raise my hand and place it back on the wheel.

"But you can't see anything. You'll cut up my legs!"

That's why you've got to position yourself on the knife, Virginie. Go ahead. Think about it.

Is that someone walking in the hallway? No, false alarm. Virginie must have thought about it because suddenly I feel her soles against my arm.

"I'll do it. Don't move!"

There's no danger. She lowers her ankles until the knife is between them, and then starts to move her legs backward and forward. I concentrate so as not to drop the knife. It's very nice to hold a knife. I never would have thought that holding a good butcher knife could be so reassuring. The nylon wire gives way.

"Yippie! Okay, let's do my hands now."

She gets up, crouches down with her back to me, and, still yawning, starts swaying back and forth again. The wire's going to snap. Yes, it's snapping. So far, so good. Now you've got to open the door for us, Virginie. Open the door . . .

I back my wheelchair all the way to the door to make her aware of my intention. I hear her steps.

"Daddy . . . Yvette . . . Elise, Daddy and Yvette are here, but they're not moving. I can't see anything 'cause it's so dark in here. I'm gonna open the shutters."

No, not that! Especially not that!

"I can't get them open. They're stuck. Daddy . . . Daddy, answer me! Don't just stare like that, answer me!"

I feel every hair on my body bristle. I'm praying she won't crawl onto his lap, but I know she will, and then she'll scream and . . . Someone's just rung for the elevator. I can hear it coming. Virginie, honey, I'm begging you!

"We've got to get a doctor. Daddy's hurt real bad. So's Yvette!"

She comes to my side. I hear her nimble little fingers feeling around for the bolt. Okay, she's pulling it, but what's she doing now? Virginie! I don't hear her anymore. Virginie, where are you? This is no time to play hide-and-seek. There's nothing but furtive sounds. I take a breath and slowly count to twenty. I hear her moving to my right, coming toward the wheelchair. Is this a new game? The worst thing about not being able to speak is not being able to yell at people, getting in their face and barking, giving orders, insulting them. What I really miss is insulting people. Ah! There's an inrush of air to my right. Well, in any case, the door's opening and—

"What are you doing here?" asks Jean Guillaume, pushing me back inside.

"She was waiting for us," Hélène answers, closing the door behind her.

Her hand rests on the back of my wheelchair and she's gently rolling me backward. I don't understand. Why has Hélène brought Guillaume here? And what about Virginie? Why isn't Hélène speaking to her?

"Yvette!" Guillaume, panic-stricken, suddenly exclaims. "Yvette!"

"She can't hear you," Hélène explains.

"We've got to get her out of here. What about Paul? Oh, my God!"

"Nobody move," Tony/Yssart orders in his sepulchral voice.

I'm in a stupor, and close to catatonia. Where did he come from? Where did they all come from? What are they doing in Benoît's apartment? And what about Yvette? Are they going to let her die on the sofa? My poor head's going to explode.

"Sit down."

I hear someone moving. Someone drops heavily onto the sofa. It must be Guillaume. Hélène must have sat in one of the armchairs. Where's Virginie? How can they not see her? After all, she's not transparent?

I still have the knife. It's flattened against the wheel. Am I next to Yssart?

"You should have made sure your gun had real bullets, Hélène," he proclaims. "Didn't you know that Benoît loaded it with blanks?"

Benoît again! Oh, yes, I remember it, Benoît's Beretta. He used to keep it in the night table. We were always arguing about it. I don't like firearms, and he would tell me it was loaded with blanks, hoping to reassure me. I'd answer, saying it served even less of a purpose that way. But why would anyone snatch Benoît's Beretta?

"You're not answering?" Tony continues, very much the master of ceremonies.

I imagine him standing here, facing us, looking so

elegant with a gun pointed our way; Guillaume huddled in a corner; Hélène raving mad; Paul's imperturbable cadaver; Yvette in her coma; and me in my wheelchair. A wild vision.

The Beretta in the night table, where there was a clock-radio . . .

"Let us leave. Yvette needs medical attention," Guillaume implores.

. . . a small glass dish where Benoît placed his wristwatch, and next to that was . . .

"I called an ambulance," Tony snaps. "Do you smell that?"

. . . his Laguiole with a yellow tortoiseshell handle!

"You're revolting," Guillaume mutters. "Can't you see that Paul's—"

"I'm not talking about Paul. I'm talking about the relics in the box there."

"The box?"

Guillaume's voice catches in his throat.

"Yes, the ebony box, on the sideboard."

I remember that. It's an oblong box, lined with satin, containing a Japanese sword. But relics? What does he mean by "relics"? I'm afraid to find out.

"Don't you want to open it, Hélène?"

"Dumb asshole."

"Hélène's always been good at repartee. Inside this box, dear Mr. Guillaume, is the memory of the murders: a pair of hands belonging to Michael Massenet, the heart of Mathieu Golbert, and the penis of Joris Cabrol," Tony says.

"Joris!"

"Yes. It wasn't the train that castrated him. As I was saying, the hair and skull of Renaud Fansten, and the dark eyes of Charles-Eric Galliano, whose retinas may still be imprinted with the murderer's sardonic face."

Guillaume belches. I hear him murmur, "Shut up!"

"It'll do no good to shut up," Tony replies. "When something exists, it exists, whether or not it's a gift from God. Haven't you ever noticed anything in common between the way most killers act and the way people into witchcraft act?

Often they remove bits of flesh, skin, or blood from their victims."

Did he use Benoît's Laguiole to cut out those eyes?

"This can't be. You're lying," Guillaume feebly protests. I can tell he's utterly confused.

"Oh, but it can. Open the box and see for yourself."

"You're crazy!"

"I certainly am. Open it!"

Silence. A click. Then a muffled exclamation: "Oh, my God! That's disgusting! Hélène, it's true. Those things are in there. You monster! How could you do such a thing? I ought to kill you with my own hands!"

"We all have the tendency to believe in magical behavior, don't we? To believe that by destroying someone we can reconstruct ourselves; that by putting the parts of human beings back together, like the goddess Isis, we can re-create a loved one."

Isis again!

"That's stupid!" Hélène interrupts.

"Is it? But if something doesn't happen, it's not because it's stupid. The ritual for obtaining the resurrection of a loved one is explained in detail in Lewis F. Gordon's *Satanic Manual,* a perfectly respectable work featured prominently in any good library. To tell you the truth, it's rarely taken seriously. Except by a few mental patients."

What's he getting at? Is he trying to justify himself?

The Laguiole that Benoît was so proud of, being used to dig into the flesh of a little face whose lips had gone blue . . .

"In fact, the process of witchcraft often has the advantage of hiding the real motivations of the devotee. That way a woman who wishes to cast a spell on the man she loves can hide her destructive, fusionist, and castrating drives beneath her desire for love. The single aim of this process is effectiveness. And because it is absolutely selfish, it totally neglects the suffering of another, who is merely a tool. This attitude is very close to that of serial killers, who live through others as objects."

Would you spare us your lecture? How can he speak so

calmly about this? It's an idiotic question, but if a man is crazy, how can he be crazy? I can't hear Guillaume or Hélène anymore. No one utters a peep. They all must be standing there, agape.

"Who can say where a serial killer will draw the line between the simple drive for blood and a magical desire to reconstitute a lost universe?"

Keep talking. The better for me to locate you. You're right near me. If I lift my arm, then I think I'll be able to plant the knife in your hip, and then . . . yes, he'll be thrown off balance. Even if he shoots, it will be our only chance.

"My theory is that ultimately the serial killer is a witch or a wizard who just doesn't know it, but that's not the question."

I'm going to count to three, and then I'm doing it . . .

One, two, three.

The blade drives into Tony's flesh as if through butter. Something hot flashes in my face, and he falls down, crying out in pain and astonishment, yet still holding his fire. Then there's a stampede.

"Don't move! Stay calm!" Hélène calls out.

I gather she's picked up the gun.

"Why did you do that, Elise?" murmurs Tony, next to me.

I imagine him holding his hip, grimacing in pain.

Why? So that I don't die here in this living room that reeks of death and madness, that's why!

"Jean, take off his tie and tie his hands behind his back," Hélène asks with composure.

Guillaume complies. I stay where I am, with the knife in my hand.

"Let go of that, Elise, you might hurt someone," Hélène says, grabbing it by the handle.

I have no desire to let it go, so I clench my fingers around it. I like the feel of the knife in my hand.

"Come on, Elise, this is ridiculous."

"Don't let go," Tony calls out in a voice permutated from pain.

This guy's definitely stranger than strange.

I hesitate. He whispers, "Elise, do you remember what I told you about enigmas?"

What does he want from me?

"Virginie didn't know I was her father."

So what does that change?

That changes everything. Virginie had no reason to protect someone she didn't know. In my head, I can hear her little voice: "Daddy's hurt real bad." So that means Tony's not lying and . . . how could I have been so stupid!

Suddenly I lift my arm to protect myself, but it's too late. The handle of the gun crashes violently on my head, while Hélène, sounding friendly, says, "It's really taken you a long time to figure it all out!"

STUNNED BY THE BLOW, I DROPPED THE KNIFE. I CAN hear Guillaume breathing heavily, making suction-like noises, as if he were choking.

"Don't just stand there, Jean. Sit down next to Yvette and hold out your hands . . . there. And don't make any sudden movements. I wouldn't want to decorate Yvette's pretty little forehead with a third eye. So is everyone here? The only thing missing is the cherry on the cake. Virginie? Where are you, honey? Virginie?"

Hearing her perky housewife voice ring out through the room, I feel every hair on my body bristle, and suddenly realize how terrifying madness really can be.

"I don't understand, Hélène . . . What does this mean?" Guillaume asks, flabbergasted.

"It means you should shut your mouth and keep quiet."

"Hélène! It can't be! Tell me it isn't so!"

"She killed them all!" shouts Tony, whose voice is at the same level with my wheels.

"Is it true?" Guillaume asks, incredulous.

"Now, that's a stupid question, Guillaume, my dear. Who did you think it was? Your dearly beloved Yvette?"

"What about Paul? What's happened to Paul?"

"Paul was very discourteous with me. He couldn't appreciate what was inside the box. He couldn't understand the value of my collection. He started to scream and shout, and said horrible things about me. I don't like it when people yell at me that way."

"What about Stéphane? Why Stéphane?" Tony calls out. "He never did anything wrong to you!"

"Stéphane? He was getting so annoying. He wanted to have me all to himself. Poor Stéphane. As if I could belong to anyone . . . Elise, I'm sure you're aware how men can be so foolishly arrogant? What's more, he was starting to get scared. And when he heard the police were looking for a white station wagon, he started to stick out, the silly thing. What he didn't know was that I'm the one who put the police on his trail. I'm the one who called the police after I left traces of blood on some of his old clothes and deposited them in the forestry shed, where I took care of Michael. I had to find a culprit, and throw him to the police like a bone to a dog, so . . . bye-bye, Michael."

"What about Sophie? Did Sophie? . . ." Guillaume stammers, aghast.

"Yes, that was me, Guillaume, my dear. Now, shut your mouth. Even like that, you look pretty stupid. Sophie knew too much. She was keeping tabs for Benoît."

Keeping tabs about what? I'm completely lost. Hélène continues, "Sophie had a big mouth. She was an incurable chatterbox. It was impossible to let her just go all over the place, tarnishing my character."

Character. She defines herself as a character. Does a true Hélène really exist?

"The simplest thing would be for her to commit suicide, wouldn't it?" Hélène continues, impishly.

"I don't understand," Guillaume stammers. "I don't think I understand. Hélène, really, this just can't be. . . . The children, Stéphane, Sophie, Paul . . . that's nine people!"

"Shut your mouth, you dumb shit!"

He cries out. I imagine she's struck him with the pistol. I could see her smashing his teeth with an offhanded blow.

A match crackles. I smell a candle. What is she doing? Why did I drop that knife?! Blood's running down my eyes.

The blow from the gun handle must have opened a gash in my scalp. I can't wipe my face. I feel blood, with its metallic odor, on my lips. It disgusts me, it's all so disgusting. I feel disconnected, too far away in fear and horror.

"They had no right to take Max away from me."

Max? Who is Max?

"I loved him so," Hélène goes on in a vindictive voice. "He was everything to me. With him, I wanted to make everything better. To forget that I was beaten, to forget the fear, to replace my suffering with love."

"And you think you're replacing suffering with love by strangling children?" Tony says, mocking.

"You're so vulgar! I wonder how I ever could have been attracted to some poor alcoholic, schizophrenic piece of garbage like you. What do you know about love? Your mother never cared about you, and your father's a bum. What does love mean to you, Tony? A hospital bed? A robotic smile from some nurse in a hurry? A little soup when it's cold out? You hold on to life tooth and nail, thinking things will get better someday, but living is suffering. Life is being in pain, always in pain. You say I killed them; I say I took away their suffering. I gave them rest—sweet, cold rest. Anyway, I'm not asking you to understand. I don't give a damn whether you understand or don't. I'm free. I don't obey your stupid rules of morality. If there were such a thing as morality, Max would be here. Everything would be different if he were here. I could have forgotten the violence, the bitter taste of violence, the salivation that comes with fear. But that didn't happen. The wheel turned in a different direction."

"Who is Max?" Guillaume asks, bemused.

"An angel. Max was an angel. A redeeming angel. He died to expiate the suffering of this world."

"A sort of Christ?" asks Guillaume, who I gather is trying to get her to talk as much as possible.

"If it'll make you happy to see things that way," Hélène says, ironically. "Enough about Max. The subject is closed. Now . . ."

She leaves her sentence hanging, as if thinking.

"Now?" Guillaume repeats, in a muffled voice.

"Now I have to go. I'm sorry, my friends, but I can't take you with me."

It may be a foolish hope, but is she leaving? Is she really leaving?

"And I can't leave you behind, either. But be assured that the fire of friendship will always burn between us."

The fire of friendship? The match . . . the candle . . . oh, shit . . .

"I'm going to take this box, whose contents our dear Tony so brilliantly examined, and I'm going to leave. So long, happy to have known you. Elise, I hope you'll suffer a lot. I've always detested you. And I'd just like to say that your hair is atrocious."

That's grotesque. Of all the things she can say, the only thing she can think of is that my hair is ugly and that she's going to burn us alive! It's enough to make me cry!

"I really don't understand what he saw in you."

He? Who is that? She still does not want to say.

"Darling, sweet Benoît. He'd decided to confess everything to you after that trip, but unfortunately he didn't have the time. And you're the one who had the privilege of being with him during his final moments!"

Confess what to me? I don't want to hear it. Benoît couldn't have . . .

"I started sleeping with him a few months after I freed Charles-Eric's soul. He wanted me to leave Paul so we could go away together. But I couldn't. Renaud was going to be eight. He used to smile just like Max, and his hair . . . his hair was so soft, so shiny. . . . You understand, I had to do it . . . so I couldn't go away with Benoît, no matter how he would beg me."

Tumult. Double tumult. She killed Renaud—she killed her husband's son. And she and Benoît were . . . Benoît was cheating on me, he was lying to me. Benoît, my Benoît with this . . .

"Don't listen to her! Benoît loved you. He could never get rid of her. She stuck to him like a leach," Tony yells.

"Shut up!"

I hear the sound of a blow being struck.

"I'm happy to know that you'll be dying with Tony. I don't know which one of you I hate more: Tony, giving all those lessons of his, or sweet, gentle Elise . . ."

"Hélène! Do you realize you've killed children? And for nothing! They're dead, for good, and nothing's left of them but small pieces of flesh that will never serve any purpose," Tony carefully articulates. "These are just pieces of the human body that are going to rot!"

"Tony, darling, you're really hurting me. You're hurting me so bad. You're always so reasonable. You don't know anything about anything." Suddenly her voice has gotten shrill. "You never understood a thing. They're not dead, you hear me? They're at peace. They're with me, they're in me, forever, and not in this dirty, rotten world. They belong to me!"

"They're dead, Hélène, just dead, and don't belong to anyone anymore."

She catches her breath and her voice becomes dangerously sweet.

"Poor Tony, I'm worried about you, I really am . . ."

She comes close, and after a thud and a crack, Tony shrieks, and shrieks again.

"Tony, darling, I do believe I've broken your nose . . . do you think it'll be all right if you don't breathe as much? In any case, soon you won't need to do that much breathing."

She laughs a high-pitched laugh, the most terrifying I've ever heard.

"What about you, Elise? Don't you have anything to say? Haven't you any contributions to bring to this historic moment?"

Benoît betrayed me.

And I'm going to be burned alive.

"You know what they say. You die from asphyxia first. Just think of Joan of Arc, our national heroine. And to think how her friend Gilles de Rais was sentenced to death for the torture and murder of more than fifty children. It's an amusing parallel, don't you think?"

That's a real scream. Elise of Arc and Hélène de Rais. A superproduction in scorch-o-rama. But this just can't be! I'm not going to die like that!

"Virginie? Come out, wherever you are, my little doll. Mommy's leaving."

Where is she? She mustn't come out. She'll tie her up and leave her to burn with us. I can sense in her voice that she's passed over into another dimension, where there's no place for human feeling. Don't move, Virginie, I'm begging you.

"Virginie! Mommy's going to be angry, and you know what happens when Mommy gets angry."

I feel tears rolling down my cheeks, and hear someone else crying in silence. I think it's Jean Guillaume. Yvette hasn't woken up. She'll be fortunate enough to die, unaware that she's dying.

"Well, too bad for you, Virginie. Mommy's leaving. Oh, I forgot my cassettes. They were fun to make. It was with one of those pocket devices, you know the kind . . . they're voice-activated."

She must be fiddling with the tape recorder. Now a voice is rising: "It's late. We've got to be going. Good night, Yvette. Good night, Elise. Good night, Jean."

Paul's voice. It's sort of funny to hear a dead man's voice speak. Especially when it's delivering such an appropriate message. The tape fast-forwards to Yvette: "So nice of you to have come. Give us a call, Hélène."

"You can count on it!" Hélène snickers. "There! The fire will free you all from life's difficulties: no more wheelchair for Elise, no more asylum for Tony, no more cholesterol for Jean. Well, bye-bye. No, Jean, come on, don't cry! Try to look a bit more courageous! I've got to go. I have a task to complete."

Something's crackling. The crackling and odor of the flames are undeniable.

"Virginie! You have ten seconds to come right here!"

"She's set fire to the flounces on the sofa," Tony tells me, in a voice distorted from his broken nose.

"I told you to shut up, you dirty pig!"

I feel her leg brushing past as she sends him a kick in the face. Tony's head bumps against the wall. He says nothing, but cannot hold back a groan. The crackling of the flames is growing louder and louder. I can feel them. They're real. I feel their heat. We're all going to die, but I DON'T WANT TO! My arm shoots out, close-fisted, and makes contact with something soft, her belly. She doubles over, and I press the forward button. My wheelchair jumps ahead, violently bumping into her legs. She tips over. I hear her tipping over, squealing with rage, and the crash of a table being knocked down. I continue forward, skating over her ankles, and suddenly she screams.

"My God, her hair . . ." Guillaume murmurs.

Hélène's crying out. Calling for air, amid the stench of something scorched. She's spinning around me.

Her hair has caught fire.

"Back up!" Tony screams.

I back up and the wheelchair brutally crashes against the wall.

And now a dull sort of detonation. Hélène cries out like an enraged animal.

"Her dress," Tony announces, as if commenting on a World Cup match. Her dress has caught fire. She's been transformed into a torch.

I have images of Buddhist monks immolating themselves . . . but she's right next to us, a woman of bones and flesh, screaming. The fire's heat is all around us, and the stench of burning flesh. . . . We've got to do something. I advance toward the door and desperately bang against it. There's got to be someone in this building who will hear it! I can't stand these shouts!

"That's enough in there, or I'm calling the police!" an exasperated voice from downstairs calls out.

Go right ahead! Call them! The heat is invading the room. The flames are brushing against me, touching me, burning me. Hélène's spinning around, screaming, knocking against all the furniture. I can feel her; I can feel her against my arm. It burns me atrociously. I can feel her flesh seething and blistering, her despair. Someone's got to do something!

Someone's touching my leg.

"Elise . . . the knife . . . I'm holding it. Take it, quick!" Tony pants.

He half rises and lets the knife drop in my lap. My hand closes over the handle.

"We can't leave her this way. Hold it straight. I'm gonna cut the knot."

Yes, he's right. Maybe he can drag her into the bathroom and turn on the shower. For the second time in less than half an hour I'm holding the knife like an automaton while he hurries, but the knot is resisting. And those cries, my God, *those cries!*

The knot gives way. Tony gets back up, leans on the back of the wheelchair, and in a strangled voice calls out "Hélène!" I guess he's trying to grab her.

Hurry up! Hélène's cries don't stop. They change in intensity, rising to pitches so high, they're difficult to sustain. They have that harsh sort of modulation one would not associate with a human voice. It feels as if my eardrums are going to burst. I'm gritting my teeth so hard they might break. I'm gripping the knife handle like a madwoman. How much time has gone by? Two seconds? Three seconds? Three centuries? Her cry tetanizes me. The flames lick me. I'd like to get up and scream. I'm going to burn as well. My hair, my hair has caught fire. I raise my arm spasmodically to call for help. Help me, help me! Hélène's spinning around, burning me—burning me! She falls on top of me. I'm burning up! I'm burning up!

Something's on my head. Someone's covering my head, pushing Hélène's fiery body aside, and swiping at me with cloth. It's Tony's jacket. He's putting out the flames on my skin. I've been saved, I've been saved . . .

The cries have stopped. Hélène's not shouting anymore. She's not moving anymore.

"She fell on top of it," Tony announces, his voice barely audible. "Thank God she fell on top of it."

On top of it? On top of me?

"Well?" Guillaume asks, with urgency in his voice.

"She's dead," Tony answers. "The blade was driven into her heart."

The blade? Oh, no . . . The knife, clenched tightly in my hand, with the blade pointing up. I killed Hélène. I, Elise Andrioli, have killed someone. The knife I'm holding in my hand was driven through the chest of another human being. The blade is covered with blood; my hand is covered with blood . . . I didn't want to . . .

The flames are still crackling in the silence that has fallen upon the living room.

"We better get the hell out of here!" Guillaume calls out.

Tony puts something on my lap, then opens the door. With delight I take in a draft of fresh air and the smell of cement in the hallway. Tony rolls me out, and Jean Guillaume joins us. I can feel Yvette's legs brushing against my cheek as Guillaume runs toward the elevator. The doors open with a wondrous hiss. Behind us is the furnace. But suddenly a question chills me to the bone: Virginie! Has Virginie stayed behind in the apartment? I lift my hand frenetically.

"She's here, in my arms. She's asleep," Tony answers as he pushes my wheelchair.

She's asleep? After everything that's just happened, she's asleep?

"I gave her an injection of hexobarbital. She won't wake up for another few hours. I didn't want her to witness what was going to happen. Hexobarbital's very effective. They shot me up with it for six years. It made me pretty calm! She wasn't supposed to wake up right away, but I miscalculated her dosage. I was looking through the apartment for Benoît's hunting rifle . . ."

Ah! That's what Hélène used to cut a gash in my scalp . . .

". . . and I found the box and what was inside. When I saw that she had woken up, but I couldn't interfere, I didn't want you to suspect I was there. I had to surprise Hélène completely to make her confess. I waited for Virginie to be freed, thanks to you, and then approached in silence while she unbolted the door. That's when I gave her her second injection."

Now it's much more clear. And to think I believed she was playing hide-and-seek. If you're a bigger asshole than me, you'll die.

Then where was she? How is it that no one saw her? This wretched man must have a sixth sense, because he answers as if he'd heard me perfectly: "When she lost consciousness, I hid her behind the big leather armchair, against the wall. You were in front of her with your wheelchair, acting as a screen."

This is all quite simple, nothing to do belly-flops over. And leaving an apartment in flames, what could be more normal than that?

I didn't even notice we were in the elevator. Guillaume keeps whispering Yvette's name over and over, with a tone of urgency in his voice. The doors open. There, we're outside. It's raining, a cold mist. Deliciously cold. Suddenly I'm feeling pain where I've been burned, and am aware of an approaching siren. I can just picture us in front of this building, with Tony carrying his daughter in his arms, Guillaume loaded down with Yvette, and me covered with blisters. With whatever Tony dropped in my lap.

"I'm gonna call the cops," Tony says, in that funny, choked voice of his. "There's a phone booth on the corner."

"You can see flames shooting out the window," Jean Guillaume announces as Tony heads off.

Then, without skipping a beat, he asks, "Do you think she'll make it?"

I'm guessing he's talking about Yvette. How am I supposed to know? I can't even see her wounds.

"If she makes it through, then I'm going to marry her."

It's good to be able to make plans for the future. I get the impression that I'll be some old rag, abandoned in her chair. All I had left were my memories of Benoît, and now . . . even that's been blown. Benoît deceived me. That whole part of my life was just a lie. Benoît is dead, I'm alone, I've just escaped a horrible death by the skin of my teeth, my best friend was a child killer, Yvette might die . . . and here we are in front of the entrance to the building, listening to Benoît's apartment go up in flames. It's insane. Now the ambulance is nearby. Tony wasn't lying, he really did call them.

"The cops are coming," Tony announces when he returns. "Someone had already notified them."

Had to be the downstairs neighbor. We wait a few more seconds in silence as the ambulance approaches with a deafening wail. Hélène's body is burning up there. How could I have ever imagined that Benoît's apartment would one day wind up as the Fanstens' funeral pyre? He met Hélène in '92. Now I understand why we were fighting so much then. Was she planning to use Benoît? To set him up the way she set up Stéphane? Is it because Benoît died that she chose Stéphane as a scapegoat? Benoît. My Benoît would have been accused of those murders! My Benoît, the traitor, the liar, the adulterer. That son of a bitch.

The ambulance comes to a halt in front of us. A big hubbub. Everyone's talking at the same time. People come flooding out of the building. It's total confusion.

"We looked all over. We took down the wrong address."

"What's going on? Why's there an ambulance here?"

"My God, there's a fire! Jacques, there's a fire!"

"Where are the injured?"

"Goddamn it, there's a fire up there! Call the firemen."

"Everyone, please step back . . ."

"Is there anyone in the apartment?"

More sirens in the distance.

"Yes, two bodies."

"My God!"

"I'm sure they're the ones who made this whole mess."

I recognize Mr. Chalier's shrill voice. He's a retired postal worker who lives on two. But I don't think he recognizes me, oh, no.

"Is the little girl hurt?"

"No, she received an injection of hexobarbital."

"Okay, no problem, we'll take her. Get me a stretcher! What happened to your nose?"

"It's all right . . ."

Vehicles come to a brutal stop and doors slam shut amid cries of outrage.

"What the hell is this shit? Mercier, you are under arrest! Put that child down on the ground right now or I'm gonna club you over the head!"

It's Gassin, wild with anger!

"Inspector, you're making a mistake. It wasn't him," says Guillaume. "You, paramedic, watch out. Easy does it, she's unconscious."

"Don't tell us how to do our job!"

"It wasn't him? Are you trying to play with me or what?" Gassin screams.

"No, easy does it, if you don't mind. That's my wife. . . . No, Inspector, it was Hélène Fansten. She confessed right in front of us."

"Hélène Fansten? Hélène Fansten was behind all these murders? Why not Cinderella? You hear that, Mendoza? And perhaps you'll be kind enough to explain all this to me, in detail?"

"Where are you hurt?"

"She can't answer. She's mute."

"She's covered with blood and blisters. Tell them we're taking burn victims. What's that box on her lap?

The *box?* That son of a bitch stuck the box on my lap?"

"That's for Inspector Gassin. Here, Inspector," Tony offers, as if giving him a box of chocolates, "open it."

"If this is some kind of trick, Mercier, I swear I'll . . . Oh, my God! You . . . You knew what was inside!"

At least I'll never see what was inside the box. But is seeing it worse than imagining it? The shriveled little fingers, the gelatinous eyes . . .

"I thought it might interest you," Tony calls out, very relaxed.

"Where did you find this?" asks Gassin, whose voice has changed in register, plummeting to a very serious tone.

"Excuse me, Inspector, but we've got to take them to the emergency room."

"What should we do about the apartment, Chief? There are two cadavers up there."

"Have you seen your nose? Inspector, this man's got a broken nose."

"Will somebody please answer me?!" Gassin screams.

"In five minutes, I'll explain everything to you, but frankly, wouldn't you like something to drink?" Tony suggests calmly.

FIFTEEN

BACK AT THE HOSPITAL. I DON'T KNOW WHAT TIME it is. They treated me, bandaged me, and gave me a mild sedative. Gassin recovered the knife. I had a hard time letting go of it. Now, it's better. It seems the hair was scorched away on part of my head. It's got to be ravishing. A mummy covered with bandages, with a clump of hair at the top of her head.

Yvette's in the treatment room. A fractured skull. They're going to put her in the scanner. All we can do is pray. Guillaume is waiting in front of the operating room, pacing up and down. Virginie is still asleep; they put her in a special room, and we're all here, in the waiting room: Gassin, me, a policeman standing guard, and Tony. They gave him ten stitches on his hip and treated his broken nose. He must have an enormous bandage in the middle of his face. This face I've never seen. When he moves, I hear his handcuffs click. He's charged with all sorts of things, for such trifling matters as "identity theft," "forgery and use of forgeries," "insulting behavior to an officer in the exercise of his duties," and "hiding evidence," not to mention the fact that he is currently serving an internment order handed down against him seven years ago.

"How did you guess?" Gassin asks, lighting a cigarette.

"I didn't guess anything," Tony answers. "Only in the end did I begin to understand. Because, you see, I didn't know whether I was guilty of the murder for which I'd been sentenced. I didn't know whether I'd killed that child or not."

"How's that?"

"I'll explain to you how it all happened. In those days, back in 1988, I was drinking so much that when the cops came for me, I honestly had to ask myself, Did I do that? Hélène said so, the cops said so, the psychiatrists said so, and me? I didn't know. I couldn't remember. But I feared I might have done it while I was zoned out. I'd done a ton of things I didn't remember. Fights. Wild episodes. I spent half my teen years in the custody of psychiatric services. I'm a regular, in a sense. But once I was interned and detoxed I got to thinking. Something incomprehensible had happened, and whether or not I strangled that child, it was too late to go back. I didn't want to spend the rest of my life in an asylum. I wanted to see Hélène again, I wanted to see my daughter. I was afraid for my daughter. In my therapy sessions I learned that people who were victims of violence during childhood are often tempted to do the same to others. I thought about my own path, in regards to violence. Hélène also had a traumatic childhood. I knew she had destructive urges sometimes. Virginie often cried for no reason at all, and would calm down only when I held her in my arms."

The police officer coughs. Tony is interrupted, but then continues, "On several occasions I found black-and-blue marks on her. Hélène said she'd fallen down. And then, one day, just as I was getting in, I found Hélène drinking a whiskey while the baby was screaming. She looked at me absently, not even intervening. I approached and saw a pin from the diaper stuck slightly into the girl's skin. 'She's sick,' is all she would say. I removed the pin with trembling hands, calmed the baby, and turned toward Hélène, furious. She criticized me for blowing the whole thing out of proportion, and called me a hysterical boozehound. I never got over it. She was letting the kid suffer, and accusing me of being irresponsible! A fit of anger came over me, I shook her, and she started to insult me, a torrent of abuses. She was beside herself. We hit each other. That was the night I broke her arm. Afterward, she told me she didn't know what had gotten into her; it was a stroke of madness, and that ever since Max's death, she had blackouts sometimes. But she never started again, never."

"Max?"

Yes, who is Max?

"Her son. The one she had when she was seventeen."

"What son? No one ever said anything to me about a son!"

"Obviously. He's dead."

"Slow down. You've lost me," Gassin protests.

"All right, I'll go all the way back to the beginning. When I met Hélène in '86, I was going through detox, while she was getting over three suicide attempts. We took part in the same group therapy sessions, and I found out that she had had a son when she was seventeen, by an unknown father, and that he had died two years earlier. The kid must have been around eight. An accident, from what I could tell. Apparently, she was disconsolate. For her, this kid was supposed to fix everything, all the hardships she had suffered as a child. And now he was dead."

"That's implausible! There's no information of the sort in any file!" Gassin says, indignant.

"Perhaps you didn't request her family record book?"

"Very funny! Don't you think we'd go through the records of everyone implicated in a murder with a fine-toothed comb?"

"Well, I see only one solution: the child wasn't declared."

"But how do you think—"

"She may very well have given birth all alone and kept him for herself and no one else. That would seem to mesh with her personality."

"What about school and everything else?"

I've just had a great illumination: What if Hélène, at age seventeen, and for x reasons, didn't want people to know that she had had a baby? All she'd have to do is have him declared by her mother. . . . That's it! Obviously, not one of my brilliant male companions has thought of this.

Gassin punches the keys on his portable phone: "Hi, it's me. Get me the Siccardi file from archives. Yes, that's right. Go through it and get me something on Max Siccardi. If you can't find anything, call up Marseilles. It's urgent. . . . Yes, call me back once you've got something."

He angrily cuts the communication.

"Where were we?"

"We were at the point when I met Hélène. Hélène and I were hitting it off. We were both just as lost as the other, coming through some rough spots. We felt close. Then Virginie came along. She didn't want to keep her, but I insisted. I thought one life had to come to replace another. . . . If only I could have known, my God, if only I could have guessed . . ."

Gassin coughs nervously.

"Go on."

"So Virginie was born, and everything more or less went okay, until Hélène met Paul. At the time he was stationed in Marseilles."

"What? You mean he was there, too?"

"I swear it's not my fault. Paul had lost his wife to cancer and he was raising Renaud, his two-year-old boy, by himself. He and Hélène met at the bank, he was working as a teller."

Paul, so young, so dashing, falling in love with this young woman in tears, who was suicidal . . . Hoping she'd help him raise his son . . . If only he could have known . . .

"What happened?"

"What do you think? Hélène was attracted to him right away. He was stable, reassuring, normal. She relished telling me that they were having an affair. But she could never choose between us. So everything continued, except I was drinking like a bottomless pit, and I couldn't stand it that Hélène was sleeping with Paul. Sometimes she gave me goose bumps. But I was mad about her. She was like a drug to me: she kept taking me back to the past, to the pain of the past."

He's talking fast, with a jerky delivery, as if there were no images left in his head besides words at his disposition.

"The blows were our secret, just like the black-and-blue marks and the feeling that you could be the brunt of anything that might happen, anytime: when you're sleeping, when you're eating—the blows could come at any moment. The belt could crash down, lashing you, lacerating you. A jail could close in around your fear, around your urine-stained legs, your hunger. . . . Have you ever gone for days and days without eating?"

"Sorry, I haven't," says Gassin. "Then what happened?"

"When the cops started poking around, she broke it off. I begged her to help me. I told her I loved her, that I'd never had anyone in my life before her, but she said it was over, that she didn't love me anymore."

Suddenly he has a great flash of inspiration: "She agreed to marry Paul, who recognized Virginie, and they left. Paul was appointed somewhere else. I thought back to all that when I was in my padded cell. It's dumb, isn't it? I thought Hélène might hurt Virginie, yet was incapable of conceiving that she might have killed that child in our neighborhood. So to make a long story short, I decided to escape and go find Virginie. I took advantage of my leave to look for them, and managed to locate them, oddly enough, by looking through the phone book. I must have slogged through every department's phone book, but I found them. And after that, it was just kids' stuff. I came here, got hired at one of Stéphane Migoin's construction sites, and realized that he knew her well. It was strange living this way, so close to them. . . . Sometimes I saw Virginie in the park, with Paul Fansten. She called him daddy. I didn't want to interfere, I just wanted to watch. It was sort of like having a family, by proxy. In fact, I think I was completely lost—and terribly jealous."

I can imagine this tall, sad silhouette, watching Virginie

laugh with the man she believed was her father; this fugitive with nowhere to go, who must feed on the crumbs of other people's happiness.

"Then I found out that Paul's son, Renaud, had just been murdered. You can imagine my stupor! And that's not all: there were other cases of children being murdered in the area, and *all of them since I'd begun to have leave!* It felt as if I were plunging back into an old nightmare. But I was sure I hadn't committed any of those murders! Or else I was completely and truly insane. I had to shed light on these murders; I had to find out the truth before I could finally be set free from all these questions."

A gurney clangs past, as stressed voices echo and elevator doors hiss open. Tony continues, "I soon noticed that Hélène was having an affair with Benoît Delmare, officially the boyfriend of the manager of the Trianon."

These words, so cold and yet so simple, gnaw at me deviously.

"Inspector Gassin, somebody's asking for you," a woman's voice calls.

"I'll be back," Gassin apologizes as he gets up.

Voices clamor at the end of the hall. The orderly, still standing, clears her throat.

"As a matter of fact, Elise, you used to see me quite often at the Trianon," Tony slips in my ear. "I love the movies, and I also had a lot of free time to kill. I noticed you because I found you very seductive."

Believe it or not, I'm dumb enough to blush at this. I live through this insane episode, and now I'm blushing because some guy who escaped from a mental institution is telling me I'm his type. Meaning that I *was* his type.

"I don't know why she had her heart set on Benoît. She met him at a party organized by the Lions Club."

That party? Benoît was trying to get me to go; he was obliged to, and I had refused, preferring to watch a movie on TV. And to think, she met him all because of that party!

"Let's get back to your investigation, my esteemed colleague," Gassin says mockingly as he sits back down. "You were telling me about Paul and Hélène."

"Yes. I decided to find out about their way of life, to spy
on them, in a way. I was sick over it. There was Hélène,
right before my eyes. I knew she was living with Paul, and
that they were raising my child, in their pretty little
villa . . . while I had been sentenced for murder. I started to
hate Paul. After all, I didn't know a thing about him. He was
always so nice, so pleasant, smooth as a pebble. I saw Paul
as the perfect child killer. And not just in Yvelines . . .
perhaps I'd been the victim of a frame-up in Marseilles,
perhaps I'd been framed by the real murderer! Who better
to have me accused than one who could get into my apartment without having to break in? Someone who hated me.
And to think, while I was pondering all this, it never occurred to me to suspect Hélène! I couldn't attribute these
acts to a woman."

"Women rarely kill, but when they do, it's most often
children," Gassin says, sounding professional. "What
about Virginie? What was going on with Virginie?"

"She seemed well nourished, and treated right, but she
looked a bit strange, absent. She was like a polite little doll,
well groomed and smiling. It occurred to me that if Paul
were mixed up in these murders, then she would know
something. Then Michael was murdered. I knew him by
sight. I knew that he and Virginie were friends. And above
all, I knew that Virginie had met Elise, and that she was
likely to confide to her some very interesting bits of information. I had to find a way to interrogate her, to be able to
lead my investigation as I pleased."

"So that's how you decided to be transformed into Yssart?"

"Yes. It was the most practical way, and I knew Elise
couldn't guess that I was tricking her."

Oh, yes, the poor little baby doll in the wheelchair . . .

"So I put on my disguise, looking to gather evidence
against Paul. I was practically sure it was him. Until a new
element entered the picture—Jean Guillaume. I poked
around and discovered that he had family in La Ciotat, and
that he and his wife went there on vacation every year. He
was in Marseilles in 1988, at the time of the murder of

which I'd been accused. I was petrified by this coincidence. So now I had a new suspect."

"So?"

"So . . . I followed the investigation, keeping Elise abreast of all recent developments."

Thanks all the same.

"I told myself that perhaps I was fixated on Paul, so I decided to systematically suspect everyone. I've got to confess, Stéphane made a very convincing suspect. But something worried me: Why was Elise thrown into the pond? Why the hell would Paul, Stéphane, Guillaume, or any murderer want to do you harm? Who could hold a grudge against you? Or maybe someone had a grudge against Stéphane, and as an indirect result you fell victim to an assault directed against him. I was completely floundering. I even thought Guillaume might have orchestrated your drowning to come off as a rescuer. Then, of course, it started to seem more than likely it was Hélène. Hélène, who was jealous of you and Benoît, and who certainly hated you. But whether or not Hélène hated you or even wanted to make an attempt on your life, it didn't mean that she was murdering the children. Let's just say I didn't want to imagine this possibility that wouldn't stop cropping up, and which I dismissed as a stupid, irksome thought."

"I don't mean to rush you, but can we get on with it? Just the outline, for starters?" Gassin suggests, a bit too sweetly.

"I'm sorry, I'm getting lost in the details. It's dumb how we can be so interested in our own lives."

"When did you start to think Hélène was the culprit?"

"When Elise was attacked with a knife. I dropped in unexpectedly and found her in blood, completely panic-stricken. The knife was there, on the floor. A yellow Laguiole. At the time, I could only think to call an ambulance. As soon as the ambulance was gone, I snuck away, on the q.t. It was drizzling outside, just a cold spray, so I walked through the rain. I wound up near the pond. But the knife was still bugging me. The form of the blade, its shape . . . everything seemed to match the different autopsy reports. So whoever had it in for Elise, and whoever was behind all these murders, had to be one and the same. Logically, it could only be Hélène."

Gassin sighs. He must be telling himself that he should have followed the same line of reasoning.

"It was like getting a bucket of cold water in the face," Tony continues, "like sobering up after being plastered for twenty years. I thought back to Max, and that photo of him Hélène always dragged around. When Max died, it drove her half-mad. I thought back to that blank expression she'd give me and Virginie sometimes—I used to refer to it as her 'night expression,' because it seemed as if her eyes could see only darkness. I thought back to it all, and for the first time I thought it really could be her. It was horrible to suspect her; it would mean that she'd purposely had me charged in Marseilles. It would also mean that she was perhaps not only a murderer, but a perverse, Machiavellian person. I wanted to have a clear conscience, I needed evidence."

"I don't understand," Gassin says, astonished. "You're almost certain that your ex is a murderer, and yet you didn't alert the police? You stayed in hiding, waiting for her to kill more children?"

"What did you want me to do? Come dashing over to the police station, so you could ship me back to the psychiatric hospital on the double, while charging me with murders committed while in the area to boot? As if, by chance, a dangerous criminal would escape and wind up in the same place where some kids were murdered? Do you think I'd be welcomed with flowers? That they would believe me when I accused the respectable Mrs. Fansten? And then I didn't want it to be her. Deep down, something inside me wanted to believe she was innocent. She's the mother of my daughter, you understand?"

"Go on," Gassin sighs.

"The idea that it could be her was driving me crazy, but at the same time I really felt it was true."

"And you weren't afraid she'd attack Virginie?"

"No. Not according to the plan. All the victims were boys. Whoever the murderer was, he was visibly fixated on little boys around eight years old. I said to myself that if it were in fact Hélène, then perhaps she was killing children who looked like Max. Max had brown hair and dark eyes. While Charles-Eric had brown hair, Michael was blond, Mathieu was a lighter brown, Renaud had brown hair, and so on and so forth. They all had different eye color. I couldn't quite make out a sequence, I was baffled."

"A sequence?"

"Renaud's brown hair, Charles-Eric's dark eyes, Michael's hands, Mathieu's heart, Joris's genitals . . ."

"A new little boy . . . ," Gassin murmurs.

"Exactly. A fantasy boy."

All nicely laid out in a box . . . shriveled little hands, the little heart, eyes set down on velvet. Eyes are really quite big once removed from their sockets. And locks of soft, silky blond hair . . . Thank you, God, for making it so that I can't see these things!

"And then what?" Gassin asks, impatiently.

"And then? The whole puzzle started to fall into place. I was in despair; I wanted to run away from it all, but I felt obliged to stay and help destroy this woman I'd loved so much, and who apparently was raving mad. . . ."

"Where was Migoin in all this?" Gassin asks, sounding slightly exasperated.

"Stéphane Migoin suspected that Hélène was cheating on Paul. He'd look at her funny. He thought that was the reason she'd come by to borrow his station wagon. But really she was also sleeping with Stéphane. Sleeping with men was her way of dominating them. Thinking back now, I imagine she must have had every guy in our neighborhood. In fact, I think she was frigid. Her father had been raping her for years, you know. For that matter, I'm persuaded that he's Max's father."

Really! Gassin must be just as flabbergasted as I am, for he doesn't say a thing. I only hear him swallow. Of course! It has to be! That son-of-a-bitch father of hers no doubt raped her, she wound up pregnant, and to avoid scandal they made it seem that Mrs. Siccardi was the mother. I'm sure of my theory.

"Where was I?" Tony continues. "Oh, yes, Stéphane. She confessed to us that she'd orchestrated everything so that he'd take the rap. She was no doubt the one who assaulted Stéphane in the park and pushed you into the pond, Elise. Because of Benoît she hated you, because Benoît preferred you to her. He'd broken it off with her. I know this because he told me so."

He *told* him?

"Yes, I knew Delmare. One day we were given a job to go repair some building—the hallways, the elevator, and so on. It was at Benoît's apartment, Elise. Figuring that as long as he had me there, he asked if I might want to paint his place—he'd pay me, of course. I agreed. I saw your picture on his night table, and said something about you. We seemed to get along. He offered me a beer, and then told me his life story, man to man. He couldn't talk about it with anyone else . . . just think, what if I'd known he was having an affair with Hélène Fansten?"

That week, when Benoît came to stay over because it stank of paint at his place—yes, I remember—he said something to me about the painter: "He's a nice guy, he's no fool." Did I get to see the painter? No, I don't think so.

So, Benoît had broken it off with Hélène. It's sort of weird to find out simultaneously that your man was cheating on you and that he broke it off with your rival. For whatever good it did me . . . How bitter, to consider that just when he'd chosen me, he died.

"Imagine what Hélène must have felt when she arrived at your house, once Paul had met you, and she recognized you. Her hatred and triumph. You, her rival, defenseless at her feet! She must have enjoyed lying to you."

Enjoyed? That's not exactly the term I'd use. Did she enjoy wishing me ill? Frightening me? Did she enjoy killing children? I don't think so. I think she was in pain, all the time. Even when she was rejoicing, she was in pain. I think back to her complaints, her sudden mood swings, her anxieties. . . . Was she aware of what she was doing? I'm not even sure. I'm sure there were times when she was convinced she was a housewife like any other, who was dogged by misfortune. She didn't seem triumphant to me. No, rather, she seemed dreadfully unhappy. Even at the last minute, when she was going to kill us, she had a certain crack in her voice. What is Tony saying?

"I don't think she was in control of her actions. It was stronger than she. If she saw a kid who reminded her of Max, then she had to destroy him, she had to hold him so tight—"

"Were you present at any of the murders?" Gassin asks, bluntly.

"It seems to me that if I'd been present at any of the murders, I'd have no doubt she was guilty," Tony replies.

I can hear Gassin turning pages a bit too rapidly.

"She confessed to you that she killed Sophie Migoin . . ."

"That's correct. I don't know if it was part of her plan, but when Stéphane fled, it served her well."

That last call from Stéphane . . . if only he'd talked to the cops!

"About Sophie Migoin . . . I found out her secret," Gassin announces in a satisfied tone. "She was fooling around with Manuel Quinson."

Talk about a discovery . . .

"But it's not what you might think, oh, no," he goes on. "In fact, he was supplying her with coke."

Manu? A dealer? Sophie? Cramming white powder up her nostrils? Why not? Nothing surprises me anymore. I've completely run out of amazement. I don't think I'd raise a brow even if they announced a nuclear explosion.

"That's why she always seemed so wired," Tony murmurs.

"What about Paul Fansten? What was his role in all this?"

"The role of the husband," Tony retorts. "You know what I mean: security, respectability, comfort . . ."

"Could he have been an accomplice?"

"Would you protect a woman you suspected of murdering your own son?"

Gassin mutters something incomprehensible. Paul knew more about it than you think, Captain Yssart, even though he didn't know what he knew! I'm thinking back now to those snatches of conversation I overheard. I'm pondering his fits of anger, his outbursts against Hélène. He took a sudden dislike to her, because deep down he must have known the unspeakable truth . . . but he lied to himself. Just like you, my darling Tony.

The chair's creaking, heels are scraping, and the policeman's jacket is giving off the odor of damp wool.

"Were you ever afraid Hélène might notice you and recognize you?"

"You know, the last time she saw me, I weighed twenty pounds more, was bloated, and had a beard and long, chestnut hair. I bought myself polarized glasses, cut my hair real short, dyed it black, and was careful never to cross paths with her, that's all."

"A dangerous game."

"No more dangerous than disguising myself as Yssart and strolling through town. When you're locked away for months and months, with no hope of getting out, and being force-fed tons of drugs that crush you—not to mention the straitjackets, shock treatment, and hundreds of hours of psychotherapy for someone else's crime—then the notion of danger becomes quite relative."

Nervous coughing. You'd think we were in a sanatorium.

"I still don't understand what her plan was in coming to pick up Elise to take her to the airport."

"My existence had been discovered. I was presumed guilty, and that was fine, but it also meant I was on her trail, and that was no good. She had to disappear. I think she decided to get rid of all the burdensome witnesses—Paul first—and then she'd start her life again, somewhere else, as she had done before. In my opinion, she wasn't following a sensible line of reasoning, but was being led by a pressing need to destroy."

A match is struck.

"Were you present at the scene of the accident?"

"Unfortunately, no. I went by to Elise's place this afternoon, but everything was locked. So I went over to the Fanstens', but it was the same story. So I headed down the roads at random, hoping to come across them. And just by the exit, where Véligny curves, I saw the car lying on the embankment, against a tree. It was empty."

"Empty?" Gassin exclaims, incredulously.

"Empty. There was blood on the backseat, and tire tracks on the grass. Immediately I thought of Elise's wheelchair. I followed the tracks and came to the shed. I saw Elise through the window. She seemed panicked and was moving her wheelchair in every direction. Hélène was standing in the doorway and looking at her, smiling. It sent shivers down my spine. Then she stepped forward and held out a glass of water for Elise, who drank and then went to sleep. I could see your chest rising and falling, and knew you weren't dead. I didn't know what to do. Should I enter? But what good would that have done?"

"Eventually it would have saved Miss Andrioli's life," Gassin suggests, acidly.

"Yes, but it wouldn't have had Hélène arrested. She had to give a confession, before witnesses, or else no one would ever have believed me. Suddenly I thought of Virginie. It was four forty-five. I thought that if Hélène had gone through the trouble of drugging you, Elise, then she wasn't expecting to get rid of you right away."

Kind of a risky gamble, don't you think, Tony dear?

"I rushed over to the school, picked up Virginie, telling them I worked with Paul, that they called me because their car had broken down, and that it was urgent because she had to be at her grandmother's house. Her teacher had been told about the grandmother, so she believed me, seeing as I was so well informed. I put Virginie into the car. Obviously, she shouldn't see what might happen. I still had a syringe and some hexobarbital on me. When I left the hospital, I took several boxes, just in case I had an attack. Basically, I gave Virginie her first injection, tied her up, and hid her in the trunk. I returned to the shed and found both Hélène and Elise. I don't know what kind of business Hélène was up to, maybe she wanted to have a little fun with Elise . . ."

"But where were Paul and Yvette?"

"At Benoît's place, I presume."

"This is unfathomable."

Now I'm going full throttle: If Hélène had drugged me in the shed, it was so that she could carry Paul's and Yvette's bodies over to Benoît's place using my wheelchair. No, someone would have seen her. . . . Even though . . . going in a straight line, the Véligny exit is a thousand feet from Benoît's apartment. Yes! All she'd have to do is take the path through the forest that runs along the golf course. But I could hardly see her making the trip two times in a row, at the risk of being seen by someone walking by.

I'm getting an idea. It's sort of a far-fetched idea, but it would explain why no one saw the accident. Because there was no accident!

When she came for us, she was alone. She was alone because Paul was already dead! His cadaver was already at Benoît's place! What about our stop at the bank? Just an illusion. All I heard were doors shutting and Paul's voice, which could have been recorded anytime on a pocket tape recorder.

Yes, I'm sure that's it. Under one pretext or another, she lures Paul over to Benoît's apartment and kills him. Then she comes to pick up me and Yvette. Oh, shit, Yvette! Yvette would have seen that Paul didn't get into the car. No, I'm so damn stupid: she knocks out Yvette as soon as we took off. The plop and sigh I heard as Yvette sat down came when she had her head split open. Which explains the blood on the backseat. She pretends she's picking up Paul, simulates an accident, and then knocks me out. And, presto, she pulls off her little scheme. Once we're in the shed, she drugs me, carries Yvette over to Benoît's place using my wheelchair, and then comes back to torture me a little. Luckily, Tony Mercier shows up. So she says to herself, "Oh, look, I'll kill two birds with one stone. I'm going to get rid of my dear Tony," and shoots him. Then she takes me over to Benoît's place, where she leaves me to go looking for Jean Guillaume. Why?

"She's out of danger," Guillaume's thick, trembling voice calls out.

Yvette's been saved!

"At least one bit of good news," Tony says. "Have a seat, old man, you look so pale."

"I'd like to see how you'd look. Her brain might have been struck."

Oh, no! One vegetable in the family is enough! Guillaume collapses into one of those plastic seats—orange, no doubt—which groans under his weight.

"Can you answer a few questions?" Gassin asks, in a hurry to be finished.

"If you insist . . ."

"Why did you follow Hélène Fansten all the way up to Benoît Delmare's apartment?"

"I didn't follow her! I'm a plumber, Inspector. I came because there was a leak in the toilet. When I got there, I saw her getting out of a car, looking all nervous. I said hi, wondering what the hell she was doing there, especially since it wasn't her car, but a gray Honda Civic."

"My car," Tony indicates.

"She blinked, and then came running over. She told me to come with her, that it was urgent, that Paul had fainted and she thought he was dead. At the moment I thought they must be visiting friends, I don't know. She was running and I followed her. We took the elevator up, she opened the door, and bang! I stumbled over Elise in her wheelchair. I was still going along with it, I didn't understand. I stepped forward, Hélène closed the door behind us, and it was very dark inside. There, in the dark, I saw Paul and Yvette. He was dead, that much was obvious; his eyes were wide open and he was covered with blood. Yvette's eyes were closed, and she was barely breathing. Blood was running out of her ears and nose. I almost got sick. . . . Well, you know the rest."

"Let's recap," Gassin whispers as he turns the pages in his notebook. "Tell me, Mercier, how did you manage to get to Benoît Delmare's place so quickly if you didn't have a vehicle?"

"On foot. I took the shortcut down the path through the forest that runs by the golf course; it's about a thousand feet. I played dead until the car had gone far enough, then got back up and hustled over. I noticed a double row of ruts—tracks from Elise's wheelchair. However, Elise had just been loaded into my car. So I deduced that Hélène had already used the wheelchair, but who was she carrying? No doubt, the person whose blood was spilled in the backseat."

My theory's got to be right! Too bad I can't enlighten them!

"You had the keys to Delmare's apartment?"

"I'd made copies of them when I came to paint the place. I thought they might come in handy sometime."

"Well, aren't you a guy who likes to think ahead," Gassin says, turning pages.

"I decided to be. I don't care to be trapped again."

"Can you explain why you claimed Virginie was at Delmare's apartment if she was in the trunk of your car?"

"It was a bluff. I made up anything that might look plausible. And as a result, when Hélène left with Elise after shooting me, I knew where she was going. What *she* didn't know is that Virginie was in the trunk of the Honda she was driving!"

That's why Hélène couldn't find Virginie when she got there. Only Paul and Yvette were on the couch. . . . My God, this is all so muddled!

"What time is it?" Guillaume inquires, audibly unconcerned with this whole inquiry.

"Ten o'clock," says a rough voice, which must belong to the officer standing guard.

"So, if I understand you correctly, Mercier, you too dashed over to Delmare's place," Gassin continues, sounding slightly nervous.

"Exactly. I saw the Honda in the parking lot. It was raining cats and dogs, and no one was there. I opened the trunk—I'd kept the key—and took Virginie. I had just enough time to hide behind the trash containers—Hélène swept out of the building like a whirlwind and took off like a madwoman, if I may say so . . ."

"Please, do go on. And then what?"

"So I still didn't know what to do. I decided to go up to

see Benoît's place. I opened up very quietly. And then I
saw."

"Saw what?"

"It was very dark, but I could make out some motionless
forms on the sofa. I came close and when my eyes got used
to the darkness, I recognized Paul, who was obviously
dead, and Yvette, who was alive, but unconscious. And
then there was Elise in her wheelchair. I put Virginie down
on the sofa, next to Yvette, and decided to wait for Hélène
to return. This time I had her!"

"What about the girl? You thought it was normal for Virginie, your own daughter, to be present for all this?"

"No, that's where the hexobarbital came in . . . but she
woke up . . . I'll spare you the details. In short, I had to put
her back to sleep. I hid her more or less behind the big
leather club chair, and then took cover behind the door."

"A regular serial novel. All that's missing is Fantô-
mas. . . . And that's when you and Mrs. Fansten entered,
Guillaume?"

"Yes, that's right," Guillaume acquiesces. "I could do
with a cup of coffee."

"Funny, isn't it? The way you're always there when
you're least expected. First you're in Marseilles, then by
the pond, and just now you were about to do repairs in Delmare's building! Who called you?"

"It so happens that someone called, asking me to come
right away to a Mr. Delmare's apartment, in building B."

"What? Are you also trying to take me for some idiot?
Is this a conspiracy?"

"No, not at all. And, besides, I had no idea Elise's fiancé's name was Delmare."

"Well, I don't see why Mrs. Fansten would have had
you come by," Gassin wonders aloud.

"Obviously, since I was the one who called Guillaume,"
Tony replies in his gentle voice.

"You?" Gassin and Guillaume exclaim at the same time.

"Before I went up to Benoît's place, I went to a phone
booth and made two calls," Tony explains. "One to call an
ambulance, as I had serious reasons to believe someone

was hurt, and the other to call Jean Guillaume. I wanted a witness that couldn't be impugned, because I was afraid Elise's testimony might be . . . difficult to understand," he concludes, tactfully.

"You could have had me killed!" Guillaume shouts, indignantly.

"Normally there shouldn't have been any problems. I was armed and knew Hélène wasn't. Obviously, I didn't expect Elise to intervene."

I'm such an asshole, I'm such an asshole, for planting that knife in his hip. First of all, I could have hit an artery, and second, I almost got us all killed. . . . From now on, Elise Andrioli, lay off the Rin Tin Tin bit.

"Nurse, would you have an aspirin?" Gassin asks.

Before she can answer, someone hurriedly steps over.

"Any news?" Gassin asks in a voice made hoarse from too much smoking.

"The bodies of the Fanstens have just arrived in the morgue. It wasn't too pretty. . . . You ever seen what hot dogs look like when you forget them on the barbecue?" a man calls out, in the mood to be nasty.

"Spare us the details, I've got a headache. Is there a lab report?"

"Tomorrow morning. What are we gonna do with this bastard Mercier?"

"Take it easy, Mendoza, we don't insult the witnesses. Mercier's coming with us."

"How come your boy's got it in for Mercier?" asks Guillaume.

"He's a little touchy, Mendoza . . . huh, Mendoza? He's so horrified that you're putting him down. You know why Mercier was so well informed about every detail in the investigation? It's because of his pal Mendoza."

"Oh, that's enough, goddamnit!" Mendoza call out as he walks away. "I'm gonna get a coffee."

"They used to meet in the bar, every morning, to discuss the sports results. I guess soccer has no more secrets for you today, huh, Mercier!" Gassin laughs.

"When I found out Mendoza was a cop and assigned to

the investigation, I did whatever I could to make his acquaintance. It wasn't that hard. I just had to rub him the right way."

"Don't ever say that in front of him," Gassin advises. "Well, I'm going. It's getting late."

A door opens.

"Your daughter has woken up, sir."

"What are you going to tell her?" asks Guillaume, with emotion in his voice.

"I don't know. That I'm her real father. And that Paul and Hélène died in a fire."

"But she knew it was Hélène. I'm sure of it!" Gassin calls as he gets up.

"So? Do you want to charge her?"

He heads toward the room where Virginie must be trying to understand what has happened. I wouldn't want to be in his place. She'll certainly need extended care. She couldn't possibly live through that and not come out unscathed.

Mendoza, who has returned, calls out "What about her?" in the tone you'd use when talking about a dog, and I realize he means me.

"I had someone call her uncle. You'll be staying here until he arrives or tells us what arrangements should be made, miss."

Yes, yes, that's fine. I don't give a damn whether it's here or anywhere else. I've got enough things to think over to last me several years. The door has just shut on Tony again. A nurse is rolling my wheelchair toward my room.

Behind me, Inspector Gassin's phone is beeping, resounding through the hall.

"Yeah, go ahead. . . . What? Well, shit, I can imagine . . . okay, ciao."

"Any news?" asks Guillaume, retracing his steps.

"No, not really. Just a Telex we just received from Marseilles. It's about Maxime Siccardi, who was born July 3, 1976, to René Siccardi, age forty-eight, and Josette Siccardi, age thirty-nine!"

Bravo, Elise! Right on target!

"What?" Guillaume mutters, without a clue.

"Hélène had a son who was officially declared in her parents' name. We're guessing she had it by her father, René."

"But that's hideous!" Guillaume exclaims.

"Like you say . . . but that's not all. You know how her son died? He was tortured to death in a basement by two teenagers who were totally strung out. Well, you know, with this world of ours . . . is it any wonder she lost her shit?"

His words fade as the nurse turns down another corridor. I feel tired. So tired. So . . .

THE RAIN WON'T STOP FALLING, LIKE HEAVY TEARS upon the glass panes in my room.

I'm sitting up in my beautiful white bed. Tomorrow, at eight o'clock, Professor Combré will attempt a last-ditch operation. My uncle has arranged it all. All I have left is hope. Yet even if it doesn't work, I know that things will be better for me from here on out.

The autopsy has determined that Paul Fansten was stabbed twenty times or more with a thin-bladed knife.

Last week, Paul and Hélène were buried in the plot he had purchased in the cemetery where his son, Renaud, already lies at rest.

Everyone found it paradoxical that the woman who killed him and his child should be buried with them, but legally they were married, and to this day, no ruling has intervened finding Hélène guilty. In any case, it suited everyone, as it cut funeral costs considerably. It's these kinds of sordid details you always forget, but which force you to return to life as usual, with its little worries and great joys, or vice versa.

Jean Guillaume asked Yvette to marry him as soon as she opened one eye. She agreed, and then went back to sleep.

Virginie's in the pediatric department, under observation. Apparently, her behavior is completely normal for a child who has lived through this sort of situation. A bit too normal, according to the psychiatrist.

"For once there's someone in the family who's normal," Tony said.

Speaking of Tony . . . Inspector Mendoza was waiting for him when he walked out of his interview with the examining judge, free as a bird—thanks to Jean Guillaume's deposition—to beat his face in. There they were, fighting like fishwives on the steps of the courthouse. It looks like Mendoza's got two split lips, while Tony's sporting a lovely shiner on his right eye.

He's chuckling about it while holding my hand, sitting at my bedside.

What am I getting myself into with this nut job?

I don't know, but I'm getting into it with no remorse. The shore of my past life is quickly fading in the distance, and there, on the other side, Benoît will stay, a silhouette that gets thinner and thinner.

I am alive.

Alive.

And tomorrow morning, I'll know if the operation was a success.